THE
CONQUEST

(Kelderan Runic Warriors #1)

Jessie Donovan

This book is a work of fiction. Names, characters, places, and incidents are either the product of the writer's imagination or are used fictitiously, and any resemblance to actual persons, living or dead, business establishments, events, or locales is entirely coincidental.

The Conquest
Copyright © 2017 Laura Hoak-Kagey
Mythical Lake Press, LLC
First Edition

Cover Art by Clarissa Yeo of Yocla Designs.

ISBN 13: 978-1942211488

To Sci-Fi Fans Everywhere

*Regardless of how TV and movies portray you, I think you're some of the coolest people I've met.
Live long and prosper. V*

Other Books by Jessie Donovan

Stonefire Dragons
Sacrificed to the Dragon
Seducing the Dragon
Revealing the Dragons
Healed by the Dragon
Reawakening the Dragon
Loved by the Dragon
Surrendering to the Dragon
Cured by the Dragon
Aiding the Dragon (May 2017)

Lochguard Highland Dragons
The Dragon's Dilemma
The Dragon Guardian
The Dragon's Heart
The Dragon Warrior

Asylums for Magical Threats
Blaze of Secrets
Frozen Desires
Shadow of Temptation
Flare of Promise

Cascade Shifters
Convincing the Cougar
Reclaiming the Wolf
Cougar's First Christmas
Resisting the Cougar

Chapter One

Taryn Demara stared at the faint blip on the decades-old radar. Each pulse of light made her heart race faster. *This is it.* Her people might have a chance to survive.

Using every bit of restraint she had, Taryn prevented her voice from sounding too eager as she asked, "Are you sure it's a spaceship?"

Evaine Benoit, her head of technology, nodded. "Our equipment is outdated, but by the size and movement, it has to be a ship."

Taryn's heart beat double-time as she met her friend's nearly black-eyed gaze. "How long do we have before they reach us?"

"If they maintain their current trajectory, I predict eighteen hours, give or take. It's more than enough time to get the planet ready."

"Right," Taryn said as she stood tall again. "Keep me updated on any changes. If the ship changes course, boost the distress signal."

Evaine raised her brows. "Are you sure? The device is on its last legs. Any boost in power could cause a malfunction. I'm not sure my team or I can fix it again if that happens."

She gripped her friend's shoulder. "After eight years of waiting, I'm willing to risk it. I need that ship to reach Jasvar and send a team down to our planet."

Otherwise, we're doomed was left unsaid.

Without another word, Taryn raced out of the aging technology command center and went in search of her best strategist. There was much to do and little time to do it.

Nodding at some of the other members of her settlement as she raced down the corridors carved into the mountainside, Taryn wondered what alien race was inside the ship on the radar. Over the past few hundred years, the various humanoid additions to the once human-only colony had added extra skin tones, from purple to blue to even a shimmery gold. Some races even had slight telepathic abilities that had been passed down to their offspring.

To be honest, Taryn didn't care what they looked like or what powers they possessed. As long as they were genetically compatible with her people, it meant Taryn and several other women might finally have a chance at a family. The "Jasvar Doom Virus" as they called it, killed off most male embryos in the womb, to the point only one male was born to every five females. Careful genealogical charts had been maintained to keep the gene pool healthy. However, few women were willing to share their partner with others, which meant the male population grew smaller by the year.

It didn't help that Jasvar had been set up as a low-technology colony, which meant they didn't have the tools necessary to perform the procedures in the old tales of women being impregnated without sex. The technique had been called in-something or other. Taryn couldn't remember the exact name from her great-grandmother's stories from her childhood.

10

THE CONQUEST

Not that it was an option anyway. Jasvar's technology was a hodgepodge of original technology from the starter colonists and a few gadgets from their conquests and alien additions over the years. It was a miracle any of it still functioned.

The only way to prevent the extinction of her people was to capture and introduce alien males into their society. Whoever had come up with the idea of luring aliens to the planet's surface and developing the tools necessary to get them to stay had been brilliant. Too bad his or her name had been lost to history.

Regardless of who had come up with the idea, Taryn was damned if she would be the leader to fail the Jasvarian colony. Since the old technology used to put out the distress signals was failing, Taryn had a different sort of plan for the latest alien visitors.

She also wanted their large spaceship and all of its technology.

Of course, her grand plans would be all for nothing if she couldn't entice and trap the latest aliens first. To do that, she needed to confer with Nova Drakven, her head strategist.

Rounding the last corner, Taryn waltzed into Nova's office. The woman's pale blue face met hers. Raising her silver brows, she asked, "Is it true about the ship?"

With a nod, Taryn moved to stand in front of Nova's desk. "Yes. It should be here in about eighteen hours."

Nova reached for a file on her desk. "Good. Then I'll present the plan to the players, and we can wait on standby until we know for sure where the visiting shuttle lands."

Taryn shook her head and started pacing. "I need you to come up with a new plan, Nova."

"Why? I've tweaked what went wrong last time. We shouldn't have any problems."

"It's not that." Taryn stopped pacing and met her friend's gaze. "This time, we need to do more than entice a few males to stay. Our planet was originally slated to be a low-tech colony, but with the problems that arose, that's no longer an option. We need supplies and knowledge, which means negotiating with the mother ship for their people."

"Let me get this straight—you want to convince the vastly technologically advanced aliens that we are superior, their crew's lives are in danger, and that they need to pay a ransom to get them back?"

Taryn grinned. "See, you do understand me."

Nova sighed. "You have always been crazy and a little reckless."

"Not reckless, Nova. Just forward-thinking. You stage the play, think of a few ideas about how to get the ship, and I'll find a way to make it work."

"Always the super leader to the rescue. Although one day, your luck may run out, Taryn."

Nova and Taryn were nearly the same age, both in their early thirties, and had grown up together. Nova was her best friend and one of the few people Taryn was unafraid to speak her fears with. "As long as my luck lasts through this ordeal, I'm okay with that. I can't just sit and watch our people despairing if another year or ten pass before there's new blood. If we had a way to get a message to Earth, it would make everything easier. But, we don't have that capability."

Nova raised her brows. "Finding a way to contact Earth or the Earth Colony Alliance might be an easier goal than taking over a ship."

"The message would take years to get there and who knows if the ECA would even send a rescue ship to such a distant colony." Taryn shook her head. "I can't rely on chance alone. I'll send a message from the alien ship, but I also want the technology to save us in the near future, too. I much prefer being in control."

Nova snorted. "Sometimes a little too much in control, in my opinion."

"A leader letting loose doesn't exactly instill confidence," she drawled.

"Then promise me that once you save the planet, you let me show you some fun. No one should die before riding the sloping Veran waterfalls."

Taryn sighed and sank into the chair in front of Nova's desk. "Fine. But how about we focus on capturing the aliens first?"

Nova removed a sheaf of crude paper made from the purple wood of the local trees and took out an ink pot and golden feather. "I'll come up with a fool-proof capture plan, but I hope you keep me in the loop about what happens next."

"I will when it's time. I need to see who we're dealing with before making concrete plans."

Dipping her feather into the ink pot, Nova scratched a few notes on the purple paper. "Then let me get to work. The staging is mostly done already, but I need to think beyond that. Since we've never tried to capture a large ship before, it's going to take some time. I think someone captured a shuttle in the past, but we'll see if I can find the record."

"You always go on about how you love challenges."

"Don't remind me." She made a shooing motion toward the door. "And this is one of the few times I can tell my settlement leader to get lost and let me work."

Taryn stood. "If you need me, I'll be in the outside garden."

"Fine, fine. Just go. You're making it hard to concentrate." Nova looked up with a smile. "And you're also delaying my next project."

"Do I want to know?"

"It's called Operation Fun Times." Nova pointed her quill. "I sense you're going to land an alien this time. You're a talented individual, except when it comes to flirting. I'm going to help with that."

Shaking her head, Taryn muttered, "Have fun," and left her old-time friend to her own devices. Maybe someday Nova would understand that while Taryn missed the antics of their youth, she enjoyed taking care of her people more.

Still, she'd admit that it would be nice to finally have the chance to get a man of her own. Most of her family was gone, and like many of the women of her age group, Taryn would love the option to start one.

Not now, Demara. You won't have a chance unless you succeed in capturing the visitors.

With the play planning in motion, Taryn had one more important task to set up before she could also pore through the records and look for ideas.

As much as she wished for everything to go smoothly, it could take a turn and end up horribly wrong. In that case, she needed an out. Namely, she needed to erase memories. The trick would be conferring with her head medicine woman to find the balance between erasing memories and rendering the aliens brain-dead. As the early Jasvarians had discovered, the forgetful plant was both a blessing and a curse. Without it, they'd never have survived this long. However, in the wrong dose, it could turn someone into a vegetable and ruin their chances.

The Conquest

Don't worry. Matilda knows what she's doing. Picking up her pace, Taryn exited the mountain into the late-day sun. The faint purple and blue hues of the mountains and trees were an everyday sight to her, but she still found the colors beautiful. Her great-grandmother's tales had been full of green leaves and blue skies back on Earth. A part of Taryn wanted to see another world, but the leader in her would never abandon the people of Jasvar.

Looking to the pinkish sky, she only hoped the visitors fell for her tricks. Otherwise, Taryn might have to admit defeat and prepare her people for the worst.

~~~

Prince Kason tro el Vallen of the royal line of Vallen stared at his ship's main viewing screen. The blue, pink, and purple hues of the planet hid secrets Kason was determined to discover. After years of fighting his father's wishes and then the ensuing days of travel from Keldera to the unnamed planet, he was anxious to get started.

Aaric, his head pilot, stated, "Ten hours until we pull into orbit, your highness."

Kason disliked the title but had learned over time that to fight it was pointless. "Launch a probe to investigate."

"Yes, your highness."

As Aaric sent the request to the necessary staff, the silver-haired form of Ryven Xanna, Kason's best friend and the head warrior trainer on the ship, walked up to him. "We need to talk."

Kason nodded. Ryven would only ask to talk if it was important. "I can spare a few minutes. Aaric, you have the command."

The pair of them entered Kason's small office off the central command area. The instant the door slid shut, Ryven spoke up again. "Some of the men's markings are tinged yellow. They're nervous. No doubt thanks to the rumors of a monster on the planet's surface."

"There is no monster. There's a logical explanation as to why our team of scientists disappeared on Jasvar ten years ago."

"I agree with you, but logic doesn't always work with the lower-ranked officers and the common soldiers."

Kason clasped his hand behind his back. "You wouldn't ask to talk with me unless you have a solution. Tell me what it is, Ryv."

"I know it's not standard protocol for you to lead the first landing party, but if you go, it will instill courage in the others," Ryven answered.

Kason raised a dark-blue eyebrow. "Tell me you aren't among the nervous."

Ryven shrugged and pointed to one of the markings that peeked above his collar. "The dark blue color tells you all you need to know."

Dark blue signaled that a Kelderan was at peace and free of negative emotions.

"You are better at controlling your emotions than anyone I have ever met. You could be deathly afraid and would somehow keep your markings dark blue."

The corner of Ryven's mouth ticked up. "The trick has worked well for me over the years."

"We don't have time for reminiscing, Ryv. You're one of the few who speaks the truth to me. Don't change now."

"Honestly?" Ryven shrugged. "I'm not any more nervous or worried than any other mission. The unknown enemy just means we need to be cautious more than ever."

"Agreed. I will take the first landing party and leave Thorin in charge. Assemble your best warriors and send me a message when they're ready. I want to talk with them and instill bravery beforehand."

In a rare sign of emotion, Ryven gripped Kason's bicep. "Bravery is all well and fine, but if there is a monster we can't defeat, promise you'll pull back. Earning your father's praise isn't worth your life."

"I'm a little insulted at your implication. I wouldn't be a general in my own right if I lived by foolish displays of machismo."

Ryven studied him a second before adding, "Just because you're a general now doesn't mean you have to talk like one with me."

Kason remembered their childhood days, before they'd both been put on the path of a warrior. Kason and Ryven had pulled pranks on their siblings and had reveled in coming up with stupid competitions, such as who could reach the top of a rock face first in freezing temperatures or who could capture a poisonous shimmer fly with nothing but their fingers.

But neither of them were boys anymore. Displaying emotion changed the color of the rune-like markings on their bodies, which exposed weakness. Warriors couldn't afford to show any weakness. It was one of the reasons higher-ranked officers weren't allowed to take wives, not even if they found one of their potential destined brides; the females would become easy targets.

Not that Kason cared. A wife would do nothing to prove his worth as a soldier to his father, the king. On top of that, being a warrior was all Kason knew. Giving it up would take away his purpose.

Pushing aside thoughts of his father and his future, Kason motioned toward the door. "Go and select the best soldiers to assist with the landing party. I have my own preparations to see to."

"I'll go if you promise one thing."

"What?"

"You allow me to be part of the landing party."

Kason shook his head. "I can't. In the event of my death, I need you here."

"Thorin is your second and will assume command. Give me the honor of protecting you and the others during the mission."

Deep down, in the place where Kason locked up any emotion, a small flicker of indecision flashed. Ryven was more Kason's brother than his real-life brother, Keltor.

Yet to contain Ryven on the ship would be like a slap in the face; the honor of protecting a prince such as Kason was the highest form of trust to one of the Kelderan people.

Locking down his emotions, Kason followed his logical brain. "You may attend. But on-planet, you become a soldier. I can't treat you as my friend."

Ryven put out a hand and Kason shook it to seal their agreement. "I'm aware of protocol. I teach it day in and day out. But I will be the best damned soldier of the group. And if it comes to it, I will push you out of the way to protect your life."

Kason released his friend's hand. "I won't let it come to that."

"Good. When shall we rendezvous?"

THE CONQUEST

Glancing at the small screen projecting an image of the multicolored planet, he answered, "Nine hours. That will give all of us a chance to sleep before performing the prebattle ritual. You can lead the men through their meditation and warm-up maneuvers after that."

Ryven nodded. "I'll see you then."

The trainer exited the room, and Kason turned toward his private viewing screen to study the planet rumored to host the most feared monster in the region. One that had supposedly taken hundreds of men's lives over the years. The story was always the same—a small contingent of men disappeared from any group that landed on the surface. No one remembered how they were captured or if they were even alive. Anytime a second party landed, a few more would be taken.

Over time, the planet had earned a reputation. Even the most adventure-seeking ruffians had stayed away.

However, Kason dismissed it as folklore. Whatever was on that planet, he wouldn't allow it to defeat him or his men. Kason would bring honor to his family with a victory. He also hoped to give his people the gift of a new planet. Keldera was overpopulated, and its resources were stretched beyond the limit. The Kelderans desperately needed a new colony and hadn't been able to locate one that was suitable. The planet on the view screen showed all the signs of being a near-perfect fit.

Even if the fiercest monster in existence resided on that planet, Kason wouldn't retreat from an enemy. Death was an accepted part of being a Kelderan soldier.

Chapter Two

A little more than nine hours later, Kason strode over to the group of twenty warriors standing in four rows of five, with Ryven in front of them. As he neared the males, Kason approved of the dark blue shade of their markings. The soldiers were calm, collected, and ready for battle.

He almost missed being a regular soldier. While he was a natural leader, his role as a prince general involved more politics than he liked. Kason much preferred planning and participating in a battle.

Maybe once his brother ascended the throne and took a bride, Kason could spend more time exploring the stars and protecting his home world. His brother's in-laws could take care of the political side of things in Kason's stead.

Taking his place next to Ryven, his friend stated, "Prince Kason has honored us with his presence and will lead the prebattle ritual."

All eyes moved to Kason. Used to the attention as a Kelderan prince, Kason merely widened his stance and extended his arms out at his sides with palms up. "For honor." He clapped his hands together and extended his arms again. "For duty." He repeated the action but added a foot stomp at the end. "To serve and protect." He clapped and stomped both feet. "We will gladly give our lives for the sake of Keldera."

THE CONQUEST

Raising his arms into the air with his fingers spread out, Kason roared to the sky. All the men joined him, and the yells echoed around the metal walls of the shuttle bay.

After thirty seconds, Kason lowered his arms and looked at the soldiers. "There may be danger on the planet below, but if we can win against the Tallarians with their mind-control abilities, we can defeat whatever monster may live on Jasvar. Our success depends on finding the enemy's weakness." He looked down all the rows of soldiers and continued, "I look forward to our shared victory."

Before Kason could hand over control to Ryven, a teenage errand boy rushed up to him. "Your highness." He held out a notescreen. "It's from the Lt. General."

Taking the small, clear notescreen, Kason pressed his thumb on the corner to unlock it and scanned Thorin's message. *Distress signal hailing from the planet's surface. Contact for more information.*

He passed the note to Ryven, waved a hand in dismissal at the messenger, and focused his attention back on the soldiers. "Begin your prebattle meditation. Trainer Xanna will return shortly to begin the warm-up exercises."

Ryven added, "I expect to find all of your markings the same deep blue as Keldera's Lake Nyvina. Anyone with even the slightest tinge of another color will be dismissed."

The men stomped their feet once in acknowledgment. Ryven clapped his hands, and the warriors moved into their meditation poses.

As the men settled into their practice, Kason motioned with his head to the far side of the shuttle bay. Once they were out of earshot, Ryven spoke up again. "The distress signal quashes any rumors of a curse or a monster. Our probes may not have been

21

able to find anything of note, but neither a curse nor a monster can work that type of equipment."

"That we know of. Still, we'll survey the surface of the planet more intently than a standard exploration mission. I want to know who or what sent that message. It could be an old one that's playing on an endless loop. Some kind of animal or force could've destroyed them hundreds of years ago, for all we know." He motioned toward the shuttle. "Double-check our supplies and weaponry. I want to be prepared." Ryven grunted in acknowledgment and Kason continued, "I'm going to talk with Thorin via the private comm unit in the shuttle bay command center, in case you need to contact me."

With a nod, Ryven walked toward the shuttle and started barking orders at the maintenance staff. Leaving the prep work to his best trainer, Kason ascended the stairs to the main command room. Five males, including the controller on duty, pounded their fist over their body in salute. Kason returned the gesture. He met the controller's gaze. "The private comm unit?"

"Currently available, sir."

Kason headed to the small room on the far side. Once the door was locked, he touched the screen and positioned his eye in front of the scanner to unlock the unit and activate the artificial intelligence system.

The comm unit asked without inflection, "What is your command?"

"Patch me through to Lt. General Thorin Jarrell."

"Connecting."

After a few beats, Thorin's face popped onto the screen. Kason didn't waste any time. "What do we know about the distress signal?"

THE CONQUEST

"The signal is weak, but it's paired with a woman's voice. She sounds frightened," Thorin answered.

"Play the message."

After a second, a woman's voice mixed with static filled the room. *"If you can hear this, please help. We've been attacked. I'm not sure how much longer the women and children will be able to fend off the attackers. Almost all of our men are dead or injured."* A boom followed by screaming. *"Please. If you can help, we're to the north of the tallest mountain."*

The message cut off after more screaming. Thorin spoke up again. "What do you wish to do, your highness?"

"What did the long-range sensors tell us?"

"Not much," Thorin answered. "There's no ship in orbit, but there are large life-forms on the planet that could be humanoid. None of our techs can find a timestamp and have no way of knowing if the distress signal is recent or not. Until we're closer, I can't tell you more than that."

The woman in the distress signal had spoken in CEL, the Common Earth Language. Jasvar was a long way from Earth, but the humans had populated the galaxy to the point of almost being pests. It was possible a few had crash-landed on Jasvar and angered someone or something.

Or, it was also possible that they were thieves and the attackers were only trying to retrieve their contraband.

Still, females were the weaker ones, especially in the case of humans. To turn his back on a female in need would be a coward's choice. Even if the women were criminals, Kason would make them face trial. If they were honorable and in need of assistance, he would make further decisions once he had more information.

Noting that Thorin was awaiting his order, Kason finally replied, "Keep me up-to-date as we near the planet. I will confer with Ryven and adjust our strategy accordingly."

Thorin stood taller. "May I speak freely, your highness?" Kason waved a hand and Thorin continued, "What if this is a trap?"

"Then the troublemakers will face the might of the Kelderan Army. They won't stand a chance."

Thorin closed his fist and hit his chest in farewell before the screen went blank.

Out of curiosity, Kason said to the AI system, "Display information on Jasvar regarding colonies or other native, intelligent inhabitants."

"Error. Nothing is known, apart from rumor. Only scientific studies from probes are available."

Kason had expected as much since he had researched the planet for years before the current mission. Since Keldera and Earth didn't have an alliance, neither one shared information with the other. "Display all known rumors surrounding Jasvar."

"Working."

As the computer displayed the first file, Kason leaned forward to read it carefully. He'd studied the files before, but he could've missed something important. It was worth doing again, especially since he might be risking his men by sending them down to the planet's surface.

~~~

Taryn adjusted her costume so that the ripped shoulder slid a little further down her arm. Satisfied with the amount of cleavage showing, she made her way around the large room.

24

The Conquest

Women and children, ranging in ages from four years to sixty, were attired in torn, dirty dresses, breeches, and various states of undress. Those who had their costumes on were either adding soot smudges to their faces or mussing up their hair with leaves, dirt, and even twigs.

According to their radar, the ship was almost to their planet. It was nearly showtime.

Despite her thudding heart, Taryn smiled and encouraged her people as she passed. While this wasn't her first time participating in a staged trap, it was her first time as leader. Not knowing which alien race was in the sky above was the most difficult aspect. However, in all the years of her people enticing ships to Jasvar's surface, only once had the aliens turned out to be violent.

Thankfully Taryn had a backup plan in case that happened again.

Nova and her sister, Celestia, darted around the room, making final preparations. Satisfied the sister team could take care of the players, Taryn searched the room for Matilda, her head medicine woman.

Spotting the older woman in the corner, helping her granddaughter with soot smudges, Taryn wove around the women and children until she reached Matilda. After applying the last dark streak on her granddaughter's cheek, Matilda said to her grandchild, "There we go, love. You will be the most desperate looking child of them all."

The little girl beamed. "You really think so, Gramma?"

"Of course. Now, go see your mother. I think she needs your help with getting ready."

The little girl nodded and ran across the room to her mother. Matilda smiled at Taryn. "Everything is ready to go, Taryn." She reached into the purse-like bag around her waist and took out thirty small vials. "These sleeping drafts for the darts are powerful. Not even the most muscular warrior aliens in the galaxy will wake up from it in less than two hours. We won't have a repeat of last time."

Eight years ago, when the previous alien ship had answered their distress call, the sleeping draft had worn off after twenty minutes. Taryn hadn't been in charge at the time, nor had Matilda been the head medicine woman, but the mistake had nearly cost them everything. Only a combination of luck and a few women waking the men up with kisses had provided enough distraction to readminister the drafts, erase and adjust their memories, and send the shuttle back to their ship in orbit.

The mistake had cost them new blood to add to the gene pool.

"I trust you, Mattie. What about the forgetful plant root potion?" Taryn asked.

"The concoction is steeping. My husband is watching over it. The memory potion will be ready in two hours."

"That's cutting it close."

Matilda shrugged. "It's the best I could do within the time frame. You know it takes a little over sixteen hours to steep."

"I know, I know. I just want everything to go perfectly."

"I've known you your whole life, Taryn. You have faced every challenge and won. I don't see why this time would be any different."

Since she wasn't good at accepting praise, Taryn avoided replying to Matilda's statement by taking about half of the vials. "You take the right side of the room, and I'll take the left. I see Nova and Celestia signaling the bird handlers, which means we're nearly ready to go, so we need to hurry."

26

THE CONQUEST

With a bob of her head, Matilda left to hand out the sleeping potions, which would be used with blow darts to knock out the visitors.

As Taryn did the same, she scrutinized every face as she went. A few women were tapping their fingers or toes, anxious to get started. Some of the older women were chatting about the staged plays that had nabbed their own husbands. The children were content to play with walking stick props or to make bets about who would be allowed to handle one of the radiant birds native to Jasvar.

It was funny to think the whole process of staging a scene and capturing alien visitors had become second nature to her people. She wondered what the original colonists would've thought about it all.

Just as Taryn doled out the last vial, Nova finally rushed up to her. "We're two minutes behind schedule. Make your speech quick."

"Of course." Taryn moved to the front of the room and clapped her hands. The noise died down to a few children murmuring with their friends.

She projected her voice. "I won't bother to tell you how important today is. Every unattached woman in this room knows it's been eight years since our last visit. We all need to stick to the plan. The better you act your part, the more vulnerable the visitors will become. Then and only then can we pounce and spring the trap."

A woman's voice asked from the back of the room, "Is it true what Nova said? That you want their spaceship this time, too? Because I don't know if we can do that."

Despite the tight schedule, the skepticism in the woman's voice needed to be quelled. "Yes, it's true. I don't know about you, but I hate the uncertainty of how we live. Not being able to

27

make a future for our daughters is heartbreaking. And what happens if it's eighty years before we have another visitor? We need to change our strategy if we're to survive. To do that, we need technology and resources we can't find on Jasvar to help us."

The same woman answered, "But Jasvar was meant to be low-tech. No one knows how to fly those contraptions, let alone how to use the fancy technology. Should we even waste our time?"

Taryn never broke eye contact. "I have plans in the works. For now, just give the best performance of your lives. With skill and a little luck, we might be able to beat the doom virus once and for all. Who's with me?" Cheers rose from most of the people in the room. "Right, then let's take our places. The visitors will be here in less than half an hour, and we need to be ready."

Murmurs of assent and nods filled the room. Raising her hand, Taryn made a fist and turned toward the exit. It was showtime.

~~~

The shuttle touched down on Jasvar's surface. From the corner of his eye, Kason took in the warriors. All were expressionless with dark blue markings.

Not that he should've doubted their trainer. Ryven would never allow less than the best to accompany Keldera's younger prince on a mission.

The outside sensor beeped twice, signaling a safe, breathable atmosphere. Kason looked to the two pilots. "What do the scanners say?"

The Conquest

The chief pilot answered, "The same as before. There is a group of about thirty humanoid life-forms just behind the slit in the rock face, in close proximity to the distress beacon."

"You two stay here on standby." Kason looked to one of the most decorated soldiers. "Jerrick, you will guard the shuttle. If anything arises, use the transmitter and let us know."

"Yes, sir," Jerrick answered.

Kason entered the code to open the outer door. As the metal slid to the side, purple trees, blue mountains, and a pink sky filled his vision. It was different from Keldera's black mountains, yellow trees, and blue-green sky.

Not that he had time to note all the differences between the two planets. Piercing cries from beyond the narrow opening in the rock garnered his attention. They sounded female.

Lifting his hand, Kason signaled his warriors to draw their weapons and to follow him down the steps to the surface. With a short sword in his left hand and a blast gun in his right, Kason moved silently toward the chaos. At the high-pitched screaming and billowing smoke, he picked up his pace. Part of him suspected a trap, but the screams of the children in particular sounded genuine. Given what he knew of children, they were hard to coach.

And since children signified the finality of marriage on Keldera, each was a precious memory. He couldn't allow the innocents to suffer. He would ensure their safety, even if their parents turned out to be deceitful pirates.

Peering through the opening, Kason took a moment to take in the scene and scout the unknown.

Eight women huddled together at the edge of the village with their children in the center of them.

Something whizzed by in the sky, leaving a trail of fire in its wake. Simple thatched houses burned as a few more women tried

29

to quench the flames with buckets of water. However, as soon as they extinguished one, another creature raced by and set it ablaze again as if the water made no difference.

The birds must possess a special type of intense burning fire.

One of the birds dove down and snatched a bundle out of one of the female's arms. The woman screamed and ran after the bird, but was unable to catch up with it before it disappeared with her child.

Gripping his sword tighter, Kason wondered what had happened to the men. Even if injured, they should be protecting their females. He was half tempted to save the women and children and then hunt down the cowardly males. Stories always spoke of humans lacking honor, but this was the first time Kason had seen it firsthand.

However, he would determine what to do with the males later. As one woman's skirt caught fire and she rolled on the ground to put it out, he decided to help the humans, albeit cautiously. For all he knew, it could still be a trap.

Kason studied the patterns of the fire creatures, looking for the best way to take them down, yet they seemed to swoop and rise at random intervals. Maybe a surprise attack from all sides would succeed in defeating them. Since there was only the narrow opening in front of him, he'd have to send two groups to climb the low-level rocks on either side and wait to jump over.

Retreating a few feet back, Kason faced his men. Pointing to a third of them, he signaled to the left. He repeated the motion for another third to take the center and the last third to take the right. He whispered, "Each side must climb into position. Everyone will fire at the flying creatures when I do."

The Conquest

He closed his fist, and the warriors moved to their places, with Kason leading the center squad.

Once everyone was ready, Kason charged into the fray and took aim at the closest fire bird. He was vaguely aware of the other flanks jumping down from the rocks to do the same. However, before he could shoot his gun, something pricked the back of his neck. The split-second distraction gave the bird time to flit away. Kason moved his arm to try to fire at another, but everything in sight wavered before he saw double.

Men on either side of him slumped to the ground. Kason lasted a few seconds longer, but as the women's cries continued in the background, the world went black.

Chapter Three

When Taryn was sure the last alien warrior was unconscious, she shouted, "End scene."

The cries and moaning ceased as the women went to work vanquishing the flames with a special mixture that could extinguish the fire of a radiant bird. The children were already at the far side, where the radiant birds landed one by one on the rock perch and waited for their human trainers to retrieve them.

One of the teenagers ran off to tell the men to assist.

With everything running as it should, Taryn dusted off her dress and headed toward the group of unconscious alien males at the entrance to the secluded valley. Nova and Celestia would check out the other two groups she'd spotted during their play.

Taryn had barely had time to notice the naked chests, tight synthetic pants, and strange markings of the aliens when she'd been pretending to be helpless, but as she approached, Taryn noted that no two sets of markings were the same. Not just because their colors ran from blue to orange to green, but the shapes and placements were unique.

She'd seen something similar before, with aliens assimilated about a decade ago. That would work to her advantage since those males were married and dedicated to their wives. They would do anything, even reveal secrets of their own world, to protect their families. Taryn would interview them later.

THE CONQUEST

Reaching the largest alien with golden skin and the most markings, Taryn squatted down and studied his face. Since he'd been leading the charge, she was pretty sure he was their leader. Even unconscious on the ground, he was huge. He had to be well over six feet tall and without an ounce of fat on his body.

Clean-shaven, his face was all angles, and his dark blue hair glinted in the sun. His hair was probably the only soft part of him. She itched to brush the blue strands to find out but clenched her fingers in her skirt. If the males were cooperative and wished to stay, Celestia would assign each one to their most compatible Jasvarian counterpart. Since touching skin to skin initiated some kind of bond with certain alien species, Taryn wouldn't take the chance of the male wanting her and then making her miserable for the rest of her life if they weren't a suitable match. While they looked like the aliens from ten years ago, she could be mistaken and couldn't risk it.

No, she would leave her future to Celestia. If no male suited her this time around, she'd find one eventually, once they had these aliens' ship under their control.

Nova's voice filled Taryn's ear. "If you don't think you can handle him, I'll have a go," she purred.

Frowning, Taryn stood and looked at her friend. "Attraction doesn't mean happiness. Let Celestia do her job and pair you with the right one."

Nova sighed. "I hate the pairing we do. I wish we could kiss a few men and find a match on our own."

"You can with any of the men born here," she pointed out.

Nova scrunched her nose. "The few I've kissed were definitely not for me. It was like kissing a cousin."

The corner of Taryn's mouth ticked up. "I know for sure none of them were your cousins. But if my plan succeeds, you just might have a wider pool to 'taste' in the future." The sound of carts creaking closer filled the air. "But enough about kissing. Who is watching your group?"

"Matilda. She wanted to ensure they were all unconscious and didn't show signs of waking up."

She nodded. "While she does that, make sure everyone has their gloves on. I don't want any sort of unnecessary bonding."

"Don't worry, I don't want a repeat of fifteen years ago, either."

The women had helped load the males onto the carts back then. Each first touch had established a bond that had ended in suicide with a few cases and more than a handful of the alien males in jail for violence. Even so, a few pairings had worked out and resulted in children. So it hadn't been a total loss.

The people of Jasvar truly understood the saying about beggars not being choosers. When a group of people faced extinction, they made the most of what they had.

Taryn took one last look at the leader's face. The lack of smile lines around the corners of his mouth or near his eyes told her he was a serious fellow. From what she remembered of the aliens from a decade ago, most weren't afraid to smile on a regular basis. Most likely, Mr. Huge Alien Warrior was going to be a tough bastard to crack.

Not that Taryn doubted her ability to do so. She just needed to clean up and don something a bit more commanding to do it.

She waved toward the leader. "Isolate and restrain him. I'll talk with him as soon as I talk with the other similar aliens in our colony and gather information. Maybe they can confirm this group is the same species."

"While I've seen the men with markings walking the corridors before, none of them were as well built as this lot."

THE CONQUEST

"The ones from ten years ago were scientists. I have a feeling these are warriors."

Nova slapped her shoulder. "You always did enjoy a challenge."

"Be grateful for that, or you wouldn't have such a wonderful leader."

Nova snorted. "Yes, oh great one."

Taryn rolled her eyes. "Just oversee the women. I'm going to head back and take some of the youngest children with me."

Nova nodded in acknowledgment and Taryn walked toward the group of children near the birds. Unable to resist, she glanced at the huge warrior one last time. Even unconscious, he radiated power. She only hoped he didn't possess some kind of persuasion ability or she would have her work cut out for her, despite her training with a few of the men and women in the colony who had inherited strange abilities from their alien fathers.

Maybe she should order extra restraints just to make sure he couldn't escape. That way, if somehow Taryn failed to resist any special powers, the extra bonds would give her people time to knock the leader out again with other medicines.

Directing three of the youngest children in front of her, Taryn walked as quickly as she could without pushing the kids too hard. She needed to find the aliens like the warriors as soon as possible and discover their weaknesses. Taryn Demara didn't like to lose, and she had no intention of allowing the warrior alien to pull a fast one on her.

~~~

Kason's head pounded as he slowly opened his eyes. The dim light was a relief over bright, but it still sent a sharp pain stabbing into his brain.

He carefully maintained an expression free of emotion and forced his eyes to stay open.

The women in distress had been a trap. And judging by his unconsciousness and aftereffects, someone had drugged him, and he wanted to know who.

But in order to do that, he needed information.

He moved his wrists, but Kason's hands were restrained behind his back. Glancing down, he also saw that his legs were chained to both the chair and a bolt in the floor, which was an old method of restraint. Most species used containment cuffs or fields for their prisoners.

Moving his gaze around the room, it looked to be a cave of some sort, lit only by a handful of candles. The cut of the wall was smooth on one half and notched on the other, almost as if a laser cutter had failed and the job had been finished by hand.

The lack of lights or any computers fit with the thatched houses and simply dressed women from the valley. Whoever was on Jasvar relied on a low-tech lifestyle.

While his blast gun was missing from his side, if he could find it, he could probably overpower the criminals and rescue his men. All it would take was some improvised armor, and their drug-tipped darts wouldn't stand a chance.

Then his eyes fell on a mirror set into the wall, and he frowned. The silver substance with etched engravings around the edge was a copy of some of the two-way mirrors inside his own shuttle.

Maybe the Kelderan scientists who disappeared ten years ago had fallen victim to the same scheming criminals as Kason and his men.

Clenching his fingers into fists, it was the only sign of emotion Kason allowed for his failure. He had a feeling the scene with the fire and screaming women had been used to lure many others in the past.

Too bad Kelderans didn't hunt down women and kill them, or Kason might've invoked the right of revenge to stop the deceitful females.

The wooden door at the far side of the room swung inward, and he made out a tall figure wearing leather pants and a tight-fitting top with leather straps crisscrossed across a chest. It took him a second to realize that the chest had breasts that could only belong to a female.

What woman would wear men's clothing? If she were married, her husband should rip off her scandalous clothes and burn them before handing her a dress or pair of flowing *kalak* pants.

The female stepped closer. The scent of human hit his nose at the same time the light highlighted her face. Despite her dark hair braided around her head and her lack of applied coloring to her face, the woman's full lips and dark eyes called to him. Maybe it was the mixture of softness and strength.

Then as he tried to shake the feeling, he couldn't help but look at her shoulders, waist, and then her thighs.

It was then he realized the danger—the only time Kason would lose focus when it came to women was because of instinct.

The human female was potentially a destined bride, which meant she was one of a handful of women who could continue the royal line. Unlike with commoners, the royal line had specific genetic complications that made bearing children difficult. Over the centuries, destined brides had been the only ones to give the kings of old children.

However, potential destined bride or not, he was going to interrogate the female, escape, and subdue the humans.

If he rid the planet of pests, then he could claim the world as his own.

The female's voice filled the room, speaking in CEL. Thankfully, all royals were forced to learn the choppy language as children for diplomatic reasons, in case Earth ever finally agreed to an alliance.

"Should I turn around so you can stare at me some more?" she asked.

The amusement in her voice only made him narrow his eyes as he replied in the same language. "It might help me better assess how to disarm you."

She raised her brows. "I would be able to take this dagger"—she touched one of the weapons strapped to her chest—"and fling it into your heart before you could blink."

Intriguing. Keldera didn't have female warriors. But he kept his surprise to himself. "If you truly want to test your skills, then untie me and let's see how you stand up against a true warrior."

She snorted. "I'm surprised you didn't mention defending my honor or some such thing. That seems to be important to Kelderans."

He wondered how she knew about his people. "Who are you?"

"Was that a hint of irritation in your voice? I thought warriors weren't supposed to show emotion."

Taking a deep breath through his nose, he studied the human a second before stating, "Maybe you heard irritation because you're looking for a weakness. I assure you, human, you won't find one. Your fate was sealed as soon as you drugged me."

Rolling her eyes, the human took out one of her daggers. "Why did it have to be warriors this time?" she muttered.

The Conquest

"This time" must mean the female had tricked males before, as he had suspected. He was believing more and more this female's people were responsible for Keldera's missing scientists.

Although ten years ago, she couldn't have been much more than an adolescent, if he judged the human's age correctly.

Still, her people had stolen from his. His resolve to escape and conquer the humans grew stronger.

If he could get the human to come closer, Kason would find a way to steal her dagger.

And once he had a weapon, the slip of a want-to-be warrior wouldn't stand a chance against him.

~~~

Taryn should stop needling Mr. Huge Alien Warrior, but his arrogance all but begged her to take him down a notch.

Thanks to the two aliens from the previous conquest she'd tracked down and confirmed as Kelderans, Taryn knew the male in front of her was more than a warrior—he was a Kelderan prince.

Prince Kason tro el Vallen to be exact, the second-in-line for the throne and a supposed general in his own right.

Provided she could keep him prisoner, he might be the leverage she needed to take over the Kelderan ship in orbit.

Not that she'd figured out how to do that just yet. All the talk of honor and how females were viewed as weaker made her job harder. But Taryn wasn't going to step aside and let a man take her place to care for her people just because another culture demanded it. The risk and challenge were hers. If she could only get the blasted man to talk, she would be better able to formulate a plan of attack.

His once-over earlier had made her skin hot, but she was intelligent enough to admit Kason was attractive and most women would have a similar reaction. However, each time his eyes found hers, it was as if he were peering into her soul. His dark blue eyes made her want to step closer and find the secrets buried in them.

And she had no idea why. She'd never felt a pull toward any of the other alien men before or even others from the same group.

Realizing she was about to step too close to the Kelderan prince, Taryn took a step back and played with her dagger, tossing it into the air and catching it by the tip. The prince finally spoke up again. "As far as interrogation techniques go, you're a novice."

She caught her dagger and raised her brows. "Is that so?" She snapped her fingers, and a small section of the door opened before a radiant bird flew around the room and landed on Taryn's protected forearm. "If I truly wanted to scare you into confessing, then I would allow my little friend here to sit in your lap. Whenever I give the command, her tail bursts into flame. I'm fairly certain that even a prince general would yelp at his balls being lit on fire."

Kason's brows moved a fraction into what she might even call a frown. "You must not have a husband because he would never allow you to speak so vulgarly."

Between the perceived weakness, the outrage she'd seen in his eyes at her wearing trousers, and his criticism of her language, Taryn was starting to wonder how the women of Keldera put up with it.

Thankfully she would never have to live in such a culture. "Are there any more criticisms you'd like to get out of the way? Maybe then you'll have something worthwhile to say."

He grunted and opened his mouth, but promptly closed it.

It took everything she had not to laugh at his near-lapse in restraint. She had a feeling Mr. Alien Prince wasn't used to people doing anything but fawning over him or obeying his orders.

Keeping her arm raised with the bird, she pointed her dagger at him with her free hand. "Look, I get that you're supposed to be a powerful warrior who has probably never seen defeat. But the reality is I have you and your men in custody. I think it's time we talked about your future."

Kason tilted his head. "If you think my people will pay a ransom, then you haven't done your homework." He lowered his voice. "This is the only warning you'll get from me—release me, and I may be able to spare your lives."

"And if I don't?"

He smiled. "Then you will be the one tied to a chair and at my mercy."

She sheathed her dagger. "That's what I expected you to say. I think it's time I paid your second-in-command a visit."

Taryn swore she saw something flash in Kason's eyes, but it was gone before she could blink.

He shrugged. "Unlike human soldiers, we don't wear identifiers for rank. Only a fool would make themselves out to be a target. My men are trained. None of them will talk."

Taryn smiled slowly. "Care to make a wager on that?"

"I don't wager with untrustworthy, immoral females who don't know their place."

It took everything she had not to draw her dagger and aim for his heart. "Suit yourself. I look forward to the day you understand your place on my planet."

Careful to keep her bird perched on her forearm, Taryn turned and walked out of the room. As soon as the door clicked closed, Nova's head popped out of the viewing room. "That was smooth, oh great leader."

Taryn lightly moved her arm, and the bird flew down the hall to its trainer. "His princely arrogance is a pain in the ass, that's for sure. But I have a few days to either break one of his men or him. If not, we'll give him the memory potion and try the ransom method."

Nova went to her side, and they walked down the hall together. "And if we can't do either before too much time passes for the memory potion to work?"

"Oh, we will succeed."

Nova raised her brows. "And how, exactly, do you expect to do that?"

Taryn smiled sweetly. "Why, with your help, of course. Didn't you just complain about not getting to kiss enough men? Well, today is your lucky day."

"If you expect me to kiss that asshole prince, then you're in for a surprise."

"Not him," she answered without missing a beat.

Nova searched her eyes. "That came out rather quickly."

"Look, do you want to help me or not? If not, I know other unattached women who'd love a chance to snag a warrior, alien husband."

"Fine, I'll drop it for now. But once I find my hot alien man and have a date lined up, I'm going to bring this up again." Taryn said nothing, so Nova continued. "So, what's your plan?"

Chapter Four

Taryn watched as the men and women, with the help of the oxen-like creatures of Jasvar, finished hauling the landing shuttle into the giant cave at the rear of their mountain settlement.

Early on, her people had discovered that the metals and natural stone of the Dianfae mountain range protected them from any sort of sensors or radar. No doubt the Kelderan ship would start searching for the landing shuttle soon, but as long as it was inside the mountain, they wouldn't be able to locate it.

Of course, that meant it was only a matter of time before they sent down more warriors. While a few helpless-looking women had managed to take down the pilots and guard of the shuttle, Taryn wasn't sure if the tactic would work again. Especially if anyone inside the shuttle had sent a warning message to the main ship before falling unconscious.

Under normal circumstances, she'd have the ability to wipe the memories of some of the warriors and send them packing while the willing remained on the planet.

Too bad she didn't have that option this time, or she'd most definitely wipe Prince Kason's memory and get him out of her hair. He may be sitting stoically in a chair not doing anything but blinking, but it was pure defiance. If Nova couldn't charm one of the other aliens, Taryn would have to change tactics. She only hoped she could accomplish her goal without relying on the prince. Killing him would definitely hinder their future, and her dagger might just slip the next time she talked to him.

As the doors to the cavern clicked closed, Taryn realized her head of technology, Evaine, was talking.

Evaine prodded, "Taryn? What do you think of my plan?"

Pushing aside thoughts of the prince, she glanced at Evaine. "Sorry. I was lost in thought. Could you explain it again?"

Since Taryn never missed anything, Evaine's curious look was warranted. However, the technology expert merely gestured toward the shuttle. "I thought we might be able to use the shuttle as, what was the old Earth myth about, oh, a Trojan horse."

"I somehow think if we fill it with Jasvarians, one, it won't ever lift off because we don't know how to fly it. And two, it'd be mighty suspicious as none of us speak their language fluently."

Evaine frowned. "I was thinking more along the lines of a few of our best fighters hiding in compartments I create. If nothing else works, we can put the shuttle back out in the open. When they come to collect it, we attack, like Maldara did with the alien visitors eighty years ago."

Taryn sighed. "Yes, Maldara's plan. Sorry, Evaine. I haven't slept in over a day, and it's starting to catch up with me."

Evaine touched her arm. "I can handle things here, Taryn. You should sleep and recharge your brain." She opened her mouth in protest, but Evaine cut her off. "I'll call Matilda if I have to."

"Right, so she can prick me with a sleeping draft as if I were a child."

Evaine smiled. "To Matilda, we're all still children. That will never change."

Taryn glanced at the shuttle. As soon as the door opened, a few of Evaine's crew went inside. "I'm going to check in with

Nova first, and I promise to sleep for an hour." Evaine frowned, but Taryn shook her head. "No more. The memory potion won't work after five days. The clock is ticking on our ability to have a secure future, especially since a second dose of the memory concoction might kill the aliens. If that happens, we may as well accept our eventual extinction as we sure as hell won't get that ship."

"You would make it a doomsday scenario."

"It is, Evaine. If you still want a partner and children someday, then we need to succeed with this."

She sighed. "I know, I know. I just try to keep an optimistic view on things."

"As do most of our people. Unfortunately, if I do the same, we might become extinct."

Evaine motioned toward the shuttle. "I'm going to study this ship and see if it's enough. Maybe we won't have to worry about ransoming anyone."

She eyed the thirty-foot-long shuttle craft. "While it may have some of the technology we need, there's no way it can have all of the medical and scientific equipment necessary to repopulate our planet and avoid luring ships here."

The tall, lanky form of Zelig, one of the Kelderan scientists captured ten years ago, strode into the room and he headed straight for Evaine and Taryn. Evaine whispered, "I'll let you know what we find from Zelig. If there's any way to survive with only this shuttle, he should know."

Zelig's markings were silver. Taryn tried to remember what that meant, but failed. She'd have to ask about the marking colors and what emotions they signaled after her nap, even though she had a feeling Mr. Alien Prince would never show his cards in such a straightforward manner.

Zelig nodded at Taryn before looking to Evaine. "If you want my help, we need to hurry. My daughter won't stay asleep long."

Taryn tried not to smile at the new father, especially since it was his fourth child. "She'll be there when you get home."

Zelig's black-eyed gaze moved to her. "With a contingent of Kelderan warriors on the planet, no one should be at ease. I'll help Evaine and her team for an hour, but then my wife and daughters need me." The former Kelderan stood taller. "I may not be a warrior, but I will protect my family." Taryn raised her brows in question, but Zelig shook his head. "I wish I could help more, but I've told you all I know about the prince. I would be careful if I were you. He became a general younger than anyone in Kelderan history."

Evaine looked to her, and Taryn pointed toward the ship. "Go ahead. Zelig and I talked earlier. He's more valuable to you right now."

As the pair headed toward the gangplank of the shuttle, Taryn quickly scanned the room. Finding everything as it should be, she headed down the corridor carved into the mountain.

Zelig gave her hope that her plan might succeed; no matter how different the Kelderans might be, it was possible for them to find happiness on Jasvar.

Speaking of which, she needed to check in with Nova and Celestia to see how their interrogations were proceeding. If the other prisoners were as stubborn as the prince, then Taryn would need to visit his royal highness and make him talk, no matter what it took. His glance had lingered on her body earlier, and if need be, she would use that to her advantage.

THE CONQUEST

~~~

Kason gently tugged at his restraints behind his back. The humans foolishly thought that the metal would keep him from escaping, but he'd nearly bent it enough to get one of his hands free. Another hour and he could put his plan into motion.

Then and only then would he finally have the chance to show the human female her place.

Still, he wasn't about to underestimate her a second time. If she succeeded in identifying Ryven, she might torture him to get to Kason, and he couldn't have that on his conscience.

He had no idea why fate would make her a potential destined bride. Kason's ideal match would be submissive and out to please.

At least Kelderans could refuse and search out another spouse, unlike some alien races who had only one shot at a future and family. Not that he wanted to take a wife. Generals never took brides because it would risk a female's safety. If Kason did take one, it would force him into retirement, and he was damned if he'd do that without proving himself to his father first. Kason may not be the heir, but without him, his older brother wouldn't stand a chance of keeping Keldera together.

Before he could think more on how Kason and Keltor's birth order should've been the other way around, the metal door slid open. Even in silhouette, he instantly knew it was the female from before.

He schooled his expression into boredom right before she strutted into the room and he blinked.

She wore a tight-fitting top that bared her light-tan and toned midriff and the top of her breasts. The straps of weapons still crisscrossed her chest, but between her cleavage and abdomen, he barely noticed.

47

Showing that much skin would've caused a riot on Keldera, but the human's boldness didn't stop there. Her upper thighs were covered a mere few inches with a leather-like material, and the rest was bare to just below her knee, where the top of her boots started. The muscles of her abdomen matched the firmness of her legs.

There was little doubt she was a trained warrior. He almost admired her discipline to reach such a state.

Then the corner of her mouth ticked up, and he banished the thought.

When he didn't speak, the human purred, "I was right."

Before he could stop himself, Kason asked, "About what?"

She took a step closer, and it took everything he had to focus on her face and not her breasts. "You know."

She reached out and traced his cheek. Not even his determination could stop the rush of heat her touch sent through his body.

Must resist. "If all you plan to do is play games, then leave me in peace. They won't work, I assure you."

Drawing a dagger, she straddled his lap. He barely noted the blade at his throat. Her heat and scent called him to do much more than kiss her.

He would enjoy dominating her in bed.

He nearly frowned at that thought. Clearing his throat, he kept his voice even. "Humans are pests. Kissing you would be like kissing a *spladert.*"

"I have no idea what that is, but it sounds like an insult." The cool blade pressed a little harder against his throat. "I think you forget that I'm the one with the dagger."

Between the combination of the female's warm bottom on his lap and the casual way she threatened him with a blade, it took

48

a great deal of discipline to keep his markings a deep blue and not red, the color of lust.

His cock, however, was waging a tougher battle.

What the hell was wrong with him? She was everything he should hate in a female.

And yet, the idea of a woman warrior intrigued him.

It was time to surprise her and hopefully scare her away. Without temptation, he could better focus on saving his men.

Raising his knees at the same time as he tugged hard at his metal restraints, the female slid against his body as he worked his hand free. Her blade nicked his neck, but the sting was minor.

Concern flickered in her eyes, but as Kason moved one of his arms around her waist and the other to her wrist holding the dagger, the look turned into surprise. In the next second, he squeezed her hand, and the dagger clanked against the floor. He half expected someone to rush into the room, but they didn't.

The female had made a mistake in coming alone.

He tightened his hold on her waist until she was flush against his chest. "Without your blade and my restraints, you will lose. Cede defeat while you have the chance."

He half expected her to whimper and plead for her life. Instead, she smirked. "Oh, I have a few tricks left."

~~~

Taryn was grateful for the guards watching from behind the two-way mirror. So far, they were following her orders to stay put until she gave the order.

She had expected Kason to try something. What she hadn't counted on was how the feel of his skin against hers awoke every nerve in her body.

So much so she'd nearly rubbed against him.

But as her dagger clattered to the ground, her lust-haze cleared. Kason could snap her neck in two if he so wished.

Still, as she mentioned a few tricks, she played her first card and leaned over to his ear. She whispered, "What about this?"

Moving her hips against his erection, Kason sucked in a breath and pulled her away from him. Taking advantage, Taryn retrieved a small syringe from her strap and stuck it into Kason's side. She'd barely pushed the plunger when he tossed her away with a roar.

Taryn crashed onto the floor. Grunting, she quickly snapped to her feet and drew another dagger. But as Kason swung side to side in his seat before taking his head in his hands, she relaxed a fraction. The precious drug looked to be working. Good, because otherwise, Matilda would have her head for wasting the truth-telling serum; it took a year to produce one vial. As it was, it'd taken ten minutes to convince the medicine woman to give up the only one she had in stock.

Since he could be playing her, she decided to test the serum's effectiveness. "Why did you come to Jasvar?"

Never lifting his head, Kason's low voice murmured, "To look for a new colony planet."

"Just like many before you." He raised his head and gave a half-hearted glare. She shrugged. "This is my planet. As a prince, you most of all should understand protecting one's people." When he said nothing, she decided to ask what she needed to know. "I want your ship. What is the best way to take it?"

Kason clenched his jaw a second but finally gave in to the effects of the serum. His voice dripped with resentment. "Threaten my life, with proof of your power, and they will do whatever you wish."

Well, well. So the prince had been lying earlier. "One more thing—who is your second-in-command and what does he look like?"

The alien prince held out a second longer than before but finally answered, "Ryven. Silver hair and light blue skin."

That could be any number of the men they'd captured. "Does he have any identifying marks?"

Hatred burned in Kason's eyes as he bit out, "A scar on his neck."

Taryn studied the prince for a second. She had a feeling his second-in-command meant a lot to him. She could play the ruthless bitch and let him think she'd hurt Ryven. But for some reason, Kason's hatred made her stomach heavy.

Before she could talk herself out of it, she blurted, "He won't be harmed."

"Says the female who uses her body to deceive."

Any guilt she'd felt fled her body. Narrowing her eyes, she mustered every bit of steel she could and said, "I'm pretty sure you only say that because I'm a woman. Well, guess what? This isn't Keldera. I'm Taryn Demara, leader of Jasvar and the sworn protector of my people. I'll do whatever it takes to ensure their wellbeing. If a short skirt and tight top distract you, then you're not going to stand a chance against me in the long-run, your *highness*."

"If you take our ship, then you'll have a civil war on your conscience."

She frowned. "What are you talking about?"

Kason sat up a little taller. "My father is the king, but he's ailing. If my brother ascends the throne without a new colony to ease Keldera's population woes, there is a growing group who will blame the royal line of Vallen. They'll try to kill my brother and marry off my sister to their new leader. They'll do whatever is necessary, and subjects loyal to the crown will fight back."

If not for the serum, she'd say he was lying.

However, the prince was under the influence of the serum, and no one had ever lied when dosed before. Add in Kason's passion, and Taryn tended to believe him.

The civil war development must be new, since none of the Kelderan scientists on Jasvar had mentioned it.

Still, letting the ship return to Keldera, even if some of the warriors stayed on Jasvar to take wives, wouldn't solve her long-term problem.

Damn it. Taryn needed to talk with Nova and figure out what to do next. First, she needed more information about both the man and his planet. She decided to find out about the man first. "Were you planning to kill me earlier?"

"I can't kill you."

She blinked. "Because I'm a woman?"

Kason narrowed his eyes. "No. Fate is a cruel mistress."

"Clarify."

The prince resisted for a few seconds but eventually answered in a low voice, "No Kelderan can harm one of their potential destined brides."

"What are you talking about?"

He gave her a slow once over and Taryn's traitorous body heated at the look. Approval flashed in Kason's eyes. "You feel the pull too. Not even the strongest mind can completely ignore instinct, as much as I may want to."

Yet more information her scientists had withheld. "I'm not Kelderan and don't have the same instinct, but you not being able to kill me is a nice development."

THE CONQUEST

The prince's eyes turned predatory, and she crossed her arms over her chest to resist a shiver. She refused to let him know how attracted she was to him.

Kason's eyes moved to her breasts, and her heart rate kicked up. His gravelly voice was like a caress against her skin. "But make no mistake—just because I can't kill you doesn't mean I won't find a way to escape." He met her eyes again. "Just like you, I have a few tricks up my sleeve."

It had been a long time since Taryn had been challenged by a worthy adversary. "Then we'll just have to see who has the best ones." Taryn motioned a finger toward the two-way glass and took a step back from Kason. "I'm going to leave you with four of my people. They have many more questions to ask you."

As three guards and one cultural recorder came into the room, Taryn added, "And don't worry, they'll make sure you can't escape."

The guards moved to better restrain Kason, and Taryn strutted out of the room. She swore she could feel Kason's eyes on her ass.

Not that she would let it matter. She might just have a way for her people and the Kelderans to both get what they wanted, even if she didn't like it.

The thought of being stuck with the arrogant prince for the rest of her life wasn't what she thought of as a happily ever after. And yet, if she could secure an alliance between the two worlds and ensure her people's survival, it might just be worth it.

However, before she could talk herself completely into it, Taryn needed a drink and her best friend. Nova would dissect her suggestion and tell her if it really was their best shot at saving the people of Jasvar.

Chapter Five

Taryn sipped her wine and asked her friend, "So? I'm still waiting for your honest opinion."

Taryn and Nova sat on the floor inside Taryn's quarters. They had started the practice of wine and floor sitting as teenagers and had carried on the tradition. It was the only time Taryn could be honest and open without everyone watching her.

Nova tapped her chin. "It's much more feasible than trying to ransom the prince in exchange for the ship, especially since we have no idea how to control that thing." Nova took a drink. "Although we'd need to keep the other warriors here until an alliance is finalized as an incentive for the Kelderans to accept your proposal."

"I was hoping you'd say it was a ridiculous idea."

"Oh, come on. The almighty prince isn't hard on the eyes, even if he does try your patience. According to Zelig, you just need him to kiss you to initiate the whole destined bride process. While having a child is the final stage in Kelderan marriage, a kiss is binding enough that he'd have to look after you for a week. The next step is having unprotected sex once, and then he'll have to protect you for the next two years."

"That runs the risk of pregnancy, and if he acts like a barbarian now, I can only imagine what he'll be like if I get pregnant with his child."

The Conquest

Nova leaned forward. "Ah, but you see, he'll have to put up with you. It's the law. That means if he makes your life hell, you can do the same."

"Isn't there some sort of law against that? The Kelderans don't exactly seem to grant equal rights to women."

"Zelig didn't mention that. But since Kason is a prince, his father probably doesn't want to create a scandal, especially if what you said about a possible civil war is true. I imagine you can have the run of the palace, as long as the public doesn't catch wind of it."

"I hate your logical thinking." Nova winked and Taryn sighed. "But in all honesty, just the thought of leaving Jasvar makes my eye twitch. Spending time in space with a bunch of aliens who view females as lesser? I'm not sure I can stop myself from gelding one or three of them."

Nova snorted. "I'd love to see you press a dagger against the almighty balls of a Kelderan warrior. They wouldn't know what hit them."

"Be serious, Nova."

"Fine, fine. Although, don't rule out the very real threat of being surrounded by strangers who mistrust you. Kason will be the key to your survival, although relying on someone else to take care of you isn't exactly your strong point. Establishing your place with the other warriors and crew will mean not belittling Kason in front of the others. You could try fluttering your eyelashes a little. That might help."

Her friend batted her eyelashes and Taryn threw a pillow at Nova, who easily dodged it. "If it were only fluttering my eyelashes, I could manage that. Unfortunately, I need to kiss him and then have sex within a week to keep his protection and the possibility of an alliance alive."

Rolling her eyes, Nova leaned against the nearest pillow. "You don't need to sound as if sex with the hot, muscled alien is such a bad thing."

"Yes, he's attractive. But by doing this, I'm giving up my future, Nova. I'll do it, of course, as it's my job as Jasvar's leader. But a small part of me is sad I'll never have a family of my own."

"You might, you never know."

She shook her head. "I don't imagine things ending well for me and the prince, even if I end up pregnant. As soon as he realizes I won't morph into a compliant wife, he'll probably keep his distance or try to keep me under lock and key. Even if he doesn't, there's still the issue of me negotiating a deal and making it back to Jasvar at all."

"Of course they'll bring you back. If the Kelderans agree to share the planet and to respect our laws when they're in our settlements, they'll need you here to make sure it happens."

Taryn drank some more wine. "I guess we have their honor to thank for not just killing us outright."

"According to Zelig, they only kill women who murder first."

"Then I guess I'll have to be careful with my dagger and not nick an artery."

Nova snorted. "There's the Taryn I know and love. Stop with all the doubting. This is probably the easiest solution we can come up with. Scratch that, I know it is. I've run through every scenario and this one requires the least amount of luck." Nova raised her glass toward Taryn. "And all because of our great leader."

"If it gives us long-term survival, then the sacrifice is worth it, especially if the Kelderan scientists can find a way to combat the doom virus."

The Conquest

Setting down her wine glass, Nova planted her feet on the ground and propped her chin on her knees. "Although there's a much more important question—will a virgin be able to handle the almighty prince's cock?"

Taryn sputtered her wine and barely prevented herself from choking. "Please tell me you haven't been peeking at the warriors' penises."

"I may or may not have spied on a few of the scientists shortly after their capture ten years ago. Let's just say that if Zelig wasn't happily married, I would've gone after him myself."

If she were acting the part of the leader, Taryn would've changed the subject. But since it was just her and Nova, she whispered, "The Kelderans don't have barbs or anything weird, do they? I know a few of the alien species do, and it's supposed to feel good, but I'm not sure I can handle it."

Nova tsked. "And here I thought you might be a bit adventurous in bed."

"Nova," she hissed.

Her friend winked. "Hey, I'm still holding out for a unique alien myself. Although if this plan goes through and we share the planet with Kelderans, I guess I'll have to settle for long cocks as the Kelderans don't have any extra bells and whistles in that department. If you give me a play-by-play of your time with Kason, then I might make a bigger effort to nab one of my own."

Taryn grunted. "If it happens at all, I expect it to be short and to the point. That seems to be his highness's style."

"Speaking of his highness, I think you should break the news before the serum completely wears off. That way, you'll know for sure if he thinks it'll work."

Standing up, Taryn placed her glass on the side table. "You're right. I guess I should change into something a little more convincing."

Nova studied her a second before saying, "No, keep your nightgown on. If you stand in front of a light, it'll show him a little of what he could have if he said yes."

"Nova, that's not how I do things. Besides, he was intrigued with my summer hunting outfit. I'll use that again."

"All joking aside, just be careful."

"Of course. As humiliating and shocking as it may be to have the guards witness my proposal, I'll have them watch me from behind the glass."

"And me. I'm going to be there too."

Even though Nova would tease her endlessly later, she would be glad of her best friend's presence. "Right, then let's hurry. We have maybe an hour left before the potion wears off and then we'll never know what he truly thinks."

~~~

Kason lay strapped to a bed and was torn between wanting to punish the human leader and to rip off her clothes and take her from behind.

Grunting, he blamed his sexual desires on the strange drug they'd administered. He'd resisted a potential destined bride before without blinking an eye and yet, the female's eyes and curves kept flashing inside his mind. Her confidence in the skimpy outfit from before was oddly appealing.

Then he remembered how he'd been interrogated and strapped to the bed and all positive thoughts of the female fled. His main goal was to find a way to escape. Even though he'd shared more about his people than he wanted, he had a feeling the Jasvarians weren't capable of space travel. He'd confirm it before leaving, but if they were planet-bound, they posed no real threat.

Besides, he intended to find a way to capture all the human descendants and still take the planet as his own. A Kelderan civil war wouldn't erupt on his watch. It was his duty to ensure that when his brother, Keltor, ascended the throne, the planet was in one piece.

Footsteps sounded outside his door, and Kason wished he could tell them to leave him alone. However, the door opened, and the light from the hall outlined the form of Taryn Demara in her alluring outfit. It wasn't hard for him to imagine the female leading a charge against some threat and he wondered how many other female warriors the planet possessed. Not that he expected any of them to be as delectable as their leader.

Focusing on his anger at being drugged, he kept his lust in check and barked out, "What do you want?"

She opened something in her hands, and a soft glow filled the room, highlighting the fullness of her lips and the confident tilt of her chin. Her demeanor was vastly different from any Kelderan female he'd met, with the possibility of his unruly sister, Kalahn. He put his sister's defiance down to being spoiled by their father after their mother's death.

The human moved to stand next to his bed. The light danced across her exposed abdomen and the sudden urge to lick her skin coursed through his body.

Thankfully she spoke before his thoughts could deteriorate any further. "I have a proposal of how we both can get what we want."

"And how do you know what I want? That wasn't one of your questions."

"I won't apologize for the interrogation. I expect you would've done the same with an unknown entity."

She was correct, not that he'd admit it. "I suspect I'll reject your idea, but what is it?"

Smiling, she placed a hand on her hip. The movement caused light to fall on the tops of her breasts. They weren't too big or small. They'd fit nicely in his palms.

Resisting a frown, he focused on the human's reply, "It may not be as disgusting as you think, given how you look at me." He kept his face expressionless and Taryn snorted. "You'll have to do more than that to fool me, Prince."

"Hurry up and tell me the plan."

She shrugged. "You're going to take me to Keldera to negotiate an alliance between our people and we can share the planet."

"And why would I do that when I can just take the planet by force?"

Rolling her eyes, she set her glowing basket on the small table next to his bed. "You seem to forget I have you in captivity." He grunted, and she searched his eyes before continuing, "But think about it—you find a planet for your people to live on, prevent civil war, reach out to Earth about an alliance and you get a destined bride to boot. What do you think of that?"

If not for the truth serum, he would've said the idea was ridiculous. And yet, the thought of taking Taryn to bed and making her scream in pleasure wasn't abhorrent.

Quite the contrary, his instinct screamed to agree to her plan.

Then logic returned to his brain. "There's just one problem. If I take you as a bride, I must give up my command. I will no longer make decisions about your people or what to do with Jasvar." He chose his next words carefully so as to be truthful but misleading. "Once I'm safe aboard the ship and the truth is discovered, my successor could decide to storm the planet by force."

"Just because we don't have the same fancy technology as you doesn't mean we don't have ways to defend ourselves. I'm confident we could defeat you again. Besides, we don't have to make it known right away. You seem like the type of guy who can keep a secret."

"Perhaps."

The lack of uncertainty in her eyes made Kason wonder what else she had planned. For a female, she was turning out to be an interesting adversary.

Taryn spoke up again. "So? What is your honest opinion about my proposal? I rather think it makes you out to be a hero for your people. I'm sure that will help your brother, come succession time."

"You were paying attention earlier."

She raised her brows. "You don't have to sound so surprised. Just because I lack a penis doesn't mean I can't listen and think for myself."

"Say we try your plan. You will have to adapt to Kelderan customs rather quickly. No bride of mine will be wearing an outfit like that."

"I'll promise not to stab anyone, but I'm not about to completely change my ways to fit your idea of normal. There need to be compromises for us both to make things work." She leaned down and it took everything he had to keep his gaze on her face. "However, all of your warriors will stay in captivity here until you return me to Jasvar."

Rather than waste time threatening her, he merely stated, "Then you're not stupid."

Anger flashed in her eyes and she leaned down until her mouth was only a few inches from his. "Call me stupid again and I'll stop asking and start taking."

As the female's hot breath caressed his lips and her scent filled his nose, Kason's decades of control slipped. "Stupid female."

"Then you leave me no choice."

Taryn kissed him.

~~~

Forcing Kason's hand had never been part of her plan, but as he taunted her on purpose and she leaned close, all she could think about was the alien's warm, full lips a scant few inches from hers. His masculine scent only made her wonder what his mouth tasted like.

When she gave him one last chance to act civil and at least pretend he wanted to discuss the future, the prince, of course, pushed her further. She wouldn't back down. After all, she needed Kason to take her to Keldera.

Not that she wasn't a little curious for herself, too. Taryn leaned down and kissed him.

At first Kason stilled, but once she lightly nibbled his bottom lip, he opened his mouth and sought out her tongue.

He wasted no time stroking hers before exploring the inside of her mouth. His taste was unlike anything she'd experienced before; a mixture of spicy and sweet and definitely not human. She wondered if his skin would taste the same.

Placing her hands on his solid chest, she broke the kiss. However, before she could move to Kason's neck, he murmured, "Devious female."

His words were like a slap to the face. Digging her nails into his chest, she looked him dead in the eye and mustered every bit of steel she possessed. "You brought this on yourself. The next step is yours. I can either force one of your pilots to message your ship and let them know you've found your bride. Or, you can agree to my terms, I'll release you, we can keep the bride part a secret, and you can radio your people, provided I'm in the room with you. Either way, you're stuck with me for at least a week, and I know you can't hurt me."

"If you're so sure of that, then release my bonds."

She tsked. "There's a lot you could do without hurting me, Prince."

"I prefer Kason."

His tone signaled that maybe the alien prince didn't want to be a prince at all.

Tucking that piece of information away for later, she added, "Fine, Kason. What do you want to do?"

"It will take a few days just to get to Keldera and maybe a few more to set up negotiations. It will take more than a week. What makes you think I won't disavow you and toss you to my soldiers after that?"

Taryn frowned. "Honestly? I don't know if you would or not. But it's a risk I'm willing to take if it means my people have a chance at survival."

Kason studied her a second before replying, "With all the talk of saving your people, no one has said why you need saving in the first place. Tell me the problem and I'll give you my answer about the next step."

She could walk away and try to contact his ship on her own. Yet if she was going to board his ship and put her life at risk, then honesty may earn her some brownie points. "There's a virus on this planet that attacks male embryos in the womb and causes miscarriages, which skews our population female. We've only managed to survive this long because of careful records and convincing alien males to stay on our planet. I want to find a way to stop this virus, but Jasvar lacks the technology to do so."

"You're originally humans from Earth, correct?" Taryn nodded and Kason continued, "Then why would they put you here with no technology or a way to fend for yourself? Were all of your ancestors originally criminals?"

"This isn't a prison planet. The original reports all declared Jasvar a safe environment for a colony. No one could've known about the doom virus until a pregnant woman stayed on the planet long-term."

"How long ago was the colony started?"

"Two hundred years ago."

"You've been resourceful," he stated.

"That almost sounds like a compliment."

"More like honesty."

For a split second, Taryn felt guilty for drugging Kason into telling the truth. But she quickly pushed it aside. She'd done what needed to be done, period. "So, what is your answer? Are you going to go along with my plan and cooperate?"

"None of my warriors have been harmed?" She shook her head. "Then I will contact my ship and set up the arrangement. However, if you want my protection for more than a week, you're going to share your body with me in the next seven days, as is our custom."

As his eyes perused her breasts, Taryn's nipples tightened. She hated the fact Kason could see how his gaze affected her, but she pretended not to notice. "I've done a lot worse to get what I want."

His heated gaze met hers. "Then we'll see if you're as confident and interesting in bed as you are with your clothes on."

Clearing her throat, Taryn picked up the glow basket and retreated a few steps. If she weren't careful, she might do something stupid, such as torture Kason's body with her touch while he was tied up.

Yes, the alien prince definitely did something to her brain. Maybe he had strange pheromones that triggered horniness. "I'll come back in the morning and we can contact your ship then. That way, I can prepare tonight and be ready to leave as soon as possible."

"Just make sure to wear something less revealing. I may not have chosen you as my bride, but I will fight any male who tries to touch you now that you are mine. That will give away our secret, which will leave Jasvar at the mercy of my second-in-command."

"I belong to no one, Prince. I'll decide for myself what to wear."

With that, Taryn exited the room. All she wanted to do was flee to her quarters to set things up for her departure, but a grinning Nova popped out of the observation room and said, "I think he likes you."

Taryn never stopped walking. "I'd hardly call not wanting to kill me for kissing him as liking me."

"Aw, but you see, the truth serum wore off about ten minutes ago."

Her step faltered. "What? It should've lasted another fifteen minutes."

"The time had been recorded wrong and one of the guards corrected it. Everything he said during the last half of your conversation was of his own free will. I think he may not kill you on his ship, especially if you 'share your body' with him, as he put it."

"I'm not taking any chances. I need to prep Zorana on everything before I leave. I hope you and her can work together to run the planet in my absence."

"I'll try. She's just stubborn, demanding, and so damn confident. In short, she's like you without a sense of humor."

"Why do you think I've been grooming her the past few years?"

"You could've picked me."

"I love you, Nova, but while you're a genius with strategy, you're too emotional to lead the planet. It involves a lot of decisions that may cause some to hate you, and you wouldn't like that."

Nova sighed. "I know, and I don't think I could handle the hatred. Still, I'll do whatever it takes to help Zorana, but just know it's temporary. I fully expect you to come back and save us all."

"I hope so. After all, that's my plan."

Her friend elbowed her in the side. "Provided you don't fall in love with an alien prince and decide to live happily ever after on a different planet."

"Right, because Prince Charming is so hard to resist," she drawled.

"At least give him a chance, Taryn. While you might be doing this to help Jasvar, I think a small part of you is doing it for yourself, too."

"Look, Nova, I have a lot to do and not much time to do it. Talking about the prince will have to wait. We'll have plenty of time once I return."

"Just make sure that you do," Nova stated.

"I plan on it."

As Taryn waved good-bye to her friend and walked down the corridor, she pushed aside thoughts of her kiss with Kason and their upcoming naked time to focus on travel preparations. She'd find out soon enough if the prince had been truthful.

Chapter Six

Kason completed his latest meditation session and opened his eyes to watch the door. His warrior's instinct was on high alert in case Taryn had been bluffing earlier and did send someone to interrogate him further.

However, his primal instinct wanted something else. No matter how many times he meditated, the instant he closed his eyes, Taryn's form flashed into his brain, and he'd proceed to undress her slowly.

While every Kelderan male knew the basics of destined brides and the process of claiming, the real-life experience was a lot more intense than he'd realized. Lust coursed through his body, true, but the desire to protect the human against every other male or enemy was also prevalent. It was almost as if he wouldn't be able to think straight until he had her warm, willing body under him, with her swearing off any other male.

If not for the fact he would lose his command as soon as the others found out about Taryn, he would look forward to having a female of his own to tame.

He could keep the secret for a time, but not forever. Even if he could no longer command warriors in the defense forces, he would coordinate the royal guards. His brother and sister would need protecting, especially if he returned to Keldera with a human bride. Not everyone would accept her.

The Conquest

Why do I care? He would use her as a means to an end, nothing more.

The door opened and his heart rate picked up at the sight of Taryn Demara wearing a flowing, floor-length dress. "You heeded my order."

She raised an eyebrow. "It's a tactical move only, I assure you. Men tend to underestimate me when I wear a dress and do this."

Fear filled her eyes as she gripped her skirts. He grunted. "Stop it. Fear doesn't suit you."

Taryn dropped the act and smiled. "I thought Kelderans liked submissive females."

"Fear should never be part of marriage. Any male who causes his female to look that way is hauled away and questioned. If there's proof he struck his female, he's executed."

"That is a rather harsh punishment, but I must say I approve."

"Females need our protection. A Kelderan male must never forget that."

Taryn rolled her eyes. "That part I do disagree with." She lifted her skirt to reveal her toned calf, knee, and then upper thigh, where she had a dagger strapped against her skin. "I believe in defending myself. All women on this planet know the basics of dagger-wielding." She lowered her skirt, and he nearly growled for her to lift it again. However, she continued before he could. "But enough about who defends who. Are you ready to contact your ship?"

"Unless you plan to carry the bed out of here, you need to undo my straps."

He waited to see if she would release him. For all that she maddened him and challenged him, hell, even tricked him, he'd made it clear he'd never hurt her. The only question was whether she would believe it or not.

Taryn approached his bed, never severing eye contact. The woman was as hard to read as one of his soldiers.

Good thing Kason enjoyed a challenge.

Rather than think about where that thought had come from—she had forced him into taking her as a bride after all—he watched her hand as her fingers brushed against his wrist. They were slightly rough, no doubt from her training. The difference from the soft hands of a Kelderan female sent a thrill through his body.

Her voice was stern when she finally spoke again. "I have several guards ready to take you down if you try anything. Are we clear?"

"You have my word that I will not harm you."

Taryn undid the buckle around his forearm first before moving to the metal bands on his wrist. Each whisper against his skin sent blood rushing to his cock. Only through thinking of the safety of his men and drawing on his years of discipline as a soldier did he keep his markings a dark blue and his cock from going rock-hard.

When his wrist was free, the female merely stood and waited. He stared back.

In the next instant, she danced her fingers against his ribcage, but he restrained himself from moving.

Taryn sighed. "It was worth a shot."

"If a Kelderan warrior can't control his body when tickled, then he would break easily under an enemy's interrogation."

She moved to the other side of his bed and worked on his other arm. "I could understand if you were in battle or on a mission, but it's just me here in this room."

"What about those watching us from the other side of the mirror?"

"There is no one there."

"If not, then you were reckless."

She smiled. "I have people waiting in the hall. If I screamed or failed to check in at the appointed time, they'd come rushing in here."

"Good. I prefer not to have a reckless bride."

"That almost sounds like a compliment." Finishing the two restraints on his other wrist, Kason sat upright, and Taryn moved to his leg. "Glad to see you're on board about having a bride at all."

"My condition still stands, human. You must tell me now that you'll share your body, of your own free will, during the next week. If you do, I'll swear an oath to bring you back to this planet in one piece."

"If I didn't already agree to your demand, you can bet I wouldn't be here, Prince. Although if you expect me to pay up now, then I may as well leave right this second."

"I won't insult your intelligence. Of course you'd wait until we're out of orbit on the way to Keldera. That's what any warrior would do."

"Oh, so I'm a warrior now? Make sure to introduce me that way to your men."

"Being a representative of a planet is a much higher prestige, and it will better ensure your safety."

"Given how you wanted to take over Jasvar by force, I'm surprised to hear that."

He shrugged. "The situation has changed. Originally, we thought you unthreatening. I know better now and adjusted my tactics accordingly."

"Fine, I'll be the representative of Jasvar. It might work to my advantage that way."

He could see the wheels turning in her head and he wanted to ask her what she was thinking.

However, he would have plenty of time to better know his bride-slash-adversary onboard the Kelderan ship. The sooner he was on his way, the sooner his men would be freed.

As Taryn undid one of his legs, he went to work on the other as he said, "If you wish to go at all, then we need to hurry. If too much more time passes, my people will send another contingent down to the planet's surface. They will be less understanding than I was."

Taryn snorted. "Can't say I want to see that." She motioned toward the door. "Come. I'll take you to your shuttle and we can get this show on the road."

He had no idea why she would describe her life and the fate of her planet as a "show," but Kason didn't want to waste more time asking about her strange culture.

His bride opened the door to reveal five guards standing outside—three males and two females. Kason could take them if he wished, but he was anxious to reach out to his ship in orbit. He may not have wanted a bride, but now that he had one, he was determined to keep her alive and safe.

As they made their way down a hallway, he watched his female's hips sway. He loved the way skirts hid just enough of a female's body that he could have fun imagining her curves underneath. Since Kason had seen Taryn nearly naked, the intrigue was lost, but he rather enjoyed watching the hips that would soon be his.

The human female had no idea what was coming.

THE CONQUEST

~~~

Taryn felt Kason's eyes on her butt. He wasn't the first man to stare, but his gaze sent a tingling sensation across her ass cheeks and between her thighs. She still believed he had some kind of special power over her libido.

She would be lying if she said she wasn't looking forward to sex with the prince. Taryn had spent most of her adult life wondering what it would be like to have a man above her. Maybe once with Kason would sate her curiosity and she'd be able to concentrate solely on the upcoming visit to Keldera.

Yes, she'd get it out of the way sooner. That would also ensure her safety. As far as she understood it, sex all but sealed the deal between a Kelderan male and his destined bride, at least until two years had passed with no children. Then the male could break it off.

In two years, Taryn should have her alliance and maybe even a solution for the doom virus. Provided she didn't get pregnant with the required unprotected first time, Kason could do whatever he wished then.

Making the final turn, they approached the door that led to a structure built adjacent to the mountain. Since the shuttle's communication systems wouldn't work inside so many feet of rock, it was ready to be pulled partially into the special room when needed.

Taryn stopped at one side of the large room, and Kason and the guards did the same. She signaled, and her people scurried to haul out the shuttle. Kason's deep voice stated, "Keeping the shuttle inside was a smart move."

She glanced up at him. "How did you know…?"

"You don't seem the type to waste time bringing me to a pointless location. Hence, the shuttle must be coming here." As two wide doors creaked open and six oxen-like creatures came into view, Kason nodded. "There it is. I'll contact my ship as soon as it's out."

She faced him. "Don't try any funny business. I'm going to be standing over your shoulder, with a few guards off to the side. I want you to speak in CEL with someone who understands it, so I can monitor your words."

He raised his brows. "And if I refuse?"

"I'll shoot you full of blow darts myself once the call ends."

"I almost would like to see you try."

"So, what will it be?"

He leaned down to whisper, "We'll save the play for later." Taryn's cheeks flushed as he stood up to his full height. "My second-in-command, Thorin, understands enough of the language to make it work. However, you're going to have to learn Kelderan if you're to survive amongst my people."

"We'll cross that bridge when we come to it." The front half of the shuttle was in view and the oxen-like creatures stopped. "Let's get this over with."

"Too bad we're hiding the fact you are my bride because if we weren't, you would need to hang all over me. It's the Kelderan custom."

She scrutinized him a second before drawling, "I'm sure it is."

"I'm being truthful. If a male accepts a bride, she wants to make as much a claim on him as he does on her."

Interesting. Maybe there was more to the Kelderan way of life than merely a man dictating how everything should run. She'd have to look into it. "Good thing it's our secret on board your ship for as long as possible, then. But in order to keep it that way, at least initially, speak in CEL and I'll keep my mouth shut."

THE CONQUEST

They arrived at the stairs to the craft and ascended. Since she had no idea where he needed to go, once they reached the interior, she stepped aside. "After you."

Without a word, Kason moved deeper inside. The sound of the guards trailing them helped to keep her heart rate under control. If she acted nervously, her guards would grow anxious and Taryn would never allow that to happen.

Kason stopped at a large, flat panel on the wall with another smaller panel below. After punching the lower panel a few times with his forefinger, the lights whirred to life and the screens filled with strange writing and a variety of shapes. If she was to learn the Kelderan language, she had her work cut out for her.

The prince looked over at her. "I'm going to send a message now. You need to stand next to me and look as leader-like as possible. It'll be hard enough for my people to believe a female can be in charge."

"I'm positive there are other worlds ruled by women."

"Perhaps, but it's easy to forget when you want to reinforce your traditions."

Kason the philosopher. Who would've known?

She cleared her throat and stood tall. "Ready, Kason."

"You must call me highness or they will see it as a sign of disrespect."

She rolled her eyes. "Your highness, then."

He nodded as he tapped a few more times on the panel. About thirty seconds later, the screen turned into a picture of a Kelderan with light blue skin and black hair. He said something she couldn't understand and Kason replied. She pinched his back, and Kason switched to CEL. "As I was saying, the Jasvarian leader only understands CEL. We'll use it for now."

75

The other Kelderan frowned. "Why disappear so long with no word?"

The other alien's accent was thicker and his grasp on CEL wasn't as good as Kason's. Still, he knew a hell of a lot more of CEL than she did of Kelderan.

Kason replied, "I was distracted. This female is actually the leader of Jasvar, and her people hold our warriors hostage. I wish to take her to Keldera to negotiate a settlement treaty."

The other alien fell back into Kelderan. Judging by his rushed, clipped tone, he wasn't happy.

Kason said something back in the same language before adding in CEL, "She has my promise to take her to Keldera and negotiate a settlement. Once this is done, we will finally have a planet to colonize."

Taryn waited with bated breath. With one move, the other alien could merely sever the connection and launch an attack on Jasvar. If he fired any type of weaponry from the sky, her people wouldn't stand a chance.

The other man finally spoke up again. "Fine. Go to original landing area. Pick you up there one hour."

The two Kelderans stared at one another for a few seconds, probably having a nonverbal conversation she couldn't understand. Once Kason nodded, the screen turned black. "Well? Did you two just plot my demise?"

"No. Thorin isn't happy, but he'll listen to my orders. However, we need to be careful. If he finds out you're my bride, Thorin will assume command, and he won't be as understanding as me."

If Kason was the understanding one, Taryn might be in over her head.

Not that she'd give up. "Let's finish the last-minute preparations and head to the site before he changes his mind, then."

Standing up, Kason met her gaze. "You may be leader here and do as you please, but onboard my ship, don't wander or be too defiant. They may decide sacrificing our warriors is worth the cost if they could contain you and use you as their own bargaining chip."

She searched his eyes. "What about your vow?"

"I will still see it through. However, not even I can defeat an entire ship of Kelderans on my own."

"And here I thought you were the mighty general prince," she drawled.

He leaned close enough that the heat of his breath caressed her cheek. "Keep pushing me, Taryn. I'll enjoy taking my payback when you're in my bed."

It was the first time he'd said her name aloud, and the deep, husky voice made her want to lean closer until her body rested against his. Of course, she wasn't going to give in so easily. "Just wait, Prince. I'll have my payback, too."

With that, she strutted down the corridor and out of the shuttle. As her guards and Kason followed, she couldn't help but smile. She was one step closer to helping her people, yes, but she was also enjoying Kason more than she could've imagined. Pushing him to the brink while onboard the ship would be icing on the cake.

Taryn picked up her pace. The next however many weeks would be unknown and hence a little scary, but with Kason on her side, she could handle it. She just needed to ensure she didn't give away their secret. The other Kelderans wouldn't be required to protect her.

Chapter Seven

As Kason waited near the fake burned-out village from his first landing, he looked over at Taryn talking with her companion-slash-advisor. The other human female was apparently in charge of technology. Judging from her pale, slightly overweight frame, she wouldn't be much of a guard. In fact, she might end up a liability.

However, no amount of reasoning had changed Taryn's mind. No matter what he'd said, the human wasn't going to allow Kason to be her only guard.

That irked him a bit.

If the situation were reversed, he would act the same way. However, prying her away from her female companion was one more obstacle he had to overcome in order to get her alone and naked.

Thorin's words earlier, about merely taking the female prisoner and forcing her to agree to hand over her planet, still remained fresh in his mind. It only reminded him of how much he needed to keep the secret about Taryn being his bride from the crew. If Thorin took over the ship's command, Kason might lose his bride and the diplomatic victory over Jasvar.

Not only that, he wanted to eventually reach out to the Earth Colony Alliance and to do that, he needed Taryn's people. As it was, a large amount of Kelderans didn't want anything to do with the ECA. But as the alliance continued to grow, Kason didn't want his people to be on the opposing side. His warriors would fight until their last breath, but any good commander would know that one planet could rarely win against the might of dozens.

Taryn's guard, a female named Evaine, spoke louder than before, garnering his attention. "This is a dream come true, Taryn. The knowledge I gain aboard this ship could help us long-term, even if the negotiations fail."

Kason grunted. "If the treaty fails, your new knowledge won't help you."

Evaine raised her brows. "We'll see about that. Some of our older technology has proven useful against other visitors."

Taryn stepped between the pair. "Let's not waste time arguing. Look, the shuttle has entered the atmosphere."

Looking up, he watched the silver ship grow larger. "As much as it pains you to do so, let me do the talking."

Taryn sighed. "I know, I know, it'll take some time for them to grow accustomed to a female doing anything but batting her eyelashes."

"Don't underestimate a Kelderan female. Insulting one will bring its own troubles."

His bride's brows raised at that, but the shuttle landed and kept her from saying anything. Once the hatch opened and the stairs extended to the ground, Kason placed a hand on Taryn's lower back. She tried to hide it, but he heard her intake of breath. Knowing his touch affected her gave him ideas of how to make her behave in public.

They met one of the pilots and a higher-ranked warrior at the bottom of the stairs. Kason nodded and spoke in Kelderan. "This is Taryn Demara, the leader of Jasvar, and her advisor,

Evaine Benoit. They have the protection of the Royal House of Vallen. Ensure you don't tread on that claim."

"Yes, your highness," they both murmured.

"Then let's depart as soon as possible. Everyone file in ahead of us. I want to ensure no one breaks my word about leaving the planet peacefully."

The warriors were trained and filed inside the ship. He switched languages and whispered to the two females, "Thank you for not defying me yet."

"The day is still young," Taryn murmured before ascending the stairs.

Once Evaine followed her leader, Kason entered the ship and sealed up the hatches. There was no turning back.

~~~

Taryn drank in the pink skies of Jasvar for as long as possible. Once the shuttle's hatch sealed shut, she stood a little taller. No matter what may happen with the Kelderans, she would find a way back home.

She spotted Evaine examining a panel. Taking her head of technology might not seem like the most practical choice at first, but Jasvar needed to learn as much as they could about their possible cohabitants. Evaine was quick with patterns, electronics, and languages. She would probably pick up Kelderan before Taryn did. And judging from the recent conversation Kason had with his shipmates, the fluid, tonal language would take her some time.

Kason ran a finger down her arm, and she kept her face impassive. "Your highness had better be careful."

"And I think the Jasvarian leader needs to follow my lead."

If she gave in to his possessive touch now, Kason would keep doing it, so she stepped over to Evaine. "I think it's time for you to give us a crash course in your ship's computer systems."

"For a society that lives mostly computer-free, I'm surprised at the request."

Evaine scrunched up her nose. "I've taken apart and rebuilt every computer I could get my hands on over the years. I was seven at my first successful attempt. I'll pick it up just fine."

Taryn bit her lip to keep from smiling. After a few days, Evaine might know more about the Kelderan system than Kason. She repeated, "The computers?"

Kason grunted. "This way. The ride back to the ship won't take long, so hurry up."

He motioned for them to follow and Taryn fell in step next to him. She whispered, "Is there anyone I should watch out for?"

"Not on the shuttle, but on board the ship, yes."

She nodded. "Point them out to me, if you can."

"Don't worry, I'll protect you."

Kason guided them into a small room and the door slid shut behind them. Not wanting to waste their precious time, Taryn avoided an argument about knowledge helping her to survive and sat down in front of a large panel, as did Evaine. Kason touched a few keys and spoke again in Kelderan. The computer answered in the same language. Kason looked to her. "State your name and rank."

"Taryn Demara, leader of Jasvar."

He motioned to Evaine. "The same."

"Evaine Benoit, head of Jasvarian technology and advisor to Taryn Demara."

The computer's flat voice answer in CEL. "Access and language preference set."

Kason said, "The AI system both here and onboard the main ship will answer your questions in your own language. Preference your request with 'computer' in your first string of requests and she'll answer, provided you're granted clearance."

"We won't have clearance?" Evaine asked.

Kason answered, "That depends on how things go."

Taryn could tell Evaine was going to argue, so she changed the topic. "How does the computer know CEL?"

The corner of Kason's mouth twitched. That was the closest thing to a smile she'd seen. "Ask the computer yourself."

Taryn looked at the panel and felt strange talking to an inanimate object, but asked, "Computer, how do you know CEL?"

"I am programmed with all languages known to Keldera."

Evaine leaned forward. "What is your processing capacity?"

As the computer listed off a bunch of words and numbers Taryn didn't understand, she had time to note the pure joy in Evaine's eyes. Taryn was glad she'd chosen her to come, even if Zorana and the others had suggested taking a male instead.

It wasn't long before something clicked outside the ship. Kason interjected at the next pause in Evaine's incessant questioning. "Computer, cease answering."

"Acknowledged," the computer stated.

Kason bowed toward the door. "We're here, leader of Jasvar." He glanced up. "Whatever you do, don't lose your nerve. Weakness will only cause complications during the journey."

Taryn stood tall and resisted the urge to palm the dagger under her dress. "Believe me, I know what's at stake."

"Good," he said before leading them out of the room and to the same place where they'd entered before. Taking a deep breath, Taryn followed Kason down the stairs. When the giant cargo bay came into view, she nearly faltered.

The room was bigger than the largest cave in the entire Jasvarian settlement. The ceiling ran so high she could barely make out where it ended. Doors and walkways lined the outer edges, all leading to a few main tubes that carried people up and down.

The lights bounced off the metal-looking sides, but none of the people walking around seemed to notice. Although, people might not be the right word as all she saw were men. Did Kelderans really not allow their women to travel? That seemed problematic on many levels, unless the Kelderans had complete control over their sexual urges. Or, maybe they didn't care about the gender of their partners. Something else she added to her list to find out.

A group of tall, shirtless men and one cloaked figure walked toward them. A quick glance at Kason's face and she noticed the slightest frown between his brows. He barked something in Kelderan and the cloaked figure tossed back their hood. Or, rather, *her* hood.

While the young woman was clothed from toe to her neckline in a flowing white dress, a few dark blue markings peeked out around her neck. Her long, dark blue hair and golden skin tone reminded Taryn of Kason.

When the woman shrugged and rattled off what she assumed was an excuse, Kason fell silent. He finally muttered something and then switched to CEL. "Pardon the interruption. It seems my sister has been hiding aboard the ship since our departure and was only discovered whilst I was away."

The female smiled at Taryn. "Forgive my brother's manners. My name is Kalahn, the sole princess of Keldera."

Interesting. Despite Kason's expression, Taryn smiled at Kalahn. "I'm Taryn Demara, leader of Jasvar, and this is my advisor, Evaine."

Kalahn's eyes widened. "A female leader. I had heard they existed, but have never met one."

Kason put out an arm. "Enough. Taryn didn't come to our ship for your amusement, Kalahn. She is here on important business."

The Kelderan male from the screen call earlier, Thorin, spoke up in broken CEL. "Take them to quarters and meet in one hour."

Kason nodded. "Taryn, this is Thorin, my second-in-command."

Taryn and Thorin nodded at each other, and Taryn carefully kept her expression neutral. However, Thorin's clenched jaw and fierce gaze told her he didn't want her aboard the ship.

While tempted to ask Thorin a question, Kason continued before she could say anything. "Thanks to my sister's foibles, it looks as if you'll be keeping Kalahn company as well. All three females will share a room. That way, it'll be easier to protect you from the males."

Eyeing Kason's sister, Taryn decided she might be able to learn more information about both Keldera and Kason from the princess. "Good idea."

Kason studied her before motioning to the door. "Come. We'll be departing soon, and the speed of our ship may be disconcerting to one who hasn't experienced space flight."

Evaine rubbed her hands together. "I look forward to it. Maybe I can even watch the crew fly the ship."

Thorin barked, "No. You guest, but with limits."

Kason said something in Kelderan before placing a hand on Taryn's back. "Come with me and remain silent."

She was tempted to tell him to stuff it, but since she would have some time to talk with his sister at the end of it, she nodded. "Fine."

As they made their way out of the large, cavernous cargo space, Taryn took in as many details as possible. It might take a few days, but she intended to learn the layout of the ship in case she needed to escape or hide. Kason may welcome her because he had to, but judging by Thorin and the other warriors' looks of disdain, not everyone would do so.

Taryn wasn't naïve. At the end of the day, she needed to be able to protect herself.

~~~

Kason left Taryn and Evaine with his sister and headed for the main conference room.

Kalahn sneaking aboard the ship was inexcusable. Once they were back home, Kason would speak to his father about keeping Kalahn in line. His father's indulgence needed to stop. Kalahn was starting to think she could do whatever she wanted, which was dangerous.

Her sharing a room with Taryn probably wasn't going to help matters, but any female aboard a warrior ship spelled trouble; only the Barren were allowed to do so to help with medical matters and sexual urges.

Most of the men were disciplined, but every once in a while, one tried to claim something that wasn't theirs. Kalahn staying with the Jasvarian humans would help protect them. No male with a sound mind would dare attack a Kelderan royal.

He finally approached the conference room and pushed all thoughts of the females out of his head. Thorin had wanted to imprison Taryn and Evaine rather than treat them as guests. Kason needed to get control of his second straight away, which required a display of strength.

Once he entered and motioned for everyone to sit down, Kason took the chair at the head of the table and said without preamble, "Some of you may be wondering why I didn't restrain the females by force. But there is a long-term goal here that requires their cooperation. If we secure a treaty and cohabit on Jasvar, we can reach out to the Earth Colony Alliance and finally form a partnership."

Thorin shook his head. "We don't need the ECA. Jasvar is the only human settlement within many light-years of Keldera. Reaching out to them would only curtail our own self-rule. We'd be at the mercy of their demands."

"We won't hand over all of our rights. We should be able to keep most of our ways, or even I will dismiss the alliance," Kason stated.

Thorin shook his head. "We shouldn't hand over any rights. We can take Jasvar in the blink of an eye."

"This isn't a matter for you to decide, Thorin. I am in charge of this mission and I vowed to take the females to Keldera. Unless you wish to face me in a public challenge, it will be as I say." Thorin's silence was his answer. Kason continued, "Good. We'll meet again in twelve hours for the daily conference. That will give me time to settle our guests."

One of the lower ranked warriors in the room, jumped in, "What about Ryven and the rest?"

"They are safe as long as the females are safe," Kason answered.

The warrior pressed on. "How did weak females manage to capture you?"

Kason answered, "On their planet, women can be warriors. It's another reason to keep your distance and leave them alone during the journey, unless you wish to be humiliated."

"At the hands of a female?" someone scoffed.

"Yes," Kason answered. "Their leader in particular is cunning."

A few men murmured their surprise but didn't ask any more questions. Kason stood. "Jerrick will take over classes in Ryven's absence. I want to double everyone's training regime. I will attend the sessions at random to ensure it happens. Dismissed."

The warriors filed out until it was just Kason and Thorin in the room. Once they were alone, Thorin murmured, "I hope you know what you're doing, your highness. This isn't your usual style."

"A new situation calls for a new approach. That is all."

With a curt nod, Thorin exited the room.

Yes, Kason was going to have to keep tabs on Thorin and any other troublemakers. Since Ryven was trapped on Jasvar, Kason was going to have to reach out and test some of his most reliable warriors until he could find one to trust completely in Ryven's stead.

In the meantime, he had a sister to question. While her presence was inexcusable, Kalahn might prove an asset in his quest to better understand and bed Taryn Demara. The only question was whether the human would keep her bargain to stay out of trouble or not.

Chapter Eight

The instant the door to their new quarters closed after Kason, Kalahn looked to Taryn and said, "Now that we're alone, I have a lot of questions for you."

Taryn glanced to Evaine, but her advisor was fiddling with the room's computer and wouldn't hear anything she said. "Answering them will probably get me in trouble with your brother."

Kalahn raised her brows. "Are you afraid of him?"

"Mostly no, although I wouldn't want to get on his bad side."

"Good. You shouldn't be afraid of him. Kason would never harm a female unless there was provocation."

"But he's not above keeping you locked up."

Kalahn moved closer to Taryn. "Yes, but that's because he's my brother. He's always been overprotective and wishes to keep me in a bubble of ignorance. He says females shouldn't worry about complicated matters. He thinks my ignorance will make me happier."

She narrowed her eyes. "Is that so?"

Kalahn waved a hand. "Yes, but every male thinks that way on Keldera. It's not just Kason."

She studied the princess. Taryn should use the time to gather information about Kason, but her curiosity about the princess won out. "Then why are you here? You had to know that you'd be caught eventually. You could even be punished."

Kalahn shrugged. "I've always wanted to see the stars. Ever since I was a child, I dreamed of piloting a spaceship. My family tried to discourage me whenever possible. It took a year of planning to get aboard this ship, but no matter what happens later, it'll be worth the pain. Traveling on a ship was everything I thought it'd be."

Taryn was starting to wonder if any of the Kelderan royalty actually wanted to rule. Both Kason and Kalahn seemed to have other dreams.

At least Taryn had become leader by choice.

"Maybe you'll have the chance one day to fulfill your dream and actually pilot a ship instead of merely being a passenger on one."

Kalahn shook her head. "Given how fragile the planet is with regards to not only resources, but also the unity of the inhabitants, changing the status quo of no female pilots is low on the list of priorities." She paused. When she spoke again, Kalahn's voice was lower. "However, if given the chance, I'd gladly give up my royal status if it meant I could explore the stars."

Her heart broke at the longing in Kalahn's eyes. "Well, I think some changes will be coming to your planet regardless of whatever else is going on. Don't give up hope. My presence alone has already changed things."

Kalahn smiled. "I look forward to seeing just how much." She leaned closer. "But enough about my planet. Will you answer some of my questions about yours?"

Taryn could easily make up an excuse about needing to settle into their quarters or not feeling well from her first space flight. But that would be lying and since she valued honesty, she decided Kalahn deserved it as well. Taryn finally replied, "I will try my best, but only insofar as it doesn't interfere with my mission. If I'm given the choice between sharing information with you or making it to Keldera to negotiate a treaty, I will choose the latter."

"Understood," Kalahn said. "Tell me, how did you win against Kason?"

While Kason had said to keep her true self hidden, she sensed it didn't include Kalahn. Tugging up her skirt, she displayed her dagger. "Women don't sit idly by on my planet." She released her skirt. "But many alien males tend to underestimate a torn dress and tears, which gives us the opportunity to pounce. It really isn't that difficult."

"So, you just make them think you're weak? That's clever. Although I don't think that tactic will help my situation."

Taryn studied the woman who had to be almost a decade younger than her, if Kelderans aged about the same as humans. "I know you mentioned the status quo, but why exactly can't you become a pilot? Is it a tradition or a law?"

"Both. Women are treasures that give life and nurture it. To go against this creed is treasonous and a sign of ultimate weakness." Kalahn scrunched up her nose. "That's what every girl is taught growing up. We may have schooling, but it's full of useless classes compared to the boys."

"What about women who can't have children?"

"Oh, you mean the Barren. They live in designated citadels and take care of our records. Sometimes they help with the sick, especially during an epidemic."

Taryn made the connection. "Because they are seen as disposable if they catch the disease."

"It's not my law, Taryn. That is just the way it is."

"But laws can always be changed."

"Maybe someday, although I doubt my father will do it. My oldest brother, Keltor, is more understanding, provided he lives long enough to take over the throne."

She tucked away the information about Keltor living long enough to take over the throne for later. She couldn't pry too quickly, or Kalahn wouldn't answer any of her questions. "You seem different than what I've been told about Kelderan women, Kalahn. How is that so?"

Kason's voice boomed from the door. "Ever since our mother's death, Father has spoiled her."

Taryn turned to look at Kason as Kalahn answered, "I wouldn't say spoiled so much as he gave me more freedom."

"Which is the definition of spoiled," Kason stated as he walked closer.

Taryn tilted her head. "Freedom should be a right, Prince."

"Using your culture as a filter for mine is the definition of bias, human."

She stood and lifted her chin, although she was still several inches shorter than him. "Not speaking up and sharing my beliefs is the ultimate recipe for disaster if we're to share the only habitable continent on my planet. If you expect me to give up everything we are and kowtow to your ways, then I may as well go home now."

He closed the distance between them until he was only a few inches from her body. "Originally, I had wished you to be more like the females of my planet."

With Kason's breath on her cheek, she forgot about the others in the room. "And now?"

"Now, I think your differences makes things interesting," he murmured.

Taryn's eyes darted to Kason's lips. "Oh, there are many more ways I could make it interesting."

Kason's breath hitched, and she smiled. Regardless of his protesting before, he enjoyed Taryn's confidence and ability to stand up to him.

Just as she met his eyes again and tried to figure out what he was thinking behind his impassive façade, Kalahn cleared her throat and said, "I think there is something you need to tell me, brother."

Shit. So much for keeping the secret about being Kason's bride. She was going to have to be more careful in the future.

Taryn retreated a few steps to clear her mind, but before she could speak, Kason did. "What happens in this room stays in the room, Kalahn."

His sister raised her brows. "Or what? I think I should get something in return."

"I'm your brother. And unless you want me to lose my command and Thorin to be in charge, you'll keep your mouth shut," Kason growled.

"Since I don't want to be locked away forever, I think we can make a deal," Kalahn replied.

"I'm not as indulgent as our father, but what would you ask for?"

"If the treaty succeeds and we're allowed to form a colony on Jasvar, I want to go."

"What?" Kason barked. "A princess's place should be on Keldera. We can't allow the traditions to fully break down or there will be war."

"Since females can't rule, it doesn't make a lot of sense as to why I need to stay, except for maybe marrying me off to a decorated warrior to form an alliance." Kalahn took a step toward her brother. "I won't be married off to further anyone's standing."

While the siblings' conversation was revealing, Taryn needed them both with cool heads. One outburst at the wrong time could derail her mission. "How about we delay this argument until we know if I succeed or not? If so, then Kason promises to revisit this discussion later."

Kason's gaze met hers. "You don't speak for me, female."

Taryn tilted her head. "I'm being rational. Deny Kalahn outright, and she'll probably just get herself into more trouble. This way, options are open and she's more likely to cooperate." She looked to Kalahn. "I'm right, aren't I?"

Kalahn smiled. "Yes. Otherwise, I may just disappear again and you'll never find me. That won't look good for the crew of this ship, and I'm sure my brother doesn't want to ruin the careers of all those men because of his stubbornness."

Kason growled. "I should lock you away until we return home."

The glimpse of Kason acting like an older brother rather than a cool, collected warrior gave Taryn a peek of who the man was. Family was important to him, for a start.

Taryn jumped in. "Then let's just decide here and now that we'll revisit Kalahn's request later, provided she keeps our secret."

Kalahn met her eyes. "I have my guesses, although no one has said outright that you're his potential destined bride."

Kason replied, "The less you know, the better. Just keep your suspicions to yourself and we'll talk about your future later."

When Kalahn nodded, Taryn sighed. "Good, that's one less thing we need to worry about. Now—"

The panel Evaine had been playing with beeped loudly. Kason rushed over, tapped a few times, and it ceased. He looked at Evaine and then Taryn. "First off, you need to learn the writing system and a few basic words so you can work some of the computers that aren't linked to the AI system." His gaze moved to Kalahn. "And you're going to be their teacher."

Taryn said, "I hope you're not going to suggest what I think you're going to suggest because I can't take a week being locked up inside this room."

"Most of your time will be spent in here, for your own safety. Only I may escort you elsewhere," Kason stated.

"And when, exactly, will you have time to do so?"

"I may not. We'll see how my schedule plays out." He looked to his sister. "Start language lessons with them now."

Before Taryn could do more than open her mouth, Kason was gone. She wondered if speaking up for him had changed his mind about sex and protecting her. If so, Taryn would have to find another way into his bed. As much as she hated to admit it, she needed Kason's help and protection if she were to succeed.

Kalahn clapped her hands. "All right, let's get you started. The sooner you can peck out things on the computer, the sooner you can learn about Keldera and who you're dealing with."

Kalahn's last words were directed at Taryn, but she wasn't about to back down. "I'm ready, although I do have one question—why isn't the AI system active here?"

Evaine spoke up. "Probably because we're foreigners and they don't trust us. I'd do the same in their shoes."

"Evaine is correct. Not even sharing a room with a princess will break that piece of protocol." Kalahn picked up a flat, shiny rectangular object. After tapping the surface, it lit up. "We'll use this for now."

As Evaine took the flat object, her eyes widened, but Kalahn took it back. "You can play with it later. First thing's first, we're going to review the Kelderan writing system."

THE CONQUEST

Taryn tried to pay attention as the Kelderan princess went over the basics, but her mind kept wandering to Kason. Would he really leave her to rot the entire journey?

Not if she had any say in it. Taryn had an idea, but she would need to get Kalahn on her side, so she leaned over and paid attention.

~~~

Kason ducked the swinging blow of his opponent, stepped to the right, and punched the male in the side and then under the jaw. He went down with a thud.

Looking up from the fallen warrior, Kason met the eyes of his training class. "Patience is more important than the first move. Any warrior who wastes energy by trying to be first for the sake of it won't make it past age thirty. Now, divide into pairs and practice sparring for the next twenty minutes. I'll walk around and give pointers after the fact. For those looking to be promoted from apprentice, this is your chance to show what you're capable of." He clapped his hands. "Begin."

As he watched the various males begin their practice, Kason helped up the man he'd knocked out and slapped him on the back. "Find a partner and try again."

With a nod, the young warrior followed his order.

There were others who could've assisted with Ryven's apprentice training class, but the lesson had provided Kason some relief. Between his sister and Taryn Demara, he had desperately needed to relieve some frustration. Doing so in an educational way was the best use of his energy.

He still didn't believe he'd agreed to revisit Kalahn's request later. Barring their father's death, she would never have the approval to join the colony.

And then there was Taryn. He'd revealed more of himself than he had intended, which had only invited the female to speak for him. Even now, she probably wondered if he'd reneged on his promise to bed her and protect her.

Not that he would do so. Taryn's strength and confidence called to him in a way he'd never felt before. A small part of him wondered if she were as defiant without her clothes as in them.

Pushing aside the thought, he focused on the males. He walked to the first fallen one. "Patience is key. Try again."

With a nod, the young man stood up and his partner took position. Kason signaled and the males began.

Fighting, tactics, laws, and tradition were all things he understood. Every male in the room had expectations of how females and society functioned. If the treaty went through and they had a colony on Jasvar, he wondered if everyone would be able to adjust.

He would have to find a way to make it work because for some reason, the thought of letting Taryn down didn't sit well with him. Kason hadn't planned on establishing the colony himself, but he might just have to. Of course, that would break with tradition, and that would look like hypocrisy to his sister.

He might just have to let her accompany him.

Then he remembered his brother's right to succession and the possible civil war that could erupt. His duty was on Keldera.

But as an image of Taryn raising her chin as she leaned in toward him to voice her opinion flashed into his mind, he didn't know if he could let her go once he claimed her.

THE CONQUEST

There was only one way to find out. He needed to seduce Taryn Demara sooner rather than later so that Kason could plan the next stage of his life.

Later in the evening, the female had no idea what was coming.

Chapter Nine

Taryn finally managed to write out the entire set of symbols used in the Kelderan writing system on her flat pad computer screen. She might not be able to do much more than read them individually with a little bit of reminding from Evaine, but it was progress. Tackling the odd shapes of swirls and lines had distracted her for the last five hours and given her time to observe Kalahn.

Her initial observation that Kalahn was different than her brother hadn't changed.

The princess nodded at Taryn's work. "You're both quick learners."

Taryn leaned back in her chair. "Evaine is quicker with languages, but what I lack in natural ability, I make up with stubbornness."

Kalahn smiled. "You sound like my brother Keltor."

Not missing a beat, Taryn replied, "I've heard the name, but no one seems keen on discussing him with me."

Kalahn shrugged. "He's the heir. Talking about him could reveal a weakness and a possible threat to the throne."

"And what about Kason? What can you tell me about him?"

"You seem to be cozy with my brother already. If you are a potential destined bride and he decides to keep you, you'll have plenty of time to get to know him."

"No one 'keeps' me."

Kalahn tilted her head. "Your planet must be so very different from mine. I think you might actually be good for Kason. If anyone can try to change something through stubbornness, it's Kason. He's a good ally to have."

"I'm sure his stubbornness hinders progress as well," Taryn drawled.

Evaine spoke up. "If he had capitulated easily, we wouldn't be here. I never would've been able to figure out this ship if we had succeeded in hijacking it."

Taryn shot a look at her friend, telling her to keep quiet. For all of Evaine's genius, she lacked the ability to keep a secret.

Kalahn's eyes lit up. "I want to hear this story."

She could see Kalahn becoming an ally. "Maybe tomorrow. This evening, I want to talk with Kason in private. Is that possible?"

"The computer's security system is monitoring access to the door. If someone tries to leave without using a special code, the guards stationed nearby will come running," Kalahn explained.

"Ah, but for a princess who managed to sneak onto a ship and stay hidden for over a week, bypassing that problem should be easy," Taryn answered.

"I'm not about to risk getting into trouble for free. I have a proposition."

Taryn had a feeling she wasn't going to like Kalahn's proposition, but she nodded. "Go on."

"If I sneak you into Kason's room without any problems, then I want you to convince him to let me join the colony."

She raised her brows. "You seem confident that the negotiations will be successful."

"None of the warriors will say it, but Keldera would greatly benefit by becoming allies with the Earth Colony Alliance. Kason knows this."

"But Jasvar hasn't had contact with Earth in over 200 years and certainly no contact with the ECA."

"So? You are an Earth colony. That and your word will be enough to start the process."

Taryn decided to try her luck and pushed. "Why do you need the alliance?"

"Except for Keldera, our corner of the galaxy is sparsely populated because of the lack of life-supporting planets. However, rumors have it that the Brevkan have been spotted at the edges of our star system in the last few months."

She frowned. "Who are they and why is that important?"

Kalahn hesitated and then finally answered, "The Brevkan are our greatest enemies. The last time they visited our planet, the Kelderans and Brevkans ended up killing half of their respective armed forces." Kalahn raised her chin. "But we were victorious in the end."

"And now they want retribution," Taryn stated.

"Yes. It's not a matter of if, but when. With overpopulation, dwindling resources, and the rise of disgruntled factions, Keldera is not as unified as it once was. The warriors would never admit defeat, but I'm not entirely sure we can win again if Brevka attacked."

"Isn't sharing all of this with me violating some kind of law?"

Kalahn shrugged. "If Kason trusts you enough to bring you on board our spaceship, I trust you enough to share a little about our planet. The more you understand, the easier the negotiations will go."

"And the greater the chance your dreams will come true."

"Exactly." Kalahn stood. "Now, do you still want to sneak into Kason's room or not? Because we don't have much time before he returns for his evening meditation."

Taryn burned to ask more questions and gather information, but seeing Kason and ensuring his protection was more important. She looked to Evaine. "Will you be okay without me?"

"Do you even need to ask? As long as I can play with one of these tablet things and work on cracking the basic commands, I'm happy," Evaine answered with a smile.

Kalahn moved to what looked like a metal wardrobe. "Then hurry up and follow me, Taryn."

As Kalahn opened the doors, she moved to the princess's side. "Are you really going to tell me that you have secret passages?"

Kalahn grinned. "The room next to a prince's room always has a secret entrance for both security reasons and discretion."

"Princesses too?"

"No. We're to be chaste until gifted to a worthy male." Kalahn shook her head. "Let's hope I can leave Keldera before that happens." Kalahn slipped inside the wardrobe, and Taryn heard a click. "Wait until I enter the security code." The princess quickly disappeared into the other room. A few seconds later, she said, "Come."

Taryn climbed inside the wardrobe and was soon inside a sparse room not much bigger than the one she'd come from. The bed, wardrobe, cushion on the floor and the entrance to a bathroom were the only things in the room. Nothing was personalized in any way. She wasn't sure if it was because of

Kason not wanting to reveal information or if it was the way of a high-ranking warrior.

Kalahn's voice garnered her attention. "No one is allowed in Kason's room except him and whomever he shares the access code with. Not even the head of security can access the logs without permission. You should be safe here."

She moved back to the wardrobe and Taryn asked, "Are you going to share the code with me?"

"No. You need to talk with Kason and I don't want you to back out."

Before Taryn could do more than take a step, Kalahn disappeared into the wardrobe and Taryn heard a faint click.

She was trapped in Kason's room.

That's what you wanted, Demara. Taking a deep breath, she paced the length of the room. All she could do was wait.

~~~

Kason took the least populated route to his room, not wanting to run into anyone until after he'd showered, meditated, and eaten. Challenging a few other males during the practice session had released most of his stress, but Taryn was still on his mind. Her room was next to his, and the longer he ignored her, the more difficult it would be to concentrate on anything.

It might be considered a weakness, but he wanted to know how her language lessons were going. Not only that, but he also wanted to see how close Kalahn and Taryn were already. Those two together would cause trouble. He needed to figure out how to contain the pair of them.

He punched in the security code for his room and entered. The lights automatically came on. While there was nothing in sight, the hairs on the back of his neck said something was different.

Drawing the short sword at his side, Kason examined the bathroom, but it was empty. Since his bed had drawers underneath it, the only other hiding spot was the wardrobe. "Come out."

The doors opened. He expected his sister to emerge, but the lithe form of Taryn Demara filled his vision. He switched to CEL. "What are you doing in here?"

"We need to talk."

Confident she wouldn't try to kill him since he was her ticket to Keldera, he sheathed his sword. "Go back to your room, human. I need to complete my evening meditation."

"Why? Will you turn into a frog if you don't?"

"I don't know what a frog is, but meditation is necessary for cleansing my mind after physical activity. I recharge and can be ready for the next encounter or obstacle."

She crossed her arms over her chest, but somehow Kason resisted looking at her plumped up breasts or he might not be able to focus on their conversation and get the human to leave. "You know, it's hard to tease you when you can't understand my jokes."

"Or maybe you're just not funny."

"I'm quite funny, I assure you. We just need to work on your sense of humor." She uncrossed her arms and took a few steps toward him. "But enough of that. You pretty much declared that you were going to avoid me, but we have unfinished business."

"Oh? You're on my ship, heading toward Keldera for talks. You are also safe and won't be harmed."

"But we both know that will only last another six days before you can toss me aside and wash your hands of me."

He frowned. "You think so little of me." He closed the distance between them and resisted the urge to tuck a loose strand of hair behind her ear. "Besides, you're the one who said you'd wait before offering your body to me."

She placed her hands on his bare chest and the heat of her skin sent a sizzle down his spine. "Maybe I've changed my mind."

As her feminine scent drifted to his nose, blood rushed to his cock. "You're walking a fine line, human. If this is one of your little games, then you need to back off now."

She tilted her head up, and the heat of her breath danced across his chin. "I want your protection, Kason. And if this is the only way to do it, I will."

Her words were like a splash of cold water, and he retreated a few steps. "I said you must come to me willingly. Your mind still isn't ready."

Anger flashed in her eyes. "How do you know what my mind wants? And believe me, if I wasn't willing, I wouldn't be waiting alone in your quarters."

"Then prove your mind is willing. Lie on the bed."

"What?"

"Lie down. If your body responds to my touch and I can make you forget your name, we'll complete the claiming."

"Fine." She muttered something he couldn't hear as she marched to the bed. The sight of Taryn's flushed cheeks and controlled movements stirred his cock a little more.

Then she plopped back on the bed and spread her arms and legs wide. The corner of Kason's mouth ticked up at the sight.

The human noticed. "What are you laughing at now? Because I assure you I'm not in the mood for you to laugh at how much different my body is than a Kelderan female."

In the next second, he stood beside the bed and stared down at her. "I have no other female in mind. You are different, yes. But I'm curious to see how different."

She rolled her eyes. "This is definitely not how I thought this would go."

He lightly traced her cheek. "What did you expect?"

"Honestly? Wild warrior sex."

His finger moved down the side of her neck and down to the neckline of her dress. He could feel her heart racing. "There are times for wild sex. However, a female's first time is not one of them."

Heat flushed her cheeks. "I don't know what you're talking about."

Dipping his fingers below her neckline, he lightly grazed the top of her breast with his nail and smiled when Taryn sucked in a breath. "It was a guess, but your cheeks give you away. You haven't given your body to any male before me. I wonder why." He stilled his finger. "Maybe you need a strong male to keep you in line."

Taryn rolled to her side and stood on her knees on the bed. "Watch it, Prince. I'm this close to cutting off your balls and living with the consequences."

"You won't. That would endanger your people."

With a growl, Taryn smacked his chest. "Stop being a logical asshole."

He gripped her hands and kept them against his chest. "I'm not the one overreacting. You clearly like the feel of my fingers. Kiss me, and I'll show you what else I can do."

~~~

Taryn tried her best to keep her nervousness masked by anger. It was bad enough that Kason guessed she was a virgin, but she wasn't entirely sure of what she was supposed to do.

Yes, she knew the basics. However, she didn't have much in the way of tricks.

Kason's voice interrupted her thoughts. "Stop overthinking it. If this is how you make all of your decisions, you will probably die untouched."

"Yes, because you're such a spontaneous person yourself," she drawled.

"Kiss me and I'll show you one area where I can be."

Between the huskiness of his voice and the heat in his eyes, she was confident he was attracted to her. Kason tro el Vallen may not have been her first choice when it came to sleeping with a man, but she was starting to think he was better than many.

With that thought, she tilted her head up. It was time to seal the deal so she could protect her planet.

Kason met her halfway and the second his warm, firm lips brushed against hers, Taryn sighed. Unlike the first time she'd kissed him, Kason didn't hesitate. His arm circled around her waist and he hauled her against his body as he stroked the inside of her mouth. At the feel of his warm, hard chest against hers, Taryn moaned and wrapped her arms around his neck.

Increasing the fervor of his tongue, Kason gently laid Taryn on her back and covered her body with his. Rather than feeling trapped, his weight on top of her caused heat to rush through her body to between her legs.

His hand snaked between them and cupped her breasts. As he rubbed his palm against her taut nipple, Taryn groaned, and Kason took the kiss deeper.

She forgot about her nervousness. Every cell in her body ached to feel Kason's naked skin against hers.

However, before she could break the kiss to tell him, there was a loud chime that echoed in the room.

With a curse, Kason pulled away and stood next to the bed. "You need to leave."

His dismissive tone cut through her lust haze. "What?"

"Go. You can't be found here."

While she knew it was the truth, his manner still stung. Edging off the bed, Taryn moved to the wardrobe. Careful to keep her voice even, she whispered, "I don't know the code."

In a flash, Kason opened the wardrobe and entered a code. The door chimed again. "Go."

Not wasting a second, Taryn climbed through the short passage and exited into her room. Kalahn and Evaine both looked up from the tablet they were working on, but Kalahn was first to ask, "So? How did it go?"

"I don't want to talk about it," Taryn murmured before rushing into the bathroom.

Shutting the door, she leaned against the wall and took a few deep breaths. Logically, she knew she couldn't be found in Kason's room. But the efficient, emotionless way he'd dismissed her had stung. The prince clearly saw their dalliance as a transaction, nothing more.

For a split second, Taryn had wondered if they could have had more in the long run, but that mistake wouldn't happen twice. She'd sleep with Kason and never think of it again. The last thing she needed was to have her judgment clouded by lust or a hope for a lifelong partner. Jasvar was her family. She couldn't let them down.

Chapter Ten

Kason smoothed his hair and spent another second thinking of war strategies to deflate his cock. He was irritated that someone would force away his willing bride. However, since having a bride in the first place was a secret, he didn't have a choice.

Once he heard the door click in the wardrobe, he stated, "Enter."

The door unlocked and opened before the tall, golden-haired form of Syzel, his battle strategist, strode into the room. "Sorry to interrupt your evening meditation, your highness. But some information just arrived from Keldera."

Kason switched into general mode. "Report."

"A fleet of ships has entered the edge of our star system. While they're still too far away for detailed sensors, it could be the Brevkan. The king has asked for you to contact him as soon as we are in range of instant communication frequencies."

"I sense there is more to the message."

"Yes, your highness. The king's advisor hinted that we may need to detour to scout the visitors and determine if they are the Brevkan before returning to Keldera. During our journey, we're to come up with various plans of attack, just in case we go to war."

"Has anyone told my father of Princess Kalahn's presence yet? Or about our Jasvarian delegation?"

"No, sir. Thorin felt it should come from you."

Of course he would. Thorin would face an entire army on his own, but would rather be skinned alive than deal with the king, all because of a past family secret. "How long until we're within reach of Keldera's short-range communications?"

"Two days, maybe a little less if Enishi can boost the engines."

Enishi was the chief engineer. "See what he can do. There is much I need to discuss with the king, and it needs to be done on a secure channel. Also, ensure this stays with the top-ranking warriors. If we end up not scouting the ships, I don't want to build up tension unnecessarily."

"Of course, sir. Anything else?"

"Set up a meeting with yourself, Thorin, Enishi, and Jerrick for tomorrow morning. I want to discuss our options. Dismissed."

With a nod, Syzel exited the room.

So, it looked like the Brevkan might disrupt his life for a second time. First, attacking his planet and killing his mother. And now, possibly threatening the alliance with Jasvar. While Kason accepted death as a possibility in his profession, he wasn't about to let the Brevkan bastards take his sister's or his bride's life.

Speaking of his bride, he needed to check in next door. Anger had filled Taryn's eyes when she'd left and he needed to educate her about the importance of keeping their dalliance a secret, especially if Keldera was to go to war. His people would need Kason's help if they hoped to win and he couldn't risk losing his position. He would just need to educate Taryn on that fact, and she should understand.

After quickly cleaning up and changing his clothes to more formal attire, which included synthetic pants and a loose, open-chested shirt, Kason entered the code at the wardrobe and went through the passage. At the exit, he opened the door a fraction and asked, "Are you decent?"

Kalahn's voice answered in CEL, "Yes, although enter at your own peril."

Curious at his sister's words, Kason opened the door and searched out Taryn, only to find the bathroom door closed. He met his sister's gaze. "I assure you that attacking me is not the best course of action, sister, no matter how upset you might be."

Kalahn glanced to Evaine and switched to Kelderan. "I can't fault you for acting Kelderan, but a certain human doesn't understand it all. You need to explain things to her, brother, or you will lose this one."

"Our connection is purely for diplomatic purposes. Neither one of us is disillusioned about anything more."

"Are you certain? Because if that were true, you wouldn't have dressed in your princely clothes for a mere visit with your sister and certainly not for an informal diplomatic meeting."

Kason didn't fidget. "Some of us remember our duties, sister. Any interaction with a leader means putting your best foot forward."

"Are you sure it's your foot?"

He grunted. "You need to start acting Kelderan or you will never find a husband."

The bathroom door opened, and Taryn's voice prevented his sister from replying, "Is he bothering you, Kalahn?"

Kason beat his sister to a reply in CEL. "My sister is fine. I came to talk with you. Will you come into my room for privacy?"

"If it's about sealing the deal for my protection, I'm going to wait until we're closer to Keldera."

He raised his brows. "I can wait, but things might be changing soon."

"What?" Taryn asked.

"I can't tell you the details," he answered.

Taryn threw up her arms. "How are we supposed to negotiate an alliance and maybe even cohabit a planet if you won't share information?" She searched his eyes. "Whatever you share with me will stay with me."

He looked to his sister and Kalahn spoke up. "I can keep my mouth shut." Kalahn looked to Evaine. "Can you keep a secret this time, Evaine?"

Evaine nodded. "I don't have anyone to tell in the near future, and by the time we return home, I'm sure the secret will be moot."

Taryn chimed in. "All of us will pretty much be confined to the room for days anyway. Who would we tell?"

Kason looked to each female in turn. "No one must know this or it might cause a panic. Understood?" After each of them nodded, he explained how the Brevkan might be entering their star system.

Taryn crossed her arms over her chest. "Kalahn explained a bit of the history between you and Brevka. But are you sure it's them?"

Kason would have to talk to his sister later about trusting strangers too quickly. "We'll know soon. But if it is them, the negotiations between Jasvar and Keldera will be delayed."

Taryn assessed him a few seconds before asking, "This was the reason we were interrupted?" He nodded. "Then let me know what I can do to help. My strategies may be different than yours, but a different perspective might spark a victorious idea."

A few days ago, he would've balked at any female claiming to know the first thing about strategy. However, after seeing Taryn's work firsthand, her offer intrigued him. "I have a meeting with some of my key staff tomorrow. Afterward, we can talk in private."

Kalahn added, "Because females aren't allowed to attend military meetings. Or anything to do with the military, except in the case of healing the warriors when the Barren are overwhelmed."

Since Taryn didn't so much as blink at the mention of the Barren, Kason had a feeling his sister had shared that, too. He would need to lay out a list of what Kalahn shouldn't discuss with the humans.

Taryn's voice garnered his attention. "That is something we're going to have to negotiate as part of the colonization agreement. Tradition or not, I won't change my advisors just because they're female. Kelderan colonists are going to have to adapt to the idea of females in nontraditional positions."

Taking in Taryn's tall posture, stubbornly set jaw, and a dare to challenge in her eyes, Kason wanted to take the female to his room and claim her straight away. Waiting a few days was going to test his ability to concentrate.

When Taryn raised her eyebrows, Kason finally replied, "Let's see if we can reach an agreement first. If so, my word holds weight and I will speak on your behalf."

Instead of a dry reply, Taryn mere said, "Thank you."

After a few beats of silence, Kalahn spoke up. "The language lessons are progressing fine. I've done as you asked, Kason. Can't you find a way to get us out of this room for at least a little while?"

"First, tell me where you were hiding this whole time."

Kalahn grinned. "The forest."

Taryn frowned. "How can you have a forest on a spaceship?"

Evaine chimed in. "Theoretically, it's possible. Some of the records back on Jasvar speak of a ship with an entire floor devoted to plant life. Not only for food but also to help with oxygen supplies."

Taryn looked back to Kason. "Then take us there."

"Why? So Kalahn can hide again?"

Kalahn shook her head. "I won't hide, you have my word. Besides, I have too many questions to ask Taryn and Evaine about their world. That will keep me mostly out of trouble."

There were a million reasons why Kason should refuse. They could be discovered. A warrior might try to steal away one of the females for his own. Or, they could run into one of the Barren and Taryn would spend the next few days questioning her, no doubt, and find another cause to fight for.

But at the curiosity in Taryn's eyes, he decided that taking the human to the forest might help ease the anger about his dismissal from earlier.

Not that he was going to do it for purely altruistic reasons. If he earned her good graces again, she might allow him to claim her sooner. He didn't want to risk another male trying to take her. He was the only one who should be tasked with her protection. "We'll go in a few hours. Kalahn, ensure they eat and then find them some clothing. I want the three of you to be as inconspicuous as possible."

"You do know we're on a ship full of males, right, brother?" Kalahn asked.

"Ask the computer to synthesize something in the correct size, preferably an outfit that isn't revealing but also disguises the fact you're female. I'll erase the logs of this room once you're done, and no one will be the wiser."

Taryn smiled. "I didn't think being sneaky was part of your personality."

"There's being sneaky and then there's being cautious. I prefer the latter," Kason said.

The human snorted and Kason almost smiled. Her attitude was infectious.

Of course, that made her dangerous.

Kason moved toward the wardrobe. "I need to complete my evening meditation. I'll be back to collect you in two hours. That should be plenty of time to eat and get dressed."

~~~

Taryn paced the length of the room as she waited. The bulky mechanic's suit was scratchy and hot. The tight-fitting cap on her head with material hanging down the sides and back of her neck didn't help matters, either. If it weren't her only ticket to a brief respite from the confines of the room, she would've shucked it off straight away.

A chime echoed inside the room, and Kalahn looked to Taryn and Evaine before saying, "Remember, keep quiet and follow my lead. Most lower-down mechanics don't speak to warriors or high-ranking staff. If you use the same gestures and body language as me, we should make it to the forest undetected."

Before either Taryn or Evaine could answer, Kalahn opened the door. Kason stood in his tight-fitting pants and bare chest, which was his regular general attire. He spoke in Kelderan, which gave her time to merely watch his mouth form the syllables. What she'd first dismissed as choppy was actually fluid, and the patterns were at least somewhat familiar to her after Kalahn's lesson.

Still, it was going to take her a hell of a lot longer than a day to learn an entire language. Evaine was close to mastering the writing system, which would help with the computer at least.

Kason stopped talking and turned back down the hall. Kalahn followed him. Taryn and Evaine followed suit.

While she had to keep her eyes cast downward so that the material hanging on the sides of her hat helped to hide her face, she did her best to study her surroundings as they walked. Unlike the large cargo bay, the corridors weren't metal but something softer looking. While Jasvar couldn't manufacture plastic or other composite materials, there were a few things still in existence from the original colonists. Maybe the corridor was made of something similar.

The sight made her homesick. She had no doubt that Nova and Zorana had things in hand, but she couldn't wait to step back on solid ground again.

For many reasons, she hoped the Kelderans didn't go to war with the Brevkan. It would delay her negotiations and her return indefinitely.

However, at least she had Evaine and Kalahn or the journey would be much lonelier. The three of them seemed to get along so far, which was good since Taryn needed all the allies she could muster.

Then she looked to Kason's broad back and imagined the dark blue symbols underneath the material. As much as her head knew she needed to wait to have sex with him, each time she learned a little more and was faced with his tall, toned body, Taryn's resolve softened.

Maybe they would one day grow close and share more than attraction or battle strategies.

She caught him nodding at another warrior and realized it would take more than fabulous sex for Kason to change his life and career. After all, she would require the same.

If only there was a way he could still lead and try to get to know her. Secrecy was exciting in the beginning, but it would strain them eventually. Taryn had seen the same thing happen with a few couples back on Jasvar.

Forget it, Taryn. You and Kason lead two very different lives. There's nothing to be done. Make the most of what time you have. Bottling up her thoughts, Taryn went back to following Kalahn's lead. If a Kelderan warrior caught her gawking at Kason's back and discovered she was female, they might suspect she was his bride.

They soon approached a giant door that had to be at least twelve feet high and ten feet across. Once Kason pressed his thumb against a panel, it slid open. Taryn blinked against the light and walked inside. Once the door slid closed, her eyes adjusted enough to see and she gasped.

Trees towered twenty feet or more toward a ceiling fitted with lights. The leaves were a mixture of yellow and a pale green, different from the blues and purples of Jasvar. More than that, their trunks curved one way and then another, creating a wiggly effect, for the lack of a better term.

Kalahn lightly patted her arm, and Taryn tore her gaze from the trees to follow her new friend. As they walked deeper into the forest, she admired the yellow grass and collection of flowers. They ranged in size and shape, in a variety of colors. Documenting them all would take years, if she tried to do it herself.

Birds chirped overhead in tones and rhythms foreign to her. There was also the sound of running water in the distance.

It was hard to believe Taryn was in the middle of space on a man-made ship. The place felt like a dream rather than reality. Maybe someday, her people could master technology to this degree.

Once they were deep inside the forest, Kason put up a hand and motioned for them to stay there. He silently disappeared into the trees. A minute later, he reemerged and spoke quietly in CEL. "The only other people in the forest are at the far edge, testing the plant life for disease or signs of decay. We should be safe here."

He met her gaze, and she answered the question she saw there. "This is definitely an improvement over my room."

Kason raised his brows. "Only an improvement? This is the biggest space on the ship, apart from the cargo bay."

She smiled. "Is everything about size for you?"

When Kason blinked, Kalahn snorted and said, "Forgive my brother. He's not one for teasing."

Kason grunted. "You don't need to speak for me, sister." He met Taryn's gaze, and she resisted a shiver at its intensity. "But if you don't care about size, then you will be content with the creek and not care to see one of the largest waterfalls I've ever witnessed inside any spaceship."

"You have a waterfall in here?"

He smiled slowly. "So size is important to you, too."

Taryn walked up to him and slapped his arm. "Let's put aside the size comment. Waterfalls are few and far between on Jasvar. Will you show it to me?"

He placed a hand on her lower back and the heat of his fingers seeped through her bulky work suit. "Come. I might actually be able to make you speechless."

They started walking again. "I was quiet on the way here, I might point out."

"Only because you had no choice. Here, with us and no known dangers, you are free to speak or remain silent. Let's see how I do."

"You're quiet most of the time, so my challenge is to make you laugh," Taryn stated.

He raised his eyebrows. "You can try."

She frowned. "Has anyone ever told you that you're cocky?"

Kalahn chuckled, but Kason replied before his sister could jump in. "You say cocky and I say confident."

Taryn opened her mouth, but they exited the forest to face a twenty-foot waterfall that cascaded into a large, blue-green pool and she forgot what she was going to say. Even though the rocks that created the waterfall had to be man-made since the real thing would probably be too heavy, they looked authentic to her.

Just as she was about to walk closer, Kason's voice filled her ear. "I think I succeeded." She barely had time to frown before he added, "Come. There's more to the waterfall than meets the eye."

She noticed Evaine and Kalahn were already standing next to the waterfall. Evaine touched the rock surface and looked to be asking Kalahn questions. Taryn was starting to think her friend may never want to go back to Jasvar.

Kason steered her toward the falling water, and she focused back on him. "What are you doing? If I get wet, this outfit will cling to my body and ruin the disguise."

"Trust me," he murmured.

Even though Taryn shouldn't, her curiosity won out. "Let's see how you do with your first test."

"This is a game now?"

"Of course. It's more fun that way."

Kason merely grunted and took her hand. Tugging her between a small crevice to the side of the waterfall, all she could see were small, glowing lights on the ceiling and the faint outline of the rocks and Kason. With another turn, they were inside a small cave with the water pouring in front of them. She looked at him. "How do you know about this spot? Have you kissed a few other warriors back here?"

"There are those who do." He tugged her up against his warm body. "But I am more interested in the female with me now."

He cupped her cheek, and Taryn's heart skipped a beat. "I didn't think you were romantic."

Leaning his head down, he laid his cheek against hers. "There's a lot you don't know about me, Taryn Demara. But for now, all you need to know is I've been thinking of this ever since we were interrupted."

Moving his head, Kason kissed her.

~~~

Kason's original plan had been to take the three females out for a brief walk, march them back to their room, and retreat to his quarters to think of ways to handle the Brevkan.

But no matter how important the meeting the following day might be, ever since he'd spotted Taryn in the ridiculous mechanic's outfit, he wanted to rip it off and expose her feminine curves again. Her gasping at the sight of the trees had zeroed in his attention to her mouth. Right then and there he'd decided he wanted to take her to the lovers' cave.

While Kason had never visited the cave since he had no interest in males and had avoided the attention of any of the Barren aboard the ship, everyone knew the location.

And now he had his bride up against his body and the sweet taste of her mouth in his.

She clutched his shoulders, and he took the kiss deeper as he backed her against the wall. It wouldn't take much to open her disguise, unzip his fly, and take her in the cave.

The instant the thought crossed his mind, he broke the kiss. Taryn's hot breath against his face almost made him rethink his decision, but he managed to hold firm. "I will kiss you, Taryn, but I won't dishonor you by claiming you inside a cave."

It was difficult to read her expression in the near darkness, but her voice was steely. "Stop treating me like a delicate flower. I'm a grown woman and I have nothing against sex in a cave. In a way, it's exciting."

"But it is your first time. It should be perfect."

She lightly tugged his hair. "What could be more perfect than losing my virginity inside a cave with a waterfall in front of me?" She rubbed against him, and he groaned. "Make our deal official, Kason."

Something about her calling it a deal irked him, but he pushed the feeling aside. He leaned back an inch and fondled one of her breasts. "Only if you promise me there will be another time in a bed, where I can see your body."

Sex was only required once to cement his protection, but Kason didn't like the idea of only claiming the human once.

Placing a hand on his chest, she nodded. "Once more, albeit protected, and that's it."

Kason had other ideas, but he bobbed his head for the moment. He stepped away from the wall and put her back on the ground. "Undo your fastenings." She looked to the water and he added, "Kalahn will ensure no one disturbs us."

120

THE CONQUEST

As Taryn's fingers flew to undo the static restraints, Kason undid his fly and freed his long, hard cock. He was done first, so he watched as Taryn's skin was exposed bit by bit.

She wore nothing but the coverall and he could see the sides of her breasts as the front parted. Clenching his fingers to keep from distracting the female, he watched as the shadows danced across her abdomen and then the patch of hair between her thighs. Kelderans and Earth humans weren't that different in overall form, except for the fact Taryn's body was toned rather than soft; the better for him to claim her and not worry about hurting her.

The instant she stepped out of her coveralls and her legs were exposed, he pulled her against him and kissed her. Her warm skin against his cock sent a rush of desire through his body and he bit her bottom lip. Taryn took a second but bit him back. With a roar, he cupped her ass and lifted. Her legs wrapped around his waist and her hot, wet center against him nearly made him come right then and there.

But Kason was no schoolboy fooling around with a Barren for his first sexual experience. He needed to ensure she was ready.

He moved his fingers between her thighs and groaned at how wet she was. Taryn may see the act as a deal, but she was attracted to him.

Breaking the kiss, he murmured, "Are you ready, human?"

She raked her nails down his back. "Hurry up already."

The sting on his back made his cock pulse. "Then let me oblige my bride."

Supporting her weight with one arm under her rear, he used his other hand to position his cock at her hot entrance. Taryn bit the side of his neck, and he thrust inside her. He swallowed her cry with a kiss and then asked, "Are you ready for more or are you too sore?"

"I'm fine. Move already."

It seemed that with human females, the first time wasn't as painful as with Kelderan women.

Then Taryn wiggled her lower body, and he forgot about everything but the female in front of him. Pulling her head to his, he devoured her mouth as he moved his hips. Her tight, wet heat gripped him perfectly, as if she didn't want to let go.

At Taryn's moan, he increased his pace. Every instinct screamed to spill inside her, but he held back. If he wanted to claim his bride properly, she needed to find her release before him.

Since he'd studied what human female records he could find earlier, he knew he could bring Taryn pleasure by rubbing the little nub between her thighs. Since the same was done with a Kelderan female's nipples, Kason would have a challenge.

Running his hand from her head, down the side of her breast, her ribcage, and finally between their bodies, he found the secret spot between her thighs. When he pressed gently, Taryn arched into his touch. He increased the pressure and speed against her, never ceasing his hips. After a few more seconds, Taryn screamed into his mouth as her center gripped and released his cock. The action drove Kason over the edge, and he roared into his female's mouth as he spilled inside her.

Once she wrung every last drop of his seed, he broke the kiss and laid his forehead against hers. "Was that satisfactory?"

Taryn smiled. "I would say more than satisfactory, but I'd rather not add to your cockiness." He frowned and she laughed. "Let's just say I look forward to what you consider a 'proper' claiming later on."

He wanted to say he would have her many more times, but he didn't want to scare her. Instead, he replied, "I might render you speechless for a second time."

"I would tease about your confidence, but after today, I think it's more than just boasting." She lowered her voice. "And I would like to see you try and make me speechless again."

For a split second, he imagined years of rendering Taryn speechless in his bed. One day she could even carry his child. Hell, she could already be pregnant in a few hours.

However, a lifetime of being a royal prince and many years as a warrior had taught him that personal desires often came second. If he could handle the enemy and secure a colony, then maybe Kason could finally go after what he wanted.

And he was starting to want Taryn.

Careful to keep his thoughts from showing on his face, he hugged her close before setting her on the ground. "As much as I'd like to discuss this with you, we should probably get dressed. I don't know how much longer the people on the edge of the forest will stay put."

She searched his eyes. "And we can't be discovered."

"Not yet. I need to handle the unknown ships first."

She studied him a second, and he wondered if she saw his quick dismissal as a rejection. He would have to be more delicate in the future, if that were the case.

Taryn replied, "Will they truly take away your rank and disregard your orders because of having a bride?"

"It is the custom. Brides become targets."

"You mean we're a weakness," she drawled.

"You are strong, Taryn Demara. But that strength wouldn't be enough to overcome a Brevkan warrior out for revenge. For once, trust me on this."

"Only if you share what you find out about the Brevkan or whoever is the threat with me. I want to help."

Kason could dismiss the female or lie to her to stroke her ego. However, he only wanted to be truthful with her. "I will. Now, hurry up. We need to leave or risk being discovered."

As they dressed and exited the cave, it took every iota of strength Kason possessed to not wrap an arm around Taryn's waist and growl at anyone who looked at her.

Kason had some tough decisions ahead of him, but first, he needed to deal with the unknown spaceships, especially if they turned out to be the Brevkan.

Chapter Eleven

The next morning, Taryn stretched her arms over her head as she stood up from her language lessons. "It's break time, Kalahn."

Evaine never looked up from her tablet. "You can take a break, but I'm going to study a little longer. I have 90 percent of the characters memorized, and I'm determined to know them all before lunch."

Taryn waved a hand. "Go wild, Evaine. Then you can help me later."

Her friend was already engrossed with the latest memory test, so Taryn looked to Kalahn, who was smiling at her. "What?"

Kalahn glanced over at Evaine and then pulled Taryn to the far side of the room. She whispered, "How long are you going to make me wait for the details? Although, nothing too graphic since it was with my brother."

She knew what Kalahn was asking but played innocent. "Details for what, your highness?"

Kalahn frowned. "My brother took you into the lovers' cave. I know what goes on there."

Taryn refused to blush at the memory, which wasn't that hard to do since she'd been blocking it all morning. Of course, the soreness between her thighs was a constant reminder of what had happened. "How, exactly? I thought Kelderan females who aren't one of the Barren have to save themselves for their husband."

The princess scrunched her nose. "Don't remind me. But just because I haven't used the cave myself doesn't mean I'm ignorant. After hiding in the forest for nearly two weeks, I saw many couples go in there. Not all of them were quiet, especially during the night hours when they thought the place was empty."

For a second, Taryn wondered if both Kalahn and Evaine had heard her and Kason. Then she pushed the thought aside. "The less you know, the better. After all, Kason wouldn't want to give up his general status, now, would he?"

"And here I thought we were becoming friends."

"We are. But how about we talk about something else? Such as the Brevkan."

Anger followed by sadness flashed in Kalahn's eyes. "They have no honor. Killing women and children is commonplace for them."

"Which is how you lost your mother."

Kalahn blinked. "Kason told you that?" She nodded and the princess continued, "Unfortunately, I don't know that much beyond the stories and what was reported in the news. As you well know, Kelderan females aren't allowed to be involved in military or political matters. It was also one of the topics my father refused to discuss with me, no matter how many times I asked."

Taryn decided to test the boundaries with Kalahn. "Surely there must be others like you, who question tradition. Why doesn't someone do something about it?"

"A few have, but the law is strict and can only change through the cooperation of the king and the commoners' representatives. My father may be lenient with me, but he thinks allowing everyone the same privilege would create chaos. My eldest brother might be open to change, but no one talks about it since mentioning my brother's future reign is borderline treasonous. In the past, some monarchs weren't above killing off their fathers to ascend the throne. Keltor would never do that, but the law is the law."

"Your people seem to cling to tradition and the status quo. Will they really be able to adjust to life on Jasvar if an agreement is reached? There's no way I will enforce such restrictive limits if any of the Kelderan colonists marry one of my people," Taryn stated.

"To be honest, I don't know. You'll have to ask Kason about it. He holds a lot of sway with the higher-ranking officials."

"Oh, believe me, I will. How much longer do you think he'll be in that meeting?"

Kalahn tapped the small locket around her neck to check the time. "It should be over any minute now."

"How do you know it's nearly over?"

"Kason always keeps his meetings to fifteen or twenty minutes, except in extreme circumstances. Imposing a time limit tends to get the men to focus quicker." Kalahn leaned against the wall. "At any rate, until he returns, I have time to tell an embarrassing story or two. There's more to my brother than merely being a warrior prince."

She scrutinized Kalahn's face. "As much as I want to hear the stories, why are you being so open with me?"

Kalahn shrugged. "In my entire twenty-five years of existence, you are the first person Kason's teased since becoming a warrior. I think you'll be good for him."

Searching the princess's eyes, she replied, "Don't get your hopes up, Kalahn. Kason and I have an agreement, nothing more."

Taryn was starting to think she wanted to give him a try for real, and not just because of the great sex. Kason was one of the few men who could stand up to her and still seemed to value her opinions. The real test would be after he returned from the meeting. If he truly wanted to hear her input, she might reconsider her decision to have sex just one more time and then forget about him.

And that wasn't even taking into consideration there was a small chance she was already pregnant, too.

Kalahn smiled. "Tell yourself it's just a transaction, Taryn, and I'll revel in saying I was right in the end."

She forced thoughts of Kason and the future out of her head. "How about you just tell me the embarrassing story about Kason for now? The more fodder I have, the more I can tease your brother."

"And that is something I look forward to seeing." Kalahn leaned close. "One time, when Kason was fourteen, he managed to gain administrative access to the palace's computer system and change the AI voice to an old woman who was barely intelligible. It took my father's men days to reverse it. In the interim, everyone stopped using the AI system because she kept mixing up the orders, unless you spoke in the old dialect. The best time was when my father asked for a soup called *surlap* to be brought to his office and instead an animal trainer brought a *supak*, which is a four-legged animal that smells of old cheese." Kalahn chuckled. "The smell lingered in Father's office for days, and no amount of cleaning would get it out any quicker."

Taryn smiled and wondered what had happened to the mischievous version of Kason. Maybe she could bring him out again.

Well, after he shared the information from his meeting. If he backed out of that promise, Taryn wasn't going to waste her time trying to know the prince beyond a working relationship.

As she listened to Kalahn tell a few more mix-ups from the AI trick, Taryn resisted looking at the time again. Kason was late, and she wondered why.

~ ~ ~

Kason gave his final order and exited the conference room. Things had gone well enough, as everyone had ideas of how to tackle the Brevkan if they turned out to be the mysterious ships, but he had had a hard time concentrating.

Taryn Demara had a habit of doing that to him.

His dreams during the night had been full of the human, mainly naked and at his mercy. But despite doing his morning meditation and then focusing on a real threat for several hours both alone and with his colleagues, he couldn't get her out of his head. If Ryven weren't being held hostage back on Jasvar, Kason would've talked with his friend to clear his mind. However, since Ryven wasn't aboard the ship and Kason wasn't entirely sure of who he could trust enough to keep his bride's claiming a secret, he had to deal with his temporary obsession on his own.

And that was all it was—a temporary obsession. Taryn was new and different from his past sexual encounters. That had to be it.

Then he remembered the way she fit around him and screamed into his mouth, and Kason admitted he was lying. He actually enjoyed not knowing how the human would act. How he'd ever thought he'd want a submissive wife, he didn't know.

His mission couldn't be completed soon enough.

It was still a day until they reached instant communication range with Keldera. If he was lucky, the ships on the edge of the star system were merely traders or pirates on the run. Those two scenarios would be easy to handle.

However, he wouldn't waste the next day wishing for it to be true. He wanted to spend time with his human during his down time.

Rather than think about why he'd said "his," Kason picked up his pace and arrived at his quarters. After entering, he checked his messages, responded to those that required it, and then went to his wardrobe to punch in the code. He needed to make sure he gave the code to Taryn, too.

Reaching the door to the adjacent room, he knocked and stated in CEL, "I'm coming in."

His sister muttered, "Fine," in the same language as he exited the tunnel between his room and hers. Searching the room, he instantly found Taryn and Kalahn conversing together in a corner. After a second, they both grinned at him. "What's going on?"

Taryn answered, "Supak."

He growled at his sister. "Unless you want me sharing your life with others, don't do the same with mine."

Taryn walked up to him. "Oh, come on, Kason. We all act out as youths."

"That is not the point. If you want to know about me, then ask me directly," Kason answered.

"Oh, is that so? Then you'll tell me another embarrassing story from your childhood?"

"That depends. Would you rather hear what happened at the meeting or about another time I made a fool of myself?"

Taryn tapped her chin. "That's a tough one." He opened his mouth, but she beat him to it. "The meeting, of course. What happened?"

He looked to Kalahn and then Evaine. "Once again, what is said in this room stays in this room, understood?"

Evaine shrugged. "Who am I going to tell?"

Kalahn then said, "Same for me. I'm the sacred princess of Keldera. Most people won't even look me in the eye, let alone listen to what I have to say."

At his sister's tone, he wanted to press her for details but decided he could do that later. "We're still waiting on confirmation, but if the ships prove to be Brevkan, we're going to attack first. That means you three will be placed on an escape shuttle when we're closer to Keldera and escorted to the planet's surface without me."

Taryn searched his eyes. "Is that wise?

"I will make my father and brother vow to protect all of you. Regardless of our disagreements in the past, I trust both of them."

"While I appreciate you trying to ensure our safety, you might need me to stay on board to help," Taryn said.

Kason's instinct wanted to scream, "No," and order Taryn not to ask questions. But if he did that, she might not talk to him again, let alone share her body.

And that didn't sit well with him.

He motioned for everyone to sit down around the table where Evaine already sat. Once they did, he looked at each female in turn. "I'll explain a little bit about the Brevkan and then I'll listen to your ideas. However, I may not use them." Taryn opened her mouth, but he beat her to it. "Not because you're female. I have more experience with these foes. I've also more than earned

131

my rank as a general. Just as you know your planet and people's strengths and weaknesses, I know mine."

Taryn nodded with approval in her eyes. "That I can understand. Now, tell us what we need to know."

"The Brevkan are technologically advanced, like the Kelderans. However, their people believe more in strength, dominance, and animal instinct to guide their society. The strongest always lead, which means lots of public challenges to the death."

Kalahn whispered, "Monsters."

"While I tend to agree, judging them one way or the other does little good. They're smart, and the rumors are they've conquered many planets over the centuries."

Taryn spoke up. "What are their main tactics when it comes to battle?"

"Decoys are a big part of their strategy, as is capturing prisoners and torturing them to prove a point. They also will attack anyone, even females and children, to ensure their threats are taken seriously."

Evaine asked, "Is there any sort of alliance or interstellar police force that tries to contain them? I read about such groups in some of the old documents back on Jasvar."

Kason shook his head. "There aren't many races out here, mostly just the Kelderans and Brevkans. Neither of us is part of the Earth Colony Alliance, and until our feud stops, no enforcement agency will agree to help."

Taryn leaned forward. "As you know, decoys and getting the enemy to underestimate me is a strength of mine. I say we should try it. The Brevkan won't be expecting it of you, right?"

He raised his brows. "Perhaps. But how, exactly?"

"You're not going to like it."

"Just tell me," he growled.

"Fine. The Brevkan probably know about your patriarchal society, right?" Kason nodded and she continued, "Then have a ship that appears to be full of women go in first as bait. Then when their guard is down, strike before they can react."

Kalahn chimed in. "We don't have female warriors. They would be sitting ducks."

"Ah, but I said *appears* to be full of women. Have some females in key positions, such as on the control deck or whatever you call it, and at the main entry points. Then, have your male warriors dress up in female attire and occupy other parts of the ship. Once the Brevkan are on board, you can strike."

Kason frowned. "Males dressing in female attire is unheard of. It will also appear cowardly to the others."

Taryn shrugged. "That may be so, but it's unexpected. Sometimes it's the split second you gain with a surprise that determines the winner."

The female was clever. Kason would be able to accomplish a lot with her at his side. "The idea has merit, but I will need to mull it over. The Brevkan have strong weaponry. One ship, no matter how much the Brevkan might dismiss them as being weak, won't be able to win against a fleet."

"That's fair. But I think I proved my point about being useful. If anything, we might need as many females as possible if you use my plan at all. I'm staying," Taryn stated.

As he stared into his human's brown eyes, he knew she meant it. "If I use your plan and can convince the others to go along with it, you can remain as long as you stay out of trouble."

She tilted her head. "Have I gotten into trouble yet?"

"No, but it's always a possibility, especially if you're becoming friends with my sister."

Kalahn rolled her eyes. "I wouldn't have to cause trouble if you'd give me more freedom."

Before meeting Taryn, Kason would've brushed aside his sister's statement. But the human was teaching him that females could do more than bear and raise children. Maybe Kalahn was more of a warrior than a mother. "I'm starting to think change might be coming to our ways, but it can't happen overnight, sister. Tell me you understand that."

Kalahn sighed. "I do." She looked to Taryn. "I'm just glad someone is getting through that thick skull of yours."

Kason grunted and Taryn laughed. "He just needed a different perspective. I'm sure being captured by a mere female opened his eyes."

He stood up. "Before all of you gang up on me, I'm going to work out a detailed plan that incorporates Taryn's idea and some of my own. If, and that's a big if, I can convince the others, we need to hurry with preparations. We'll be cutting it close for Keldera to send over some shuttles of females and to have the computer make enough clothing."

"What about the Barren?" Taryn asked. "I think there are about fifty or so onboard the ship. That should be enough for my idea."

"Using the Barren would be unwise. They have a stigma attached and most of the officers won't agree to accepting their help."

Taryn also stood. "So your warriors will sleep with them and allow the Barren to tend to their wounds, but won't ask for or accept their help in other areas?"

He put up a hand. "Getting the others to agree to use women at all is going to take a lot of convincing. Add using the Barren to the mix, and it will never happen."

Evaine touched Taryn's arm. "Pick your battles, Taryn. We can tackle the Barren later."

Taryn clenched her jaw before finally replying, "Promise me we'll revisit the Barren later and I will grudgingly agree to still help."

The fact the human had so much passion for a people she barely knew only raised her in his esteem. If he could convince Taryn to be his bride for good, then Keldera had no idea what was in store for them. Even if he and Taryn lived on Jasvar, he was positive his human would find a way to enact change on Keldera.

If his father thought Kalahn was a handful, he would be in for a surprise with Taryn.

Kalahn asked, "Why are you smiling?"

"Never you mind," Kason replied. "Taryn Demara, I promise to try helping the Barren, although I can't guarantee things will change. That will require changing the hearts and minds of the people."

"I understand that. But just know that I won't forget your promise."

The corner of his mouth ticked up. "I'm sure you won't. When you set your mind to something, you see it through."

Taryn raised her brows. "That almost sounded like a compliment."

"Perhaps."

Taryn's tension eased from her body, and she sighed. "If not for everything that needs to get done, I would tease you back."

He wanted to say she'd have many years to do that, but resisted. He didn't want to scare or anger her. "Then help me with my plans. We can work in private in my room."

"I hope you truly mean work, Kason."

"Of course. You'll fulfill your promise to me once I take care of the ships at the edge of the star system. Let's call it a form of motivation."

"For you or for me?"

He smiled. "Both."

Kalahn jumped in. "You do realize Evaine and I are in the same room? Hurry up and go next door. Then we won't have to put up with the flirting."

Kason put out his hand. "Come, Taryn. We'll get more done without my sister's constant interruptions."

Taryn looked to Evaine, and the other female said, "I'll be fine. With you gone, Kalahn can speed up my language lessons."

"So I'm just slowing you down?" Taryn asked.

"Yes," Evaine answered.

"I love your honesty, Evaine. Have fun. I fully expect you to be my interpreter before long."

Taryn placed her hand in his, and he gripped her rough fingers tightly. He didn't want her to change her mind.

As Kason tugged Taryn through the wardrobe and into his room, he tried not to think of how much he was coming to admire his human. Keeping the secret about her being his bride was going to become trickier, especially if she helped with the possible threats and the other males saw her worth.

In that second, he decided that as soon as any threats were vanquished, he was going to claim Taryn Demara publicly. She was his and the sooner everyone knew that, the better.

Chapter Twelve

Taryn crossed her arms over her chest and studied Kason from across the table in his room. "What if the other ships can't come to aid the bait fast enough? I still say you should train the women for the positions they'll be playing. It will make it that much more convincing, not to mention it will give them a little bit of protection in case things go wrong."

Kason shook his head. "My father would never agree to send the females if he knew we were going to train them."

She shrugged. "Then forget to tell him that part. I'm sure he'll forgive you once you've won."

"Confidence isn't enough to win."

"Ah, but a lack of confidence ensures defeat."

"Perhaps."

She rolled her eyes. "It shouldn't be so hard to admit that I'm right."

He grunted. "If I do it too often, you'll get cocky."

She grinned. "That's the pot calling the kettle black."

"I have no idea what that means."

The slight frown between his brows was almost adorable. She enjoyed unsettling the big warrior across from her. "Just that you're one cocky bastard and I have a long way to go before I catch up to you."

She leaned forward and placed her arms on the table. Kason's eyes darted to her cleavage, sending a rush of heat through her body. She'd mostly been able to block what had happened in the cave.

If not for the possible upcoming battle and wanting to convince him of her ideas, Taryn might've encouraged him to kiss her again.

However, there wasn't much time before he would be meeting with his fellow officers again and she needed every minute she could get to fine tune their plans.

She pointed a finger toward her face. "My eyes are up here."

His heated gaze met hers, and her heart skipped a beat. The huskiness of his voice made her shiver as he said, "I wish we had time for a break."

"Even if we did, I don't think we'd be resting." The dark blue markings on his skin flashed red for a split second before returning to their usual color. She raised her eyebrows. "That's a first. What does the red mean?"

"It reflects desire."

Her cheeks heated. "Oh."

"You should feel honored. The color of my markings hasn't wavered in many years." He reached out and traced the skin of her forearm. "And yet, a human female easily rattles my control."

"Only because I'm your bride."

He never ceased stroking her arm. "Perhaps."

As they stared into one another's eyes, Taryn saw them together when they were old and gray, arguing over how to protect their people.

And not just their people, but their children, too.

Get a grip, Taryn. There are more important things to worry about.
She cleared her throat. "You say 'perhaps' a lot. Is that common
in Kelderan?"

He removed his hand, and Taryn nearly reached out to pull
it back as he answered, "Yes. Ambiguity prevents arguments and
strife."

"It also means you never get to say what you really mean."

"Perhaps."

She snorted and Kason grinned. The combination of his
white teeth, lines around the corners of his mouth, and the
lightness of his eyes made her suck in a breath. She tried to make
her mouth work, but Kason beat her to it. "That's twice now I've
made you speechless. It's becoming rather easy to do."

Clearing her throat, Taryn found her voice again. "Just be
glad your grin doesn't make me scream and run the other way.
For a while there, I wondered if you could even smile or tease."

He reached out and took her hand. Taryn didn't pull away.
"There isn't much opportunity to do so when you're a general
giving orders and inspiring men to follow you."

"Being a prince hasn't helped, either, I would think."

"No. But we are each born to find our place and purpose.
The royal family gives Kelderans someone to look to for
guidance, strength, or even hope. If sacrificing a few freedoms
means an entire planet is happier, is that not worth it? Even
though you're not royalty, I think you understand."

"Yes, I do." She hesitated about how much to share, but
Kason squeezed her hand in encouragement, and she added, "I've
done the same for my people. That's why I'm here in the first
place."

He nodded. "Then we should understand each other, Taryn
Demara. In a way, I think that is why we will work and live
together well."

She blinked. "What?"

He released her hand. "Think about it. Because while you seem determined to sleep with me, obtain your agreement, and go back to your life as before, the question is—do you really want to? Or, would you rather co-rule Jasvar with me and always have someone watching your back?"

~~~

Kason had slipped up twice. First with his markings and then with telling Taryn he wanted a future with her.

But he wasn't about to take it back. Most of his life he'd been dedicated, obedient, and had done his duty. For once, he wanted to combine duty with his own wishes. If Taryn didn't want the same thing, he needed to know sooner rather than later. That way he could plan his next steps without her, if need be.

He waited until his female finally spoke again. "I will think about it."

Only through years of training could he keep his markings from showing his hope at her statement. "At least it's not a no."

"No, but it's not yes either. How about we take care of the threats and cement our plans for your colony first? No one should make a life-altering choice right before you might die."

He growled. "We won't die."

"We will if we don't train the women."

Taryn's steely gaze told him she wasn't about to give up. "Let me talk with my men first and then decide if I want to deceive my father, the king. Is that amenable to you?"

"Just because we disagree doesn't mean you have to be cold and put distance between us again."

"I didn't realize I was."

She smiled, and it eased his concern a fraction. "We'll have your language skills in top shape before long."

"Speaking of which, you need to get back to your lessons."

"You want me to go?"

"If I'm honest, no. But I need to meditate and prepare for my next meeting."

She tilted her head. "You seem to meditate a lot. What does it entail? Answer that and I'll go back to bothering your sister."

Sharing a warrior's meditation practice with a female was strictly forbidden. But considering how many barriers Kason had already broken, he decided one more wouldn't be much worse. "Come, sit on the bed." She gave him a skeptical look, and he added, "I'm not going to ravish you, if that is what you're afraid of."

Taryn moved to the bed and plopped down. He smiled at her lack of grace. "Now, close your eyes." She obeyed, and he leaned down to whisper in her ear. "Imagine your mind in the black vastness of space with tiny pinpricks of light. Nod when you're ready."

He watched Taryn's face as her eyes moved beneath her eyelids. He noticed a freckle near her eye for the first time. It took everything he had not to reach out and lightly stroke the mark.

Thankfully, the human nodded, and he was able to focus again. "Now pick one of the lights and imagine who lives there, how they protect themselves, how they fight. Then imagine their strengths, weaknesses, and what you would do if you have to protect your family from them. Next, how you would forge an alliance. By the end of the meditation session, you should have a fresh look on life, new ideas on how to do your best as a warrior, and a calm, focused mind."

"That is a lot to do."

"Shh. Just focus on your session. I will watch over you until you're done."

Taryn raised her face an inch. She took a deep inhalation and then went still.

As he waited for her to finish, he studied the curve of her cheek, the slightly unevenness of her eyebrows, her light tan complexion, and then focused on the shape of her lips. The upper one was much thinner than the bottom one, but it just meant he would have to focus his attentions there until her lips were swollen from his passion.

Aware he had a meeting soon, Kason pushed past his desires and studied his human again.

Her face was relaxed. Combined with her silence, his human looked younger and more carefree. In the moment, it was difficult to imagine she was a leader or strategist. While he knew the meditation would help her understand him and maybe even herself, he liked her better when she was lively.

After about five minutes, Taryn's lips curved up, and she opened her eyes.

"Well?" he asked.

"I rather enjoyed that."

"Enjoyment is usually not the objective."

"Perhaps."

He smiled. "I see you're picking up my linguistic cues."

"Perhaps," she murmured as she winked.

Shaking his head, he took her hands and helped her to her feet. "Beyond enjoyment, what else do you feel?"

"Calmer, for sure. And maybe even a little overwhelmed since I've never given much thought to those who occupied the stars."

He tucked a piece of hair behind her ear. "Good. The meditation should make you both at ease and uncomfortable. We must always be reminded that others are out there, but with strength and determination, we can usually coexist. If for some reason we can't, then we aren't afraid to face them."

She gently laid a hand on his chest, and he reflexively put his own over hers as she replied, "There is more to you than I originally guessed, Prince."

"I can say the same about you, human."

They smiled in unison and Kason merely enjoyed the moment. No matter what happened, he would remember this sense of ease and lightness for the rest of his days.

Standing on her tiptoes, Taryn gave him a quick kiss on the mouth before whispering, "I better go, or neither of us will get much done."

She tugged her hand, and Kason reluctantly released her. Just as she opened the wardrobe, he said, "I'll update you once I know more."

"You had better." She waggled a finger before grinning. "*Tushaun.*"

It took him a second to realize she'd said "good-bye" in Kelderan, but she was gone before he could answer.

Looking around his room, it seemed cold and lifeless without his human. The feeling motivated him to sit down and begin his meditation. He had his work cut out for him to convince the others of their plan, and he needed all the strength and wisdom he could muster.

~~~

Kason stood at the head of the table inside the conference room and waited for the others to respond.

Thorin was the first to speak up. "Never in our history have we used females during a battle, beyond nursing the wounded. Why would you suggest this? Is it because of the human?"

Kason was careful to keep his face neutral as Thorin studied him. "As I learned firsthand, females can defeat others much stronger than them, and we should consider every option available to us if we fight and wish to defeat the Brevkan."

Thorin tapped his fingers against the arm of his chair. "Since you were recently defeated, I'm not sure we should take your advice."

Syzel chimed in. "We've all suffered defeat at some point in our lives, Thorin. I remember you losing to your fair share of warriors during our training years."

"Training is one thing, being bested by females is quite another. We can't risk the upcoming battle with our greatest foe, if those ships turn out to be the Brevkan," Thorin replied.

"We don't even know if it is the Brevkan." Kason looked to Syzel. "Let's put past defeats aside for the moment. You're our chief strategist, Syzel. What do you say?"

Syzel nodded. "The idea has merit. The Brevkan wouldn't expect it. However, my main concern is convincing the others to cooperate. Many of the younger warriors will be offended at working with the women, almost as if they aren't strong enough to do it on their own. Asking them to wear women's clothing would be the last straw. We could end up with a mutiny."

Jerrick, one of Kason's best soldiers, said, "If they were provided an incentive, such as a promotion, more may agree than not. And those who won't can be sent back to Keldera when we pass by it in a day or so. That should prevent a mutiny."

Thorin shook his head. "Even if some of them would agree, what about the people of Keldera? This goes against

144

tradition and everything we've been taught since we were children. The antimonarchy faction could use the change to their advantage, and we could end up facing a revolt."

"The revolt might come anyway, Thorin," Syzel pointed out. "However, if the Brevkan finally finish what they started all those years ago, there won't be a monarchy for anyone to try to overthrow."

Kason looked his second-in-command straight in the eye. "What is more important? A future free of our greatest enemy? Or preserving a tradition and not having much of a future to enjoy? Even if the antimonarchists try to use the situation to their advantage, a victory over the Brevkan will return us to favor with the people."

Enishi, chief of engineering and Kason's weapons specialist, finally chimed in. "How about we quietly talk with a few of the best and most trusted warriors? If it looks as if no one will participate, we carry on with our previous plan. If we can convince them, then we'll try the new plan. Either way, I will have our weapons at the ready."

Kason looked at Enishi. "What is your personal opinion on the matter? Would you be willing to train females?"

Enishi shrugged a shoulder. "Considering some of the halfwit males I've trained in the past, a few females might brighten up the place. It's not easy being stuck in the bowels of the ship for most of the day."

Syzel sighed. "You like it there."

Kason ignored Syzel and answered Enishi. "Good to know you'd be on board." He looked to each male in turn. "For the next few hours, I want each of us to quietly seek out the best and most trusted of our crew and speak with them. We'll meet back here in three hours. That will give us enough time to finalize our plans before we enter instant communication range with Keldera and possibly discover the threat. Dismissed."

Kason watched each of the men leave and paid special attention to Thorin. While his second-in-command's markings were a steady, deep blue, Kason's gut said the other man was unhappy with his request.

Maybe once they dealt with the unknown ships, Kason could seek out a better fit for his second.

Then he remembered that he would soon no longer be a general.

After having Taryn once and getting to know the female, Kason wouldn't hesitate to claim her publicly once the threat was vanquished. However, if she didn't want to co-rule Jasvar, provided an agreement could be reached, then he wasn't sure what he'd do with his life. He'd been bred and trained to lead. Sitting on the sidelines, even if he was blessed with a family, would soon drive him crazy.

Pushing aside his doubts, Kason stood tall and exited the conference room. The next three hours could change his people forever. He needed to concentrate on that, and the rest could wait.

Chapter Thirteen

Taryn sat with Evaine and Kalahn in silence as they each focused on their tablets. She'd lost track of time, but it felt as if a day had passed since Kason had left. It took everything Taryn had not to tap her toes in impatience. She didn't like being in the dark.

Kalahn never looked up from her screen as she said, "He'll come when he's ready. Remember, the plan you proposed challenges our way of thinking. It's as if I asked you to make a law so only males could rule. Would you give it up so quickly?"

Taryn shook her head. "That's not the same. The men can still be warriors. The women would just help."

"Ah, you might think so," Kalahn said. "But if it goes well, women might demand the right to become warriors as well."

"Then why aren't you jumping for joy? You could probably become a pilot after all."

"Princesses don't have professions. That is an entirely different issue I hope changes one day," Kalahn answered.

Evaine finally looked up from her review lesson. "There's no reason to make it happen someday. If you don't take the first step, then it may never happen."

Just as Kalahn opened her mouth to reply, a knock sounded from the wardrobe. Taryn's heart rate kicked up. After taking a deep breath, she said, "Come in."

Kason emerged from the wardrobe in his general's attire, which meant tight pants and no shirt. She took a second to appreciate his toned abs before asking, "Well? What happened?"

Kason grunted and she met his eyes. "Just enough men agreed to the plan so we can go forward, if need be. It was a close call, though."

Taryn clapped her hands. "See? I knew it was a good idea."

"Perhaps. There is some dissent that I'll deal with as soon as all of this is over. Besides, it may not be the Brevkan after all. We'll know tomorrow morning."

Kalahn said something in Kelderan and Kason replied. Once they fell silent, Taryn raised an eyebrow. "Care to tell me what you just said?"

"You need to study harder," Kason replied.

Taryn raised her chin. "I'm sure even his mighty highness took more than a day to learn CEL."

"Perhaps."

With a sigh, Taryn looked to Kalahn. "I don't have the patience to wheedle the information out of your brother. What did you talk about?"

Kalahn smiled. "I won't always be here, you know. You're going to have to work on getting Kason to elaborate. I'm sure you can think of ways."

Taryn's cheeks flushed, but she did her best to pretend nothing had changed. "Well, right now you're here. Consider it your duty. After all, you need an agreement with me so that Kelderans may colonize the planet."

Rolling her eyes, Kalahn replied, "Fine. Kason asked me to help him with the women."

She whipped her head to Kason. "Really? I thought you were going to send her back to Keldera."

148

He shrugged. "Having Kalahn here will help tame tempers among the males since many of the warriors will want to impress a princess. Females also look up to her, even if she doesn't like it, and if they see her trying hard, they will too."

Kalahn bobbed her head. "I think it's a great idea. However, you're forgetting Father. He'll never agree."

"Leave it to me," Kason said. "But it's only if we need to fight. If the threat is minor, such as pirates, then you're going back to Keldera along with Taryn and Evaine." Taryn opened her mouth, but Kason beat her to it. "No, I won't negotiate on that. Consider it your duty as a diplomat."

Evaine spoke up again. "Remember why we're here, Taryn. Nova and all of the others back home are counting on you."

Under normal circumstances, Taryn never would've forgotten her duty. However, Kason tended to make her forget everything else, which was both a good and bad thing. "Well, we won't know until tomorrow, anyway. There's no use arguing about something that might never happen." She tilted her head. "How many hours until we know what's out there, Kason?"

"We'll hit instant communications range in about twelve hours from now, which is the only time my father can transmit a secure message without fear of someone else listening in. Soon after I know, I'll tell you." He paused and asked, "Are you done with your lessons for the day?"

"Yes, why?"

He put out a hand. "Then come with me. There's much to discuss, and I'd like to do it in private."

Kalahn snorted. "I'm not sure how much discussing will go on."

Kason growled. "Mind your own business, sister."

To prevent the pair from arguing, Taryn took Kason's hand. "Do you want to argue or do you want to 'discuss many things' as you put it?"

He met her gaze, but it was unreadable. "Come."

Kalahn asked, "Will you be back tonight, Taryn?"

But before she could answer, Kason had tugged her through the wardrobe and into his room. She expected him to release her hand, but instead, he guided her to a table and chairs on the other side of the room. "You're going to have dinner with me and tell me about your ways."

She blinked. "I wasn't expecting that."

He smiled at her. "Did you expect me to ravish you?"

"Er, yes."

"Maybe later. For now, I want to get to know my bride. Who knows when I'll have the chance again."

"You're serious about what you said before, about a future together, then?"

He raised his brows. "Why would I lie about that, especially given the consequences once I proclaim you mine?"

She slid into one of the seats. "About that, I don't want you to give up your general status, Kason. As much as you may think you want to be with me, I have a feeling you'll come to regret the decision eventually and blame me for ruining your life."

"I don't blame others for my decisions. You need not worry about that."

She looked at him askance. "That's easy to say now."

"I swear on my sister's life that I will bear sole responsibility for my decision to take you as a bride." She opened her mouth to argue, but he spoke as he sat in the other chair and crossed his arms over his chest. "You wish to rule Jasvar on your own, without me."

THE CONQUEST

She blinked at his topic change. "I don't know. There's so much changing so quickly, and unlike you, I don't have the chance to gauge my people's opinions on the matter."

"You like facts, so here it is: Without Keldera's help, your people will be at the mercy of whoever comes to your planet. You don't seem like a woman who likes that kind of uncertainty."

Taryn hated that Kason knew her so well already and could use it to reason against her. "This conversation is moot until after tomorrow anyway, so how about you ask me what you want to know about Jasvar? That will distract us both."

He studied her a second, and she wondered if Kason would ever open up to her. If he didn't, their future would be a frustrating one.

Her prince finally spoke up. "While I know that males are scarcer on your planet, why did none of them help you with the capture? That seemed odd to me."

Deciding she'd try to pry more information out of him later, she shrugged. "Unlike Keldera, men on Jasvar help in all aspects of marriage, including childrearing and chores. They were taking care of the others while we sprung the trap. The heart of my people is the ability to judge strengths and use them to our advantage. It's not about whether a person has a certain set of genitals or not, but rather about how they can best contribute to our society."

"And that will be part of your negotiations, to maintain that practice?"

"Of course. And judging by what happened with Kalahn, there are plenty of Kelderan women who would welcome the change. I'd suggest that people open to the idea of women doing nontraditional Kelderan roles should be the ones to join the colony. That will lessen the chance of revolt."

Kason remained silent for a few seconds before he finally said, "If I'm honest, I never would've considered it before meeting you, Taryn. However, you have a way of convincing people to change their minds."

She leaned forward. "At least I no longer need to use a dagger to get you to agree to anything."

He chuckled. "I was shocked to the extent you probably could have bested me if you'd tried. You were like a warrior goddess."

"I don't have any special powers to merit the goddess aspect, but I'll take the warrior one." She lowered her voice. "I even brought my outfit with me, in case I need it."

Heat flashed in his eyes. "You will save that for me."

"Is that an order? Because we know how well I handle those."

He growled. "Consider it a request, at least until everyone knows you're mine."

"Too bad you asked rather than dictated. It would have made quite the impression on Keldera during negotiations."

"More like you would've given my father a heart attack. As much as he and I may disagree, no one is ready for him to step down yet."

She searched his gaze. "You and Kalahn speak of your father, but I don't know much about him except that he sounds like a traditionalist."

"He is the king," Kason answered. "When my mother was alive, he made a token effort to spend time with his children. However, once she was killed during one of the Brevkan attacks, he focused all of his energy on his people and left childrearing to the female servants."

Taryn tilted her head. "Do you think it's because you remind him of your late mother?"

"Perhaps. My father and I don't have heart-to-heart conversations."

She smiled. "I could try to fix that."

Kason shook his head. "No, meddling with the royal family can be dangerous. Even though you're not from Keldera, one wrong word or sentence could label you as a traitor. I'm not sure even I could save you if that happened."

"I'll keep that in mind. Although I hope I don't have to be so careful around your brother."

Kason's eyes shuttered. "Keltor and I aren't very close. You'll have to ask Kalahn about him."

Okay, so it seemed Kason's family problems ran deep. While she'd heed his advice about not meddling for the present, she'd have to see what she could do later. "At least your family is still alive. All I have is my grandmother and her memory is failing."

"Family isn't always because of blood. You seem to have friends who care about you. I will also become your family."

"You seem pretty certain of that."

"Yes."

She snorted. "I must admit that your honesty is growing on me. Although, it is ultimately my say or not."

"Then tell me what I must do to convince you and I will do it."

The more determined Kason became, the fewer reasons Taryn could come up with as to why she should refuse him.

Maybe, just maybe, things would work out between them.

She reached out a hand, and Kason took it. "For now, focus on the negotiations and the possible threat. That's all I ask."

He stood and tugged her against his chest. "You are levelheaded, practical, and as stubborn as any male. I can't wait to claim you as mine in front of everyone."

Lowering his head, he kissed her.

~~~

It had been a long time since Kason had talked with a female about his family, let alone the troubles he had with them. If he had had any doubts about Taryn Demara being his bride before, they had vanished.

When she merely asked him to focus on what was important rather than try to impress her, his restraint snapped. He needed to taste his female.

The second her soft breasts crushed against his chest, he descended on her lips. Taryn didn't hesitate in opening to him.

As he stroked her mouth, he ran a hand down her back to her rear and rocked her against him. She moaned, and his cock screamed to take her. However, he managed to linger a few seconds more before breaking the kiss and murmuring, "Tomorrow will be a long day. You should go."

She blinked. "What?"

"It's not what I want, but we both need to rest. The fate of your world and mine hangs in the balance over the next few days."

Placing a hand on his chest, she said, "If I have to go back to the other room, I'll lie awake thinking about you. We should share a bed."

"I want that, but if I can only take you once more, then I want to do it without distractions."

She traced some of the markings on his chest. "I'm starting to rethink the 'once more and I'm done' decision from before." Her finger stilled. "As it is, I could already be carrying your child. I think the time for distance is over."

"But I don't have any sort of birth control to use since only the Barren are onboard the ship, and there's no chance of pregnancy. If I take you, it could increase the chances of pregnancy."

"Is that such a bad thing?"

He pulled her tighter against his body. "No."

"Well, then let's share a bed, Kason. Who knows, we may come up with our best ideas yet after a little sex and we don't want to waste that opportunity, now, do we?"

He smiled. "That sounds like an excuse."

"But it's a good one, isn't it?"

Lowering his head, he stopped when he was an inch from her lips. "Maybe I should reward you."

"Maybe? I think you should."

With a growl, he scooped up Taryn and carried her to his bed. "Just try not to scream too loudly or someone might hear you."

"I would think the walls would be soundproofed."

He laid her gently on the bed. "For the most part, but I plan to be very attentive."

And for the next few hours, Kason was.

Chapter Fourteen

Kason lay awake listening to Taryn's even breathing at his side. Since he'd never allowed a female to spend the night before, it was both a strange and comforting sound. Different from his days as a young warrior, when he'd had to share quarters with three other males, but in a good way.

She snuggled into his side and he hugged her close. It was hard to believe their lives could change forever in the next day, and not necessarily in a good way. He rarely worried about a possible battle, but with Taryn in his life, he was afraid for her.

Not that he was going to send her away. She'd probably risk stabbing him with a dagger so that she could stay.

Leaning over, he was about to kiss his warrior's forehead when his comm unit beeped and he mentally cursed. Carefully slipping from his bed, Kason moved to the unit. Thankfully, the screen faced away from the bed. He pressed the receive button, and Thorin's face appeared on the screen. "The king will be ready in fifteen minutes. We need you in the conference room."

He nodded. "I'll be there."

Thorin studied him a second before replying, "You look well-rested despite the upcoming challenges."

"Anyone can do the same with enough meditation."

Thorin searched his eyes. "If you say so. I'll see you in the conference room."

The screen turned blank, and Kason looked to the bed, where Taryn was awake. She said, "Thorin suspects something."

"Probably, but he won't probe until after the threat is assessed and handled."

"He seems an odd choice for a second-in-command. You two don't appear to get along very well."

"He is a good warrior. I thought that was enough."

"But no longer?"

He smiled at her. "A certain female makes me question everything now and then I wonder how I can improve it."

Taryn sat up, and the sheet fell to expose her upper body. When she cleared her throat, he met her eyes again and she replied, "All of that doesn't matter right now. Just promise me that you'll tell me the news as soon as you can. Waiting around is going to kill me."

He moved to the bed and brushed Taryn's cheek. "If I could have you at my side in the conference room, I would."

"But now is not the time to challenge yet another tradition." She sighed. "I know."

After giving her a quick, rough kiss, he murmured, "Patience, my bride. Try meditating a little before you go back into Kalahn's room. That will help to pass the time."

"Is that a good idea? I don't want to risk someone coming in here while you're gone."

"Only a handful of people have the code and they will all be busy."

She nodded. "Okay. I'll try meditating, but I doubt it'll make time pass any quicker."

"It might surprise you." He gave her another kiss and then changed his clothes before exiting the room.

As he walked down one corridor and then another, he tried pushing thoughts of Taryn to the side. However, whenever he passed another warrior, he wanted to growl and proclaim the human his.

The meeting with his father couldn't end soon enough.

He finally made it to the conference room and found more than Thorin sitting around the table. Enishi, Syzel, and Jerrick were there, too. He would admonish Thorin for inviting the others to the meeting without his permission later.

Kason took his seat at the head of the table and looked to each male in turn. "I will discuss the details of our plan with the king, if needed. That's an order." Each of the men nodded, even Thorin. "Good. Signal the king that we're ready to receive his transmission."

Enishi tapped a few commands on the computer panel, and the king's face appeared on the screen. While his father's hair had been white for many years, Kason swore the lines on the king's face were deeper and more pronounced. He would have Kalahn reach out to Keltor to find what was going on.

The king spoke. "I'm not going to waste time on formalities. Our scout ship discovered two pirate ships at the edges of the system, but after probing further, the crew also discovered two battleships. While unlike any of the Brevkan ships we've encountered in the past, it's possible they've commandeered or engineered new prototypes. You need to investigate the vessels and find out who is commanding them. Send any of the sick or injured to Keldera as soon as you can and then be on your way."

Kason was one of the few who could challenge his father and avoid punishment. "Were the pirates working with the other ships? Or not? That will determine our strategy."

"The scouting ship couldn't tell."

THE CONQUEST

While Kason hadn't wanted so many people in the room when talking with his father, he made the best of the situation. "One more thing, Father. The humans on Jasvar proved to be a worthy opponent. They sent a delegation to negotiate a colonization agreement."

One of his father's brows raised a fraction. "I thought it was uninhabited."

"It wasn't. As soon as we assess and handle the threats, I will bring them to you for a meeting. Your advisors can put together a team to discuss the terms of the colony."

He expected his father to admonish him, but the king merely asked, "Do you plan to sacrifice them if the battleships turn out to be enemies? That would solve all of our problems as we could take the colony planet by force."

Leave it to his father to pretend as if Jasvar had never been cursed in the first place, let alone how Kason had proved that point. "Sacrifice should be unnecessary. Their presence may help if the battleships are related to the Earth Colony Alliance."

"Do as you see fit. Just make sure you succeed."

Kason nodded. "We'll change course directly and I'll send word when it's safe. Just make sure to send two other fighter ships to wait near the closest moon at the edge of the star system. They need to be ready for my order, in case we need them to join us."

"It will be done." The king cut the transmission. Since he hadn't asked about Kalahn, his father must not know she was missing yet.

However, the strangest part was that his father had acquiesced so quickly. Even a year ago, the king would've pressed Kason for every last detail. His health must be declining quickly.

While he may not be close to the king, Kason vowed to take care of the threat and bring Kalahn back to Keldera before their father's health could deteriorate further.

Thorin spoke up. "Since the threat is unknown, has your plan changed?"

"No. Regardless if it's the Brevkan or someone else, the possibility of using the female ruse could be useful. Request about forty competent females be sent to our ship when we pass by Keldera in a few hours. Give the excuse of keeping the Jasvarian delegation company. We'll also send the unwilling males back to the most isolated military base to be watched. Make sure you contact the right people. I don't want the order to be leaked and cause a panic."

"As you wish, your highness," Thorin said before exiting the room.

His gut told him he needed someone to watch Thorin. Kason looked to Syzel. "Go with him. Since you have all of the details and numbers we need, make sure he requests the right number and ensure everything goes smoothly."

Syzel nodded, and Kason trusted the male to keep an eye on Thorin, too.

He looked to Jerrick and Enishi. "Start making preparations for training the females. Jerrick, you're going to have your hands full. I'll check in once the females arrive."

Jerrick asked, "What about Princess Kalahn? Is she still going to help me with the females?"

"My sister will help with the females, as will the Jasvarian leader, although not necessarily together. Vow to me you will protect both of them with your life."

Jerrick made a fist and thumped his chest. "I swear it. No harm will befall them as long as I'm still breathing."

"Good." Kason stood. "I'll meet you all in the cargo bay when the shuttles arrive. If you need to contact me before that, use a secure comm unit."

Once the two males nodded, Kason exited the room. He was taking a huge chance by going forward with the plan, even if the ships were unknown. However, three warships had to be either the Brevkan or related to the ECA. There were no other forces with enough resources to command such ships nearby.

In either scenario, Taryn's help would be invaluable.

He just needed to ensure preparations happened without a hitch.

~~~

Taking a deep breath, Taryn opened her eyes again. Each time she completed one of Kason's meditations, she felt stronger and better prepared. By the time Jasvar had spaceflight capabilities, she should have a multitude of ideas to address any aliens she encountered.

Of course, not everyone on Jasvar was going to appreciate the changes. But thanks to the doom virus, living a low-tech lifestyle wasn't much of an option anymore. Maybe she could send the low-tech diehards to form another settlement near the main one. That might be easier to handle than constantly easing egos and fears. Or, worse, a rebellion.

As she stood, the door slid open to reveal a woman wearing a brown, flowing dress and an intricate tattoo on her forehead. Unless Kason had already brought aboard more females, it had to be one of the Barren.

Not wanting the woman to flee, Taryn tugged her into the room and shut the door. Even though the woman probably couldn't understand CEL, she whispered, "It's okay. You don't have to run."

The woman tilted her head and said, "Human."

"Yes. Do you understand me?"

"A little. Why here? Prince room."

"Do you understand what a secret is?" When the woman looked confused, Taryn grabbed her hand and tugged toward the wardrobe. "Come with me."

She punched in the code and brought the woman through the wardrobe. On the other side, Kalahn and Evaine both looked at them. Kalahn said something in Kelderan and the female in the brown dress replied. After about a minute, Kalahn sighed and switched to CEL. "Now we're going to have to deal with her."

Taryn glanced at the woman. "Who is she? And is that a problem?"

"Her name is Vala Yarlen. She's one of the Barren and I hope she doesn't become a problem."

Taryn faced Vala and smiled. Pointing at her own chest, she said, "Taryn." Pointing to the woman, she said, "Vala."

Vala smiled. "Hello, Taryn."

Greetings were one of the things Taryn knew. "*Urani*, Vala." Taryn looked back to Kalahn. "How does she know any CEL at all?"

"The Barren have a lot of time on their hands. When not onboard one of the ships, they live at one of the citadels and spend their time reading books and researching. Vala must've studied CEL."

Evaine spoke up. "Well, we can't keep her prisoner forever. What can we do?"

Kalahn talked with Vala. All Taryn could understand was "yes" and "no." Eventually, Kalahn explained, "Vala will keep the secret of finding you in Kason's quarters provided she is assigned to look after us. Since at least one of the Barren must accompany us in the halls when Kason or one of the other high-ranking officers is unavailable, I don't see it as a problem."

Taryn studied the woman who couldn't be much older than she. "I think I've just discovered a reason to really work on my language lessons."

"Why?" Kalahn asked.

"As much as I appreciate you interpreting for us, I want to ask Vala some questions myself. After all, I need to learn all about Kelderan culture, and the mysterious Barren should be part of it. Maybe Kason will even allow her to join the colony, if she's interested."

Kalahn frowned. "I'm not sure if that would be a good idea. As you can see, the tattoo tells every Kelderan her status. Some might be upset that a Barren is allowed to join a colony even though they can't help populate it."

"Then they can stay with the Jasvarians and become teachers, if they wish. It'll be a good learning experience for all."

Evaine asked, "Do any of them study technology or programming? Engineering? I would love to meet any who do."

Kalahn shrugged. "I don't know. Little is known about what goes on at the citadels." She talked with Vala and then added in CEL, "Some do, although getting Vala to admit it was tough. She's used to living in the shadows. All of this attention can't be easy."

Taryn eyed the tattooed woman and gently placed a hand on her arm. "Don't worry. I will keep you safe."

Taryn smiled, the universal sign everything was okay, and Vala smiled back. "You nice."

As she tried to think of what to say that Vala might understand, Kason strode into the room. The instant the door shut behind him, he glanced at Vala and then at Taryn. "What's going on here?"

"She walked into your room, and I needed Kalahn's help to talk with her." Taryn waved toward the woman. "This is Vala."

He grunted. "I know who she is. She cleans my room and brings my meals." He gave his sister a piercing look. "What did you say to her?"

"Don't take that tone with me, Kason. All she asked was to be our escort, if needed. Since Taryn has taken a shine to her, that shouldn't be a problem."

Kason sighed. "Fine. We can talk more about this later. Right now, we need to discuss what I learned." He made a motion with his hand, and Vala bowed her head before exiting the room. Once she was gone, he continued, "We don't know if the Brevkan are waiting for us or not. But there are two pirate ships and three warships, so as a precaution, we're going to prep for our plan."

"Pirates as in space pirates?" Taryn asked.

"Yes. Provided they're not mercenaries hired by an enemy, a few goods will encourage them to move on. The warships could be anyone, maybe even the Earth Colony Alliance. Although why they would be out here, I don't know."

Evaine chimed in, "I might know." All eyes turned toward her, and she shrugged. "I read somewhere that my predecessors launched an experimental beacon ten or twenty years ago, with a brief message asking for help. Given the hodgepodge of our technology and its age, no one believed it was more than a rumor, let alone that it would reach Earth if it were true."

Taryn frowned. "Why didn't you ever tell me about this?"

Evaine put up her hands. "I wasn't even part of the technology team when it was sent. Much like the others in the department, we thought it was a rumor since no one could find out who had sent it."

"Placing blame or focusing on the past won't help," Kason interjected. "Either way, you all are staying aboard to help. If it is the ECA, your presence will be more important than ever before."

"Well, we'll see how it goes. My people left Earth 200 years ago. I have no idea what to expect."

"I understand. Now, here's what we're going to do."

As Taryn listened to Kason's plan and schedule, she forgot about Vala and what the future might entail. All that mattered was handling the present so she could see through all of her grand plans for Jasvar and Keldera.

Chapter Fifteen

The next few hours flew by in a flurry for Taryn, filled with last-minute essential phrase lessons and ensuring that there were enough supplies synthesized by the computer for the coming females. When it finally came time to head to the cargo bay, Taryn downed one last energy drink, adjusted her new outfit that walked the line between concealing curves and allowing movement, and then nodded at Evaine and Kalahn. "Here's to hoping this works."

Kalahn replied, "Since I usually only give hope-filled speeches about nothing, I'm excited to be useful."

Evaine spoke up, "Not only that, I think after this, women on your planet might start demanding change."

"Maybe. But we can think about that later. We only have a few days to train the women and ensure they can handle the pressure," Taryn added.

As they exited the room, they found Vala waiting for them in the hall. After Taryn waved hello and they all walked down the corridor, she continued, "Speaking of handling the pressure, where did Kason and the others find them?"

Kalahn shrugged. "Just because females can't participate in the military or politics doesn't mean they can't hold other professions. Most are high-ranking entrepreneurs, educators, and even law clerks, which is the closest thing to a lawyer they can be on Keldera."

"In other words, strong, intelligent women who should pick things up quickly," Evaine pointed out.

"Exactly." Kalahn guided them down another corridor. "There are even a few engineering assistants, which will probably be working with you and Enishi."

Evaine rubbed her hands together. "I'm curious to meet him, especially since he's open to training women."

"He knows some CEL, which will help." Kalahn looked to Taryn. "Jerrick doesn't, however. So try your best with the guard and sentry training."

Taryn raised her chin. "There's a lot you can do without words when it comes to defense and attack techniques. I actually look forward to trying to best the warrior."

Kalahn smiled and lowered her voice. "Just don't get too cozy or Kason might punch the male. That will draw suspicion and the rest will come out soon enough after that."

Taryn rolled her eyes. "Once this is over, it'll be nice not to have to worry about my every action." She touched Kalahn's arm. "I hope you can come to my planet in the end."

"Me, too. I'm not sure I can go back to being cooped up with little interaction with others beyond the servants or the Barren. Being a princess isn't all that grand and not a fate I would've chosen." Kalahn stopped in front of a large metal door. After placing her thumb on a panel, it slid open to reveal the cavernous cargo bay. "Here goes nothing."

Kason and several other important-looking and bare-chested men stood to one side, their heads together and talking. Taryn recognized Thorin, but none of the others. However, one had to be Jerrick and another Enishi, not that she could tell who was who since they were all muscled and wearing almost identical outfits of tight pants, boots, and weapons holstered at their sides.

They were only halfway across the floor when Kason looked up and met her gaze. The lack of heat or any emotion for that matter was strange to see, even if she understood the reason behind it.

All too quickly, she'd become accustomed to him looking at her as if she were the most beautiful woman in the world.

Stop it, Taryn. We have much more important matters to worry about. Straightening her shoulders, Taryn gave her most distinguished, take-no-crap expression as they closed the distance. One of the warriors spotted her and the corner of his mouth ticked up. He might be a potential ally. Especially since Thorin didn't hide the disgust from his eyes as he looked at each of the four females. He nearly sneered when his gaze flicked to Vala.

To her credit, Vala ignored the look. It was sad to think the Barren might endure such disgust on a regular basis. She hoped it was just Thorin's reaction and not the norm.

They reached the males and Kason spoke up in CEL. "The females will be here in the next few minutes. Evaine, this is Enishi"—Kason waved toward a man in his late-thirties with golden hair and light blue skin—"you're going to work with him."

Enishi smiled. "Welcome."

Evaine moved to Enishi's side. "If possible, I want to work with the engines."

"Engines?" Enishi echoed. "If you have right touch, maybe."

Before Evaine could ask another question, Kason waved to the black-haired, golden-skinned man who had smiled at Taryn. "This is Jerrick. Taryn will be working with him."

They nodded at each other, but before Taryn could think of what to say, Kalahn interjected, "And me?"

"You and Vala will be working with Syzel. He's going to train you in how to pilot and use the communication systems."

Kalahn's eyes lit up. "Really?"

"Yes. Those will be some of the most vital roles, and I'm hoping your presence will encourage the others." A beeping sound echoed inside the room. "That would be the ship with the females approaching. Just one last thing for Taryn and Evaine— you've temporarily been granted access to the AI system to assist with the language barrier. While she can do some interpreting, it will be delayed, so try to rely on yourselves as much as possible."

The cargo doors opened, but due to the force field across the entrance, Taryn could see the ship and space beyond it without being sucked outside.

Even the small glimpse of the vastness with pricks of light was beyond words.

Maybe someday Kason could take her to see a planet from afar.

Then the shuttle stopped inside and the craft's rear door opened. Once the stairs extended, a male warrior descended and soon was followed by a steady stream of women.

Each of them gaped at the cargo bay, much like how Taryn had done. However, the lead warrior barked an order in Kelderan and the women picked up their paces. When the Kelderan females spotted Taryn, Evaine, and then Kalahn, many of them stopped in their tracks.

Kason said something and they started walking again. Kalahn leaned over and whispered into her ear, "He told them to treat all of us as friends. I doubt it'll happen straight away, but try not to display any signs of anger or disappointment unless absolutely necessary. As many have said, change can't happen overnight. It's scary for them to be aboard a starship, let alone with one full of men."

Kason and the warrior from the shuttle talked for a minute longer before the unknown warrior directed the women to each of the leaders. Kalahn gave her arm a squeeze before heading over to Syzel. Taking a deep inhalation, Taryn moved to where Jerrick stood.

"*Urani*, Taryn," he said, and she returned his greeting.

Thankfully the group of females assigned to them arrived and prevented Taryn from trying to communicate with the warrior. Still, she was grateful it was Jerrick instead of Thorin.

She didn't think it was a coincidence that Kason had kept her, Kalahn, Evaine, and Vala away from that man.

Once the group of forty or so women each had a place, Kason raised a fist, and the cargo bay fell silent except for the sound of a few cargo bay staff running around in the background.

Taryn watched Kason's face and gestures as he gave a booming speech. Whatever he said made the women nod and stand taller. Even at her side, Kalahn stood a little straighter.

With a clap, Kason turned from the crowd and walked up to Taryn. He tugged her to the side and whispered, "I'll check in later. I'm counting on you to help Jerrick. If anyone can convince a female that she can win against a male, it's you."

She smiled. "Watch out, or you might have a mini-army that can take you and your men down."

"Unless they have poisoned darts, I'm not worried."

"I might just have a few."

He nearly smiled. Taryn had a feeling if they had been alone, he would've laughed. "We'll talk later. Good luck, Taryn Demara."

"Luck? More like 'I rely on your skill, oh great human.'"

Shaking his head, Kason murmured, "Human females."

She bit her lip to keep from grinning. She needed to be more distant with Kason in front of the others.

Clearing her throat, she made a fist and thumped her chest, like she'd seen the Kelderans do earlier. "I won't let you down."

THE CONQUEST

With a nod, Kason headed to Kalahn. Taking that as her cue, Taryn walked back to Jerrick. They acknowledged each other, and he motioned toward the exit. As Taryn took up the rear, she ran through several training options inside her head. Prepping the women in a few days to full-fighting force was impossible, but even a few well-rehearsed moves could trick the unsuspecting.

No matter, she would succeed. Not just for Jasvar's future, but for her own, as well. There was no way in hell she would let Kason down.

~~~

Kason stood with Thorin inside the cargo bay command center. They watched from behind a glass wall separating them from five females, who sat in front of individual computer panels. Each one was studying the basics of cargo bay mechanics. While it was impossible to teach them everything, he just needed them to fool the enemy if they boarded the ship.

Thorin changed the position of his arms over his chest. Since they were alone in their section, and the walls and glass were soundproofed, Kason decided he'd put off the conversation with Thorin long enough. "I know you don't approve. However, I need to know if you will follow my orders. I can't be second-guessing my second."

Thorin glanced at him. "I've always followed orders."

"In the beginning, yes. But recently, you've been making decisions that you should've cleared with me first."

Looking back to the females on the other side of the glass, Thorin replied, "You are the one who should be careful. I'm close to proving who the human female is to you. Once that happens, I can assume command. Then I'll call off this ridiculous exercise and implement a winning strategy."

"I don't know what you're talking about. Speak freely."

Thorin raised his brows. "Are you sure that's wise?"

"Threats aren't wise. I'm one of the few who knows the true identity of your father. You were lucky that you inherited your mother's looks. If our superiors knew you were half-Brevkan, you never would've been allowed into the army. You owe my father for your mother's pardon and the fake birth register."

"I am Kelderan. I claim no allegiance to the dishonorable animals who raped my mother and left her to die. And let's not forget it happened while she was trying to save your aunt, I might add."

"My father has repaid that debt already. So let's just make sure your allegiance is true for this mission. Do your duty, avoid gossip, and I will find you a position so that you can command your own ship. Try to betray me or usurp my place, and I will ensure you are banished and never employed as a warrior ever again. Understood?"

"As long as you speak the truth once the battle is complete, then I will go against my better judgment and follow your plan." Thorin met his eyes. "However, the crew has a right to know the human is your bride."

"If that is true, the people will know. Dealing with the upcoming threat is all that is important."

"The female has made you soft."

Kason wanted to punch the bastard for insulting Taryn, but resisted. "Your loyalties?"

"I vow allegiance, your highness."

Thorin's words dripped with disdain, but Kason was going to give him a chance. "Good. Then oversee this work while I check on the others."

THE CONQUEST

Without another word, Kason left the room and exited the cargo bay. Bringing up Thorin's secret was risky, but his second needed to understand his place. Until Taryn had boarded the ship, Kason had never had reason to question Thorin's loyalty. He suspected Thorin was acting this way partly due to his own future, or lack of one. While his appearance seemed Kelderan, there were other signs that could reveal his Brevkan father during a sexual claiming.

In other words, Thorin may never find a bride of his own. No Kelderan female would want to be associated with a half-Brevkan male.

Of course, joining the colony might solve that problem. Kason would have to think about it.

As he finally reached the training room, he opened the door and stepped inside. Taryn stood in front of the class and was repeatedly saying, "Volunteer?" in Kelderan.

As no one stepped forward, Kason answered, "I'll do it."

Her eyes met his and her lips curled up ever so slightly. Yes, sparring with his human bride would be a good way to forget about Thorin for a little while.

The females cleared a path for him. Out of the corner of his eye, he noticed their looks of awe. Kason's status as a general was well-known, but apart from mandatory celebrations, he tended to stay out of the public's eye.

Watching a human female try to best him was unthinkable to his people. He hoped none of the Kelderan women would suffer heart attacks.

He reached the front and waited. Taryn finally said, "Computer, interpret into Kelderan until I tell you to cease."

"Understood."

Taryn faced Kason. "When facing an opponent who is bigger than you, the key is to focus on their weaknesses." Once the computer caught up, Taryn continued, "Even the strongest warrior has vulnerable spots. However, your greatest advantage is playing on their arrogance. Most men will see a cowering female and expect her to be an easy target."

Motioning him to come at her with her hands, she ordered, "Try to tackle me."

He wasn't going to pass up the chance. However, Kason approached slowly, and they circled one another. Eventually, Taryn tripped and tumbled to the ground with a smack.

Afraid she had broken a bone, he rushed down to her. As he checked her for injuries, she kneed him in the groin. Pain shot through his body and Kason rolled to the side. Taryn then kicked him in the kidney.

As Kason tried to gather his wits, Taryn said, "Cowering is good, but so is feigning weakness. This may not work on all enemies, but it's a start and gets you thinking outside the box. Now, work in pairs and think of how to attack a vulnerable part of a male as they try to attack you."

The computer translated, and Taryn crouched down beside him. While his balls still throbbed, he found his voice and murmured, "Was that necessary? The Brevkan won't fall for your injured female trick."

"Maybe not, but it broke the tension. Look at the others."

Kason managed to roll to his side. The women were busy pointing out places to attack or discussing how to disarm someone in a less than honorable fashion.

Taryn's voice filled his ears again. "See? Your pain has a purpose."

He wanted to tell her she had payback coming, but Jerrick came over to him and asked in Kelderan, "Are you all right, your highness?" Jerrick glanced to Taryn and back. "She's quite the feisty one."

174

Kason sat up and answered in the same language. "Believe me, I know." He slowly stood and forced himself not to cup his genitals. "What do you think of the women? Will they be ready?"

Jerrick looked to the crowd. "I was skeptical at first as no one would even speak. However, the human seems to understand them better than me."

"She is clever, but you understand the Brevkan. Make sure to cover their strengths and weaknesses, too."

"Of course, your highness."

Both watched as Taryn walked among the women. As Jerrick's gaze drifted down to Taryn's rear, it took everything Kason had not to punch the male in the face.

Their mission couldn't be over soon enough for many reasons.

Kason spoke up. "Then I'll leave the training in your capable hands. I'll check back later if I can. Otherwise, you can report everything at the meeting at the end of the day, before evening meditation."

Jerrick made a fist and pounded his chest as he bowed his head. Kason did the same and exited the training room.

For once, he was glad of Taryn's language barrier. It gave him less competition.

Chapter Sixteen

Vala Yarlen stood at the perimeter of the main command area and tried her best to blend in with the wall.

From the day her genetic scan had signified her inability to bear children at age six months, she'd spent her life in the comfort of the citadel with the other Barren. There no one treated her differently or tried to hide their pity. She was simply part of the Barren family.

However, last year, she'd petitioned to assist on one of the starships and had been accepted. Since then, her existence had consisted of her blending into the background and only speaking when required. Others in her group dallied with the warriors, but Vala had never worked up the nerve.

Besides, her main assignment had been caring for General Kason tro el Vallen, the younger prince of Keldera. To say he was intimidating was an understatement.

However, after meeting the human female named Taryn, Vala had finally mustered some of her confidence and asked to be assigned to her and the other two females.

She'd never envisioned being treated as an equal of the other women.

Syzel, the warrior instructing them, came over and murmured, "You either need to participate or leave. It's your choice."

His words were neutral, which was an improvement over Lt. General Thorin's disdain earlier.

Taking a deep breath, Vala moved to one of the consoles at the back of the area. After typing in a set of instructions, she brought up the flight simulator. As she controlled the computer, guiding the ship through an asteroid field, the rest of the room faded away. Like most of the Barren, she'd spent a lot of time with simulators since their access to the outside world was restricted. She easily reached the target at the end and smiled.

To her surprise, Syzel's voice filled her ears again. "You've done this before." She nodded but never met his eye. He ordered, "Bring up level 15."

She did as he asked and again guided the ship. This time, it was through a debris field that also included five other vessels, one of which fired at her and she had to dodge the blasts. When she reached the end, the male spoke again. "How would you feel assisting the other females?"

Daring a glance, she whispered, "Must I?"

"I can make it an order if need be, but I'm asking you to do it. You're ready for real-life flight instructions, and I need to get the others up to speed. That way we can try a few short shuttle flights."

Her lips parted at the thought of flying for real. "We're going to take a shuttle out?"

"Provided enough of you are ready, yes." He studied her. "Will you help?"

Syzel didn't look at her with desire or hatred. All she saw was curiosity.

Even though facing the women wasn't going to be easy, this might be her only chance to feel and act as a non-Barren female. For years, she'd convinced herself she was content with her life.

But the thought of flying a ship and not blending in with the wall sent a little thrill through her body.

It might only be for a day, but she could pretend she was normal.

She bobbed her head. "I'll try."

He smiled. "Good. Go to Fia. She needs the most help."

As Syzel left, Vala met Kalahn's gaze. The princess tilted her head in question, but Vala gave an imperceptible shake of her head. She could fill the princess in later.

Vala walked over to the female named Fia and forced herself to keep her head high. Even if all of the females hated her or treated her as lesser, Vala would soldier on. This could be the only opportunity in her lifetime to fly a shuttle, and she wasn't going to pass it up.

Stopping next to Fia, Vala cleared her throat and said, "I've been sent to help."

The female looked up at her and blinked. "But you're one of the Barren. How do you know how to fly a ship?"

She kept a smile pasted on her face. "I just cleared level 15 of the simulator. Syzel ordered me to help. Will you let me?"

Fia searched her eyes. "What's your name?"

"Vala."

"Well, Vala, I can use all of the help I can get. I run a set of shops on Keldera and this is completely different from what I'm used to."

The woman's occupation enlightened Vala as to why the female was speaking to her—the Barren purchased many goods and any store owner would want their business.

A small voice inside Vala's head said maybe it was because the woman was kind, but she pushed it away. After all, Vala had been burned too many times in the past when she'd trusted someone too early.

Bringing up the flight simulator, Vala focused on instructing Fia on how to maneuver the ship. She may not be able to control how her life would play out long-term, but for the foreseeable future, she was determined to fly. Helping Fia was her top priority.

~~~

As the last woman filed out of the training area, Taryn faced Jerrick. She blinked. The warrior was grinning at her.

Before she could ask the computer to interpret, Jerrick did, and the computer said in CEL, "Good job today. But before you leave, let's have our own sparring session. I want to see how good you are."

Since she didn't have a reason to refuse, she nodded. Jerrick made a motion with his hands for her to attack.

They circled one another. Since she knew he wouldn't fall for any of the tricks she'd taught the women, Taryn kept an eye on his feet. If she wanted any chance at winning, she needed to get him on the ground.

Jerrick rushed at her, but Taryn stepped to the side and whipped around. However, Jerrick was already facing her again. Damn, he was fast. She would have to try something else. If only she had her daggers, she would have a better chance at besting him. Sadly, Kason had forbidden her to bring them to the training class.

They each waited for the other to attack. She feinted left and then dove headfirst between his legs. She managed to punch his testicles as she slid through, but he barely grunted. Before she

179

could get back to her feet, Jerrick pinned her down and flipped her onto her stomach. With who knew how many pounds of muscles on top of her, Taryn knew she was trapped.

She had much to learn about hand-to-hand combat with a fully trained warrior when both her weapons and her element of surprise were gone.

The computer translated Jerrick's words. "I wish to claim my prize for defeating you. Have dinner with me."

She muttered, "I'm pinned to the ground, and you want dinner? Such a lady killer."

Even without her asking, the computer translated and Jerrick chuckled. Again, the computer interpreted, "I have always admired strong women, even if it's not the norm on my planet. I want to better know the leader of Jasvar. You may just convince me to join the colony."

"If an agreement can be reached."

Before the computer could say anything else, Kason's voice was curt. While he spoke in Kelderan, even Taryn could tell he gave an order. Jerrick slowly stood up and released her.

Once Taryn was upright again, she looked between the two males. While Kason's gaze was stoic, the tightness of his jaw told her he was barely restraining himself from doing something stupid, such as punching his new trainer.

Taryn walked up to Jerrick and put out a hand. "Thank you for the match, but I must postpone our dinner. There's much to do, and I couldn't give you the attention you deserve."

The corner of Jerrick's mouth ticked up as the computer finished her words. Then it interpreted his. "I will call upon you at a more convenient time, warrior ruler of Jasvar."

Jerrick bowed, and Kason touched her shoulder. The prince muttered, "Let's go."

With a final wave, Taryn followed Kason out into the hallway. Aware of eyes and ears everywhere, she remained silent until they reached her quarters. Before the door slid shut, Kason darted his eyes toward his room and back. He wanted to talk with her.

Wanting to keep him in suspense, she shrugged and shut the door.

Kalahn's voice filled the room. "I hope you don't keep him waiting too long. Otherwise, his temper will be awful."

Taryn faced Kalahn and noticed Evaine was nowhere to be found. "I'll talk to him eventually, but he needs to cool down a fraction before I do. Where's Evaine?"

"She messaged to let me know she's staying with Enishi for a few more hours. Apparently, she wanted extra sessions."

She smiled. "Evaine may not let him go until she's gleaned everything she can from him." She sat across from Kalahn. "How did yours go?"

"The flight simulations went pretty well, for the most part. I was second in the class. Surprisingly, Vala was first."

Taryn moved to get a clean dress. "Vala did better than you?"

Kalahn nodded. "Yes. Apparently, she's been practicing with a flight simulator for years. She even helped one of the other women with her training."

"Did that go okay?" She asked as she changed clothes. "Considering what I know of the Barren, they usually keep to the shadows."

"She was uneasy but managed to last the entire session. I could tell she wanted to bolt a few times, though. It was the first time I realized how isolated the Barren must be."

"Good, then you can help me with them later, after I've secured an alliance and a colonization agreement. Given what I've

181

heard about unrest and factions on Keldera, I'm sure your father and brother will need the Barren on their side. We need to ensure they will stand with them as soon as possible, or one of the other factions may beat us to it. That most likely means a change in how they're treated."

Kalahn raised her brows. "You seem pretty confident that we can change things."

"Oh, it'll happen. After my interactions today, I think a lot of people will want to move to the colony and forge a new path. The Barren will be welcome on Jasvar, so others will have to accept that if they wish to live on my planet."

Kalahn leaned forward. "Is that why Kason was clenching his jaw as if it would break? Did Jerrick mention wanting to join the colony?"

"After he defeated me in a sparring session, Jerrick said I might be able to convince him, and then he asked me to dinner."

"Then you'd better talk to Kason straight away. No male is to touch another's bride until the marriage is announced publicly, and while you two were merely sparring, it would still be considered touching you. Kason not punching Jerrick is a miracle."

She sighed. "I can't wait for all the secrecy to be over."

Kalahn motioned toward the wardrobe. "Go see my brother. Only you can calm him down. Also, don't worry about hurrying back. I expect Kason to claim you at least once to sate his instinct."

Taryn eyed Kalahn. "I'm not sure I could talk about a sibling's sex life so casually."

"Kelderans are open about it. After all, none of us would be here without it," Kalahn stated.

She snorted. "That's true." Taryn moved to the wardrobe. "I don't think Jerrick will come looking for me, but make excuses if he does."

"Of course."

With that, Taryn went through the wardrobe and emerged inside Kason's room. Her prince stopped pacing and rushed her. In the blink of an eye, he had her pinned against the wall.

His breath was hot on her face as he growled, "I don't like that you kept me waiting."

She raised her brows. "If you think I'm going to heed your every beck and call, then I should leave now."

"No. You'll stay."

"Ordering me to do so won't help your case."

"Then consider it a request—please stay with me."

"Wow, you said 'please.' That must've been tough for you."

He leaned a fraction closer. "No more teasing. Tell me why Jerrick asked you to dinner."

She wanted to roll her eyes, but the fierceness of Kason's gaze warned her it was a bad idea. "Maybe he's just curious about humans and Jasvar? He mentioned maybe joining the colony party, if it's approved."

"He never expressed interest before."

"Sometimes meeting someone from a far-off land convinces you to go there."

"Perhaps."

"You have another theory?"

"He wants you as his own," he bit out.

She arched her back until her body touched Kason's. "Stop worrying about that. The only one I want is you, okay?"

With a growl, he took her lips in a rough kiss.

She opened her mouth, and the urgency of his tongue against hers told Taryn how close to the edge he'd really been.

While they had agreed to wait until after the attack to have sex again, Kason needed her now.

Not that it was a hardship for her to get naked with her warrior prince.

Pulling back, she whispered, "Take me to bed, Prince, and then you can tell me about your day."

"If you're in my bed, there won't be much talking for a while."

She raised an eyebrow. "Is that a promise?"

He grunted and squeezed her hip. "Such sass." He nipped her neck. "I think it's time to make you speechless again."

Taryn bit her lip as he continued to nibble her neck. She was already having trouble stringing two thoughts together, and she still had her clothes on.

Clutching Kason's shoulder, she whispered, "Try it, Prince. I dare you."

In the next second, he stepped back, swooped her up, and laid her on his bed. "With pleasure."

She expected him to rip off her clothes and take her, but he merely stood back and studied her body.

~~~

Kason wanted nothing more than to claim Taryn until she was a boneless heap from too much pleasure.

However, with the upcoming battle, he needed to ensure she wanted him and only him. That way he would have a clear mind and perform his best.

He would take his time and make his human beg.

He lightly traced her cheek, down her neck and to the neckline of her dress. Taryn squirmed as he stroked the soft skin there. While she didn't have runic symbols to tell him her emotional state, the rush of pink to her chest told him all he needed to know.

Leaning down, he blew across her flushed skin and her nipples tightened under the thin material.

Taryn growled and he looked up. Her voice was husky as she asked, "What are you waiting for?"

He lightly strummed her taut nipple. "Hard and fast is good sometimes but so is slow and torturous." He pinched her peak and Taryn's legs opened. "You'll soon understand."

Before she could reply, he scooped her breast out of her dress, leaned down, and took her nipple into his mouth. Taryn cried out as he sucked and nibbled. With a Kelderan female, he'd continue to torture a nipple until she came. But Taryn was human, and he was eager to bring her to orgasm by licking between her thighs.

Releasing her, he ran his hands down her ribs, her hips, and to the hem of her dress at the ankles. Slowly lifting the material, he stopped when he could see the special place between her thighs. He looked up and the sight of one of Taryn's breasts exposed with the other concealed made his already hard cock even harder.

Without saying a word, Taryn opened her legs further. At the sight of her swollen, pink flesh, he lost some of his restraint. He lowered his head and flicked out his tongue.

As he groaned at the musky taste of Taryn, she clutched the sheets and arched her hips. Taking it as an invitation, he thrust his tongue into her core.

She was so tight and wet already but tasting her was only part of it. Running his tongue upward until he found her hard little nub, he then circled the sensitive spot. Each pass made Taryn arch her back a little more.

185

Removing his tongue, he lightly flicked her nub with his finger. Taryn murmured, "Yes," and he did it again. He loved how such a secret hidden spot could make his bride thrash about in pleasure.

It was time to make her come.

He pressed against her hard nub and rubbed back and forth until he found what Taryn liked. Once he did, Kason increased his pace until Taryn cried out and closed her eyes as she tilted her head back. He watched her face as waves of pleasure broke over her.

It took every iota of strength he possessed to not plunge into her heat with his cock and find his own release. However, he wanted her coherent and with him when he claimed her again, especially as he needed to do the honorable thing and ask her a question first.

Once Taryn slumped onto the bed, Kason moved until he was eye level and covered her body with his. After giving her a slow, lingering kiss, he smiled. "Can you take any more or shall I stop now?"

She frowned. "You would stop if I asked?"

Nuzzling her cheek, he murmured, "Of course."

Her arms went to his back, and she lightly scored her nails down his spine. "The more time I spend with you, the more you break down my original opinion of you being an arrogant ass of a prince."

He chuckled and met her gaze. "I would say the same of breaking your commanding, bossy self, but that seems to be who you are." She slapped his back and he added, "I jest. You merely state your opinion and fight hard for those you care about. I could not ask for a better bride."

"Even though I'm not submissive?"

186

"I think my life would've turned out boring if I had taken a submissive bride. Your fire calls to me."

She lifted her hips against his erection, and he hissed. She grinned. "It seems the call has been unfulfilled still. Maybe I should take care of that."

"Careful, human. My restraint has its limits."

She searched his gaze. "Why are you restraining yourself?"

"Because I don't have anything to prevent pregnancy."

She traced his jaw. "The fact you remembered tells me more than you know."

"So I guess that means I'll just have to make you cry out again with my fingers and tongue."

"As much as I'd like that, I want to ride you even more." She kissed him. "I'll chance pregnancy if you get on your back and let me take you at my own pace."

"I've never done it that way before."

"That doesn't surprise me." He opened his mouth to reply, but she beat him to it. "But neither have I. I only know what I've seen in books and pictures." She traced down his jaw until she reached his chest. "However, I think I'll figure it out. So? What will it be?"

He didn't hesitate to roll over and take her with him. She straddled his chest, but he wanted one thing. "Take off your dress for me so I can watch your beautiful body as you move."

Taryn slowly tugged the material over her head and tossed it to the side. He took his time memorizing each curve and the little dark spots humans called freckles.

She finally cleared her throat, and he met her gaze. "Then watch me as I do this."

Taryn took his cock in hand, and he hissed as she squeezed gently. She lifted her hips and guided him to her entrance.

However, she didn't take him but merely stayed that way for a few seconds. At the sight of him so close but so far, his cock released a drop of liquid.

He was close to begging for her to take him when she gently lowered. At the noises Taryn made at the back of her throat, he checked her face for pain, but didn't see any.

Once he was completely inside her, he reveled in the tight heat of her core and waited to see what she'd do.

~~~

Taryn was still reeling from Kason's thoughtfulness as she finally took him to the hilt. Her tough warrior prince had thought of her and her desires above his own. Considering what she knew of Kelderan culture, it was a huge step.

In more ways than one, he was slowly winning her heart.

However, as Kason stared at her and palmed her breasts, his touch sent a new rush of fire through her body. She would have plenty of time to ponder her feelings later. For the moment, she wanted to tease and drive her prince crazy.

Placing her hands on his chest, she marveled at the flash of colors. Some of the symbols on his skin were red, others blue, and yet more were pink. She traced the closest one and Kason squeezed her breasts in response. His gravelly voice filled the room. "How long will you torture me, human?"

She met his gaze. "Maybe as long as it takes you to use my name."

The corner of his mouth ticked up. "Oh, Taryn Demara, great leader of Jasvar, how long must I wait for you to drive me to orgasm?"

Taryn tried her best not to blush. "Soon enough."

She leaned down and took his lips in a rough kiss. With each stroke of her tongue, Kason tortured her breasts and nipples a little more. If he kept it up, she'd never get the chance to try out a few moves of her own.

Pulling back, she took his hands in hers and threaded her fingers to keep him secure. She whispered, "Let me take control for a little while."

For a second, she couldn't read his expression and worried that the warrior in him wouldn't allow Kason to cede control to a female. However, he squeezed her fingers and murmured, "I will as long as you start in the next minute. Otherwise, I roll us over, flip you on your stomach, and take you from behind."

The image of Kason holding her hips as he thrust into her core from the rear sent a rush of wetness between her thighs. Kason chuckled. "I think we're going to try that later."

"Perhaps."

He winked. "I've taught you well."

Aware of how easily Kason distracted her, Taryn maneuvered his hands to above his head and released them. "Keep your hands to yourself for now. Do that, and I'll let you do whatever you want to me later."

His symbols flashed red and he nodded. "Deal."

Kason gripped his forearms above his head, and she leaned onto his chest. More than accustomed to his size now, she moved her hips forward and back. She bit her lip at the way his hardness stroked inside and sent little waves of pleasure through her body.

Noticing how tightly Kason gripped his arms, Taryn knew she needed to hurry or she'd miss her chance to be in control. Focusing, she rotated her hips a few times until Kason groaned. When she dug her nails into his chest, he arched his hips and reached even deeper inside her.

"Stay still," she hissed.

To prevent Kason from speaking, she started a steady rhythm, moved forward and back but adding a swirl of her hips every once in a while. She barely noticed the flashing symbols on his body as each pass brought her close to another orgasm.

Maybe he had special sex powers. She kept forgetting to ask him.

Taryn increased her pace as the sound of flesh slapping against flesh filled the room. Kason's symbols were solidly red, and judging by his heavy-lidded expression, he was drawing close to his own release.

Clenching her inner muscles as she moved, Kason moaned. "Just a little more, *zyla*."

Taryn had no idea what *zyla* meant, but the gentleness of his voice told her it was a good thing.

Digging her nails harder into Kason's skin, she focused on moving her hips, gripping him tightly, and pushing back her own orgasm. She wanted Kason to come first for once.

After a few more seconds, Kason roared as he bucked his hips. He was so deep inside her that Taryn felt his hot release.

Biting her lip, she still kept herself from going over the edge. However, as Kason slumped into the bed, he reached out a finger and lightly brushed the bundle of nerves at the juncture of her thighs. Lights danced before her eyes as waves of pleasure coursed through her body.

When she finally came down, she mustered the strength to say, "You were supposed to keep still."

He drew her down to his chest and engulfed her in his arms. "I waited until I was done, *zyla*. And I intend to claim my prize later."

The Conquest

Too tired to argue, Taryn merely snuggled into his chest and gripped the top of his shoulders. "Let me catch my breath first."

His muscles tensed under her cheek. "Are you hurting? Do you need a doctor?"

She smiled at his concern. "I'm fine, just a little tired. A long day, topped with great sex, tends to wear a person out."

He relaxed and hugged her tighter against him. "I suppose 'great' will do for now. I prefer 'fantastic.'"

Snorting, she looked up to see his eyes. "Are you always this competitive?"

He raised his brows. "Aren't you?"

She grinned. "You have a point."

Moving one hand to her cheek, he traced her skin. "Thank you."

"For what?"

"For allowing me to take you early. I might have endangered the entire ship with my possessiveness if you hadn't."

She propped her chin on his warm chest. "I could claim I was doing it selflessly, but I'd be lying. It's hard for me to pretend you're not mine in front of the others, too."

Taking a piece of her hair, he rubbed it between his fingers. "We just need to make it a few more days, *zyla*. Then two planets will know the truth."

"Even if it threatens the alliance and a possible colony?"

"It won't. The implications of refusing a treaty or pursuing a colony are too great for Keldera. Even if my father is stubborn, my older brother will convince him it's the right path."

"You don't speak much of your older brother."

Kason's expression shuttered. "He and I are two very different males."

"Care to elaborate?"

Kason grunted. "You can see for yourself when you meet him." He took her chin between his fingers. "I'd much rather hear about your family."

Taryn sighed. "There's not a lot to tell. All I have is my grandmother, but her memory is fading by the week. I don't remember much about my parents since they died when I was younger, during a research expedition to the Forbidden Continent."

"That sounds ominous."

"I suppose. To date, no one who has visited it has returned."

"So maybe they are alive and trapped."

"For a while, I had thought so, too. But my parents would've moved mountains to come home to me. The only reasonable explanation for their silence is that they died."

Kason stroked the soft skin under her chin. "I will look for them myself when we get back to Jasvar and settled in. It will be my wedding present to you."

For a brief second, hope flared in her heart. But Taryn cleared the emotion from her throat and said, "Don't. I appreciate the intent, but I don't want to lose you, too."

His expression softened. "Why is that, *zyla*?"

"What does '*zyla*' mean?"

He shook his head. "Answer my question first and then I'll answer yours."

As she searched his eyes, the words spilled from Taryn's lips, "Because it's getting harder to imagine living my life without your princely self."

He smiled wide and her heart skipped a beat. The man was beautiful when he revealed his true feelings.

The Conquest

Kason gently kissed her forehead and whispered, "The word '*zyla*' means 'dear heart' in CEL. You have wormed your way into mine, and I'm not letting go."

Chapter Seventeen

Kason managed to keep his symbols from turning yellow and displaying his nervousness to his bride.

He hadn't planned on calling her *zyla* or letting his symbols change colors. Both opened him up to being vulnerable and to being viewed as weaker.

At least, that was the case on Keldera. He wondered if it was the same with Jasvarian humans.

Not that he would take it back. Taryn was turning out to be his match in all ways, from ally to bed partner. He didn't want to hide that fact from her any longer.

Taryn finally took his face in her hands, and he relaxed a fraction. After kissing him, she said, "Then we both have yet another reason to try to win, if it comes to a battle."

Placing his hands on her hips, he nodded. "But maybe we should have another few orgasms. Each one will only strengthen our determination."

She snorted. "That sounds like an excuse to me."

He rolled them over and ran his hands down her thighs until he could press her ankles behind him. "It's also the truth." He gently rocked his hips and Taryn moaned. "So what do you say?"

Mischief danced in her eyes. "As long as it fulfills your promise about flipping me over in the process, I'm open to the idea."

He kissed her jaw. "Knowing how much you want to try that position means I'm saving it for last."

"Kason—"

He bit her neck, and she made a noise in her throat. His husky voice rolled over her as he murmured, "I love making you speechless."

"I rather thought you enjoyed making me scream."

With a growl, he moved his head until it was a whisper away from her lips. "My little wanton warrior wants to play."

"Call it whatever you like." She moved her hips. "Just stop talking for once. I want action."

He pulled mostly out of her core and was about to slam into her when the door chimed.

Cursing, he gave Taryn a gentle kiss before pulling out and grabbing a blanket to wrap around his waist. He whispered, "I'm sorry, *zyla*, but you're going to have to go for now."

For a second, he thought she might interpret his words as a rejection. But his doubts evaporated as Taryn nodded and gathered her things. Wrapping her dress to cover her breasts to just above her knees, she said, "Find me later," before disappearing into the wardrobe.

Taking a deep breath, Kason stated, "Enter."

The door slid open. One of the apprentice warriors stood there. Judging by the young male's expression, he was trying not to appear nervous.

"What?" Kason barked.

"Lt. General Thorin needs you. Two battleships are nearly within weapons range."

"How did they escape the sensors this long?"

"I don't know, your highness. One second they weren't there, and in the next, two large ships appeared out of nowhere."

Kason grabbed his clothes. "I'll be there as soon as I dress. Go next door and inform Princess Kalahn of the situation. I want her and the two humans to join us in the main conference room."

Despite the curiosity in his eyes, the apprentice merely nodded and left.

Kason dressed as quickly as possible, grabbed his weapons, and headed out the door.

There were rumors of spaceships that could hide their appearance from sensors, but there had never been any in Keldera's star system. If the battleships turned out to be enemies, victory would be tough since Keldera didn't have the same capabilities. Not impossible, but it would take every strategic maneuver he could come up with to win. It may even take a few ideas from Taryn and his senior staff, too.

He entered the elevator and prevented himself from tapping his fingers. Displaying impatience to the others might start doubts or even a panic. Kason needed to be calm and collected, even if for the first time he had something precious to lose if he failed.

Not his life, as any warrior was prepared to lose it. No, he'd just found his bride and even cared for her. She might even carry his child.

In other words, Kason was on the verge of having his own family and woe betide anyone who tried to take that away from him.

~~~

Taryn stumbled from the wardrobe and headed straight into the bathroom without saying a word. Kalahn would ask a million questions, and she'd answer some of them, but Taryn wasn't about to do it while half naked.

As she cleaned up and got dressed, it was hard to push aside Kason's words about not letting her go.

Maybe all the years of waiting and the frustration of not having a chance with any man had been her fate, to bring her to Kason.

Well, if she believed in fate.

Taking a deep breath, Taryn did her best to bundle up her new feelings and exited the bathroom. However, as soon as she entered the main room, Taryn blinked. Kalahn was at the door talking with one of the warriors from the training class earlier.

His gaze darted to hers before he left. Once the door slid closed, Kalahn spun around. "Good, you're dressed. Kason wants us in the conference room."

"I thought females weren't allowed."

"Well, it seems the rule is being broken in this instance. Are you going to stand here and question it or come with me?"

Taryn grabbed her straps of weapons and fitted them over her dress. "Let's hurry up before they change their minds."

With a nod, Kalahn led her out of the room and down a set of corridors. Both warriors and Barren were running around shouting orders. It almost seemed like they were prepping for battle. She asked Kalahn, "What else did that young man tell you?"

"All I can say out here is that the entire ship is on red alert. The details will come out in the conference room."

Kalahn took her up an elevator and down one last corridor to a door guarded by two warriors. Both bowed their heads before pressing their thumbs to pads at the side of the doors. Once open, Kalahn and Taryn entered.

Inside was a long table. All of the higher ups from earlier—Thorin, Enishi, Jerrick, and Syzel—were there, along with Kason. Evaine was missing, which meant she was probably helping down in engineering.

Every set of eyes looked at her and Kalahn. Thorin motioned toward them and said something in Kelderan.

Kason answered in CEL. "They're here to help. Taryn for her ideas, and Kalahn to help with the females."

Thorin replied in the same language. "The females aren't ready. They had one day of training."

"Regardless, we might need their help. They can at least pretend to know what they're doing as a ruse." Kason looked to Taryn and Kalahn. "Sit down. Kalahn, you can interpret for Taryn."

Once they both sat, Kalahn translated Kason's words, "The two battleships still haven't answered our messages, and their oblong shape doesn't match anything in the records. A battle should be the last resort. Any ideas how to get through to them?"

Syzel answered, and the princess continued to interpret. "Not all species use words. Even though we're broadcasting in all known languages, we might need to send images as well, of both our species and anything that can represent peace and the desire to talk."

Taryn spoke up. "We should include pictures of humans, too. That might help since humans are known across the universe."

Kason nodded and told the others her idea. While Thorin raised an eyebrow in question, the others didn't protest.

THE CONQUEST

Kason continued, and Kalahn's voice filled Taryn's ear. "While we do that, I want all stations to be at the ready in case of attack. Some of the females might be confused, afraid, or just overwhelmed. Kalahn will help get them ready for their roles, if we end up needing them. Taryn will help on the command deck, just in case the battleship wants to talk with a human. Everyone will keep each other updated with any problems or concerns. Understood?" Everyone nodded and Kason clapped his hands once. "Dismissed."

All of the men except Kason left the room. Kason walked up to Taryn and Kalahn and said in CEL, "I know I didn't ask for your help on the command deck, but we might need you, Taryn."

She missed his Kelderan endearment but understood that the present circumstances were more important. "The fact you want me there at all means the world to me. Shall we go? I'm anxious to see images of the ships and see if sending our own pictures will do anything."

Kason grunted in agreement. "Yes. And no matter if Thorin glares at you the whole time, if you have an idea, you tell me. Understood?"

"Of course. It's hard for me to keep quiet when lives are on the line."

"Let's hope it doesn't come to that."

They walked out of the conference room and toward the elevator. It was time to see how Kelderans handled problems in space. Taryn had no experience with space battles but hoped she could help in some small way, if needed.

~~~

Kason took his position in the raised chair in the center of the command deck. "Any updates?"

One of the young males toward the back at the communications station answered, "We just started sending images. Other than that, there's still no word from the ships."

"You included pictures of humans too, correct?" Kason asked.

"Yes, your highness."

Kason motioned for Taryn to sit next to him. He didn't care if anyone thought it odd. Having his bride close was a comfort and made him more determined to succeed.

The small screen on his chair console beeped and he hit Receive. Enishi's face appeared on the screen. "Some sort of sensor just passed along the ship. It didn't do any damage that I can tell, but I thought you should know."

"Anything else?"

"All engines and weapons systems are ready."

"Good." Kason tapped off his screen and looked to the two oblong ships on the front viewer.

They were sleek with few corners. If there were windows for quarters, they weren't visible. Whoever designed the ship cared a lot about aesthetics. Of course, the sleek design could also help navigate through difficult areas or tight spots.

The main question was who were they and what did they want. He didn't think the Brevkan had advanced so quickly in the twenty-odd years since the end of the war on Keldera. Maybe the ships were related to the Jasvarian distress signal Evaine had mentioned.

Before he could think more on it, the communications officer spoke up. "We received a message in CEL. It says to have one of the two humans reach out to them via a secure line. They must do it alone."

"Are they with the Earth Colony Alliance?" Kason asked.

"I don't know, your highness. They didn't say."

"Clever," Kason said. "If they end up attacking us, we can't pin it on the ECA when our black box is retrieved by Keldera." He looked to Taryn and switched languages. "They want to talk to either you or Evaine."

Taryn touched his arm. "Let me do it."

Kason answered, "I don't like leaving you alone, but I trust you, Taryn. Come with me." He looked to his officer and switched languages. "Tell them one of the humans will reach out in a minute."

As the warrior followed his order, Kason guided Taryn into the private comm unit off the main command deck. Once the door slid shut, he spoke again. "If all they wish to do is travel through the star system, then I give you permission to grant it to them, provided they fly under a flag of truce. If they want more, then I need to talk with them. It's okay if you're in the room with me, but I need to represent my people, especially if there are demands."

Taryn touched his cheek. "Thank you for trusting me."

He lowered his voice, even though the room was secure. "It may only have been a short time, but you've earned my trust, *zyla*. We both want what's best for our people, and I don't expect you to give them an inch." He took her chin in his fingers. "But if you need my help, hit this button,"—he motioned toward the green button that would signal his command deck chair—"and I'll come running."

"Let's hope I don't need it."

He stroked her soft skin. "Even so, I will always have your back, *zyla*."

As Taryn searched his eyes, he wanted to tell her how he wanted to always have much more than her back.

201

Yet the private comm unit room reminded him of why telling her how he felt would have to wait. "I should go."

"Er, if you could set up the comm unit for me before you go, that would be extremely helpful."

He smiled at her sheepish tone. "I think my sister isn't doing a very good job at teaching you Kelderan. I may have to take over your lessons."

He set up the secure video line as Taryn answered, "I might be further along if I hadn't spent so much time in someone's bed."

Grunting, he finished the setup. "Maybe I'll combine the two." He motioned toward a button at the bottom of the flat console. "Tap this to turn on the feed and again to turn it off." He moved to kiss Taryn gently. "My people are in your hands, Taryn Demara. I hope you can help us."

She cleared her throat, and for a split second, he wondered if she'd cry. Then his warrior leader raised her chin and said, "I won't let you down."

After one last kiss, Kason left the private comm room and returned to the command chair.

Even a week ago, he would've scoffed at the idea of a female speaking for all of Keldera. But Taryn wasn't just any female. Besides, if she could negotiate a peaceful solution, it would make the meeting with his father and older brother that much easier. It would be hard for them to turn down her suggestions for the colonization agreement when she'd proven so useful.

For the time being, Kason remained still in his chair and studied the two ships on the view screen. He had faith in his bride, but Kason needed to be ready in case things went south.

Chapter Eighteen

Taryn took one last deep breath. She had no idea what was on the other end, but there was no use in putting it off. She pressed the button Kason had shown her.

A man in his fifties with graying black hair and brown eyes appeared on the screen. His light brown skin and features looked human to Taryn, but his clothing was a strange synthetic-looking material that shone faintly in the light.

However, she barely had a chance to note more than that before his deep voice spoke in CEL, albeit with a strange accent. "State your name and place of origin."

She figured giving her name wouldn't hurt. "I'm Taryn Demara, the leader of planet Jasvar. Who are you?"

"Jasvar? What are you doing on a Kelderan ship?"

She shook her head. "I won't answer until you tell me who you are."

He raised one gray brow before answering, "My name is Dextrell Jennings, originally from Planet Charlen but now working as a representative for the Earth Colony Alliance. Now, tell me why you're on that ship."

Taryn had no way of checking the man's story, but she didn't have the leverage to bargain for more just yet. "I persuaded the Kelderans to take me to their planet for a cohabitation colony agreement."

The man tapped something in front of him and then looked at her. "Jasvar is a low-tech colony. The ad hoc distress beacon only confirmed this when the ECA received it a year ago. How did you reach out to the Kelderans?"

"That is a story for another time. I want to know why you're here and why you didn't answer the Kelderans' original communications message."

Dextrell steepled his fingers in front of his body. "The last we knew, the Kelderans were at war with the Brevkan. The ECA has no desire to become involved. However, when images of humans flooded our screens, we scanned and found two on board. It's the ECA's mission to protect all humans, hence why I'm talking to you now."

"I'm in no danger, if that's what you're concerned about."

"What about your planet? The message was short, but something about a virus that was slowly killing off the population."

"That's true." She leaned forward. "What were you going to do to help me?"

"That depends. We need to meet in person to discuss the details further. Once you and your human companion board our ship, we can talk about relief efforts."

She paused a second before stating, "You don't trust the Kelderans."

He shrugged. "All we know is they are a patriarchal society and that they make fierce adversaries. There are also no humans on Keldera. It isn't the ECA's concern."

"Ah, but you're wrong."

The older man frowned. "I don't have time for guessing games, Taryn Demara. Tell me what you mean."

She hesitated a second but then remembered Kason had given her free rein to negotiate with other ships, up to a point. She might be pushing her luck a little, but hopefully Kason would understand. "I will be sending a few representatives to Keldera, once an agreement is reached. Also, many Kelderans will be living on Jasvar with my people. Some Jasvarian humans have already married Kelderan males and have had children. They should be your concern since the ECA is supposed to care for half-humans as well."

"There is much you aren't telling me."

She lifted one shoulder. "Even you should know that negotiations take more than five minutes to complete. You and your representatives should come aboard, and we can talk further."

"No. You and a Kelderan representative may come aboard our ship via a shuttle. We can talk more then. I'll give you five minutes to decide. Send your answer via your communications. If you do decide to come aboard, you have an hour to prepare and come to our ship. After that, we'll turn and leave you to fend for yourselves."

The screen went blank.

For years, Taryn had wondered if the Earth Colony Alliance would rescue her people. Every scenario had been one of heroes coming to the rescue with medical supplies and a vaccine for the virus.

The reality was much harsher.

Not that she had time to think about it. She had five minutes to convince Kason to go with her.

Taryn exited the room and went looking for her prince.

~~~

Thirty minutes later, Kason closed the distance between his shuttle and the oblong ECA ship. He had two hours to talk with the ECA representatives and send a transmission to his people. If he missed the deadline, Thorin's orders were to return to Keldera.

His sister hadn't liked the plan, but reminding her that she needed to look after the other females had quieted down most of her protests.

Taryn's voice filled the shuttle, and he focused on his bride. "Before you dock the shuttle, I'm going to ask one last time. Are you angry with me for making this decision?"

He sighed. "I already said no. Thorin was upset, but it's the same decision I would've made."

Taryn placed a hand on his arm. "Just know that whatever the ECA representatives propose, I won't say yes if it doesn't include plans for a Kelderan colony on Jasvar."

He leaned down and kissed her hand. "Keldera is lucky to have you on their side."

She smiled. "Someone's going soft. I almost miss the tough, prickly warrior I first met."

"Oh, he's still in here. And once we start living together, I'm sure he'll come out every so often."

Taryn snorted. "He still won't be a match for my daggers."

As they grinned at one another, the urge to pull Taryn into his lap and never let go coursed through his body. However, they'd agreed that their relationship needed to remain secret, even to the ECA, until negotiations were complete. Otherwise, Thorin might claim command of the Kelderan ship, toss aside their plans, and go with his own, which wouldn't include negotiating with the ECA.

THE CONQUEST

As Kason maneuvered the shuttle into position to dock, he murmured, "I look forward to it, *zyla*." The shuttle locked into position. "Now, let's create the best future for both Keldera and Jasvar."

With a nod, Taryn unbuckled her seatbelt and followed Kason to the airlock. The light signaling it was safe to debark was steady, so he reinforced calmness in his mind, ensured his markings were dark blue, opened the door and exited the shuttle.

Three individuals stood in shimmery clothing that fitted their bodies and left nothing to the imagination. However, after Taryn's initial outfits, they were tame in comparison and Kason could easily keep his expression free of emotion.

Kason scanned the contingent of guards with what looked like blast guns in a semi-circle behind the three leaders. He had a feeling the armed guards were there for him, given what Taryn had told him earlier about the ECA only knowing about Keldera's war with the Brevkan.

An older man with graying black hair and light brown skin stepped forward and spoke in CEL. "Welcome aboard, Taryn Demara." He looked to Kason. "And you must be Prince Kason tro el Vallen. My name is Dextrell Jennings." He motioned behind him. "Come, let's not waste time."

The human named Dextrell turned and walked toward the largest exit. His two companions followed him. It seemed odd to Kason that he wouldn't introduce his compatriots.

Yet as Taryn moved, Kason did, too. He took the opportunity to study the unknown ship's interior.

The cargo bay was small and could accommodate no more than three shuttles. That told him the ECA crew didn't trust them to see more of their ship, which could reveal some of their secrets.

Kason's respect rose a notch.

While having them trust him easily and giving in to his and Taryn's demands would be nice, it would make him suspicious. Every time something had fallen into place too quickly in the past, it had spelled danger and possibly a trap. Their caution meant the ECA might be sincere.

As they went down one long, empty corridor, he noted that the upper halves of the walls were covered in view screens. For the moment, they displayed a lush forest while the halls echoed with faint animal noises.

Of course, the images and sounds weren't merely for soothing nerves. It was clearly a display of power and wealth. Kason's people were decades from having the same technology so readily available on a mere starship.

For a brief moment, he wondered what would've happened if the ECA had made it to Jasvar a few months ago, ahead of Kason's arrival. He may never have gotten to know his bride, let alone win her.

He itched to place his hand on Taryn's lower back, but resisted. He didn't want to give the ECA anything to be used against him as a weakness. After all, they cared for humans and half-humans. Kason was onboard the ship purely because of association. He wasn't about to take it for granted.

They finally reached a large door with two guards. Dextrell nodded, and the guards opened the doors. Inside the room was a large rectangular table with chairs mounted to the floor. Dextrell and his two comrades sat at one end. Dextrell motioned toward the other. "Have a seat."

He let Taryn take the seat at the end and he sat to her left. Taryn spoke up first. "Now that you've shown us your advanced technology, your guards, and control over the situation, how about we cut to the chase? You were clearly heading toward Jasvar to help us. What were you going to do?"

Dextrell answered, "Nothing until we confirmed the situation. Since the planet was cleared for colonization, I'm curious about this virus."

Taryn didn't waste time replying, "It disproportionately kills off male embryos in the womb. We've resorted to integrating alien males into our society to prevent extinction. However, our technology is old and failing. When it does fail, we won't be able to reach out to any alien race. We need a better long-term solution."

In that moment, Kason was extremely proud of his bride. It was easy to see why she was a leader.

Dextrell waved a hand. "Finding a vaccine should be easy enough. How do the Kelderans factor into all of this?"

Taryn looked to Kason, and he took his cue. "We wish to form an alliance with Jasvar and establish our own colony. Until you appeared, we were also going to work on a cure to the virus as a sign of good faith."

The woman to Dextrell's right finally spoke for the first time. "You wish to help them for more than an alliance."

Kason's gaze moved to the female with long, blonde hair nearly to the floor, green eyes, and faint purple swirls on the sides of her jaw. "Who are you?"

She inclined her head. "My name is Geneva. I have minor empath abilities and can sense there's more that you aren't telling us."

He wanted to know what her nonhuman half was, but focused on the more important things. "Bringing an empath to a discussion without stating the fact is viewed as deceit on my planet."

Dextrell stepped in. "Since all we know about the Kelderans is their penchant for war with the Brevkan, we had to be careful."

Kason was tempted to cross the room and show Dextrell how Kelderans treated threats, but Taryn touched his arm and said, "Kason only wishes to help me and his people."

Geneva looked to Taryn. "I sense why, but also that it must remain secret. No one will share your connection outside this room. You have my word."

Kason frowned. "Dextrell will follow your orders?"

"Yes, he will," Geneva stated. "I am the captain of this ship. I'm sure you can understand why I didn't want to advertise that fact from the beginning, given that Kelderans are a patriarchal society. But after seeing the way Prince Kason has allowed Taryn to speak for all, I think he has accepted that women can handle being in charge. Am I right?"

"Yes, Taryn has shown me that a female can be a capable leader." Kason could feel Taryn's eyes on his face, but he focused on Geneva. "But now it's my turn to ask—what do you plan to do? Spare me the flowery language and false promises. My own people are anxious for our return. I don't wish to keep them waiting."

Geneva nodded. "I understand. But I also can't make a split-second decision without all of the facts. Provided there's peace on Jasvar, we will leave some observers there to report back to me. In exchange, you will offer a few hostages to live on my ship. If after a few months my people on Jasvar give a positive report, we will head back this way, return the hostages, and assist Jasvar. If not, especially if war breaks out between the new Kelderan colonists and the Earth descendants, my people will leave and we'll never return. That should be reasonable."

Kason didn't like the assumption his people would start a war, but thankfully Taryn spoke before he could. "Why hostages? You have my word that no one will be harmed."

Geneva shook her head. "As much as I'd like to trust your word, especially as I sense you're an honest person, it is ECA's policy. The practice has saved many ECA representatives' lives in the past. If you refuse, we can't help you." She motioned toward a door on the side of the room, different from the one they'd entered. "You may go in there to discuss the offer privately. I'll give you five minutes."

Taryn stood. "Thank you."

Kason wanted to growl, as five minutes wasn't enough to make any long-term decisions, but at Taryn's stern look, he followed her into the room. When the door clicked closed, she faced him.

~~~

One look at Kason and Taryn could tell he was barely hiding his anger. While his markings might be blue, the tightness of his jaw told her all. She placed a hand on his chest, taking as much comfort from his heat as he hopefully took from her touch. "I know the situation isn't ideal, but there is always the chance your scientists can't find a cure for the doom virus. The ECA's help would be invaluable."

He grunted but placed his hand over hers. "I don't like the fact they hold all the cards. I've heard things about some ECA ships in the past. The female captain seems harmless, but empaths can be tricky to read since they can funnel others' emotions and portray them as their own."

"Then we'll just have to work quickly to ensure the Kelderan settlement becomes a reality. That way, you can help me in case things go awry."

"Of course I'll help you. But there's one point I don't like—the ECA will be on Jasvar when you're not there, and I don't think they'll wait until you finish negotiations to make the journey."

She searched his gaze. "I would guess that your father and brother won't leave the planet unattended to meet with me on Jasvar, either."

He shook his head. "Not with the antimonarchy factions gaining strength." He squeezed her hand. "But there is one card we can play. Ryven and my other warriors are still back on your world. If a small ship of warriors takes Kalahn to Jasvar, Ryven will trust any message she delivers. They can ensure the ECA doesn't try anything in your absence."

She sighed. "I hate planning all of this without asking Kalahn first."

"She will agree. After all, she's the one who wants adventure. If I don't mention she's missing to my father, then he probably won't notice. At least until she's already gone and he can't do anything."

Kason proposal required a lot of trust. Yet as she studied her warrior prince, she didn't need empathic abilities to know she could trust him. After all, she'd trusted him with her body, and he was also close to capturing her heart. The next step was allowing him to help her people. "Okay, we'll try your suggestion. Still, I want to finish the settlement negotiations as quickly as possible. My people take strength from my presence."

He brushed her cheek. "Of course. Now, let's see if we can get those people to agree to our plan and get off this ship."

She nodded. Just as she opened the door to the conference room, the entire ship rolled to one side, and danger warnings echoed in the room.

Geneva stood and shouted, "Computer, what just happened?"

The computer answered, "An unknown projectile took out one of the main engines. The ship moved until balance could be restored with backup thrusters."

"Can you pinpoint the source?"

"From the direction of the Kelderan ship on starboard," the computer stated.

Geneva shot Taryn and Kason a look. Taryn barely managed, "It can't be," before Geneva tapped something on her wrist. "Guards, secure the visitors and lock them up. Captain to bridge, lock a tractor beam on the Kelderan ship."

"Aye, aye, sir," an unknown voice answered.

In the next second, the guards came in and surrounded Taryn and Kason.

Taryn looked to the captain. "There's no way the Kelderans would fire on you."

"For the moment, that's what appears to have happened. Until I figure out the truth, you'll be staying a while." Geneva motioned at the guards, and something pricked her skin. In the next second, the world went black.

Chapter Nineteen

Vala was in Princess Kalahn's room when the ship lurched for a second, and the lights flashed red alert.

Before she could ask anything, Kalahn was tapping on the flat panel at the far side of the room. With anyone else, Vala would remain silent and stay out of the way. However, Kalahn had made her promise to speak up, so she asked, "What's happening?"

Kalahn never looked away from the words on the screen. "The ECA ship has us locked in a tractor beam. But why?" She tapped a few more times before standing up with a growl. "Thorin won't answer me." She turned. "Come on. We're going to the command deck."

Vala frowned. "With your brother gone, I'm not sure Thorin will allow it."

The second it was out of her mouth, Vala wondered if she'd crossed the line by questioning a princess's decision.

However, Kalahn smiled and touched her bicep. "It's okay to ask questions, Vala. I've never been fond of people agreeing with everything I say. It's rather boring."

She resisted letting out a sigh of relief. The princess might view it as weakness and second-guess her decision to bring her along. "Then my concern still stands. Lt. General Thorin doesn't like females in the way."

"So you've noticed that as well? Too bad for Thorin. My brother could be in danger, and I'm going to do whatever is necessary to help." She took Vala's hand and tugged her toward the door. "Let's hurry."

As they wound down one corridor and then the next, Vala was aware of people staring at her. Her brown dress and tattoo on her forehead made her stick out. Her Barren sisters had said it marked her as special. But in the moment, it only highlighted how out of place she was in the traditional Kelderan order.

Maybe someday she would grow accustomed to the attention.

She blinked at that thought. Once the prince and princess's mission was complete, Vala would go back to her normal routine and goal of being a shadow. There wasn't any other choice, unless she wanted to end up imprisoned inside the citadel for the rest of her life.

Before she could think too much on it, she and Kalahn were inside the elevator on the way to the command deck. The princess leaned over and whispered, "You only take orders from me. You don't have to listen to Thorin."

She paused a second before asking, "But isn't he acting general?"

"Perhaps. But a princess outranks everyone on the ship right now, and I might need your help with a plan, if Thorin won't listen."

The elevator doors opened, cutting off Vala's reply.

Warriors rushed to and fro as Thorin barked orders. From what she could see on the view screen, the ECA ship was damaged toward the back, and a bright yellow light beamed straight at them; it must be the tractor beam.

In any other situation, Vala would love nothing better than to stand at the back and watch the activity. She'd never witnessed the command deck during a crisis.

However, Kalahn took her hand and moved toward Thorin's chair. The princess stood tall and demanded, "What's going on?"

Thorin's gaze flicked to Kalahn before meeting her own. Some emotion flared in his eyes, but she couldn't pinpoint what. Kelderan male warriors were difficult to read.

Thorin looked back to Kalahn. "A missile came from behind us and hit the ECA ship. They think we did it."

"Then tell them it wasn't us."

"It's not that easy. The missile's shape and components matched the ones we use. It's almost as if someone wanted to set us up." He nodded toward the door. "Now, go. I have much to do and don't have time for your meddling."

Kalahn bowed her head. "Of course."

As they left, Vala managed to keep any sort of expression from displaying on her face. Once in the elevator, she whispered, "Why did you give up so easily? That seems contradictory to your character."

Kalahn snorted. "It is. But I have a plan."

"What plan?"

"You'll see. After all, you're a big part of it. But first, we need to visit Jerrick."

The elevator stopped. As the princess took them toward Jerrick's training area, Vala wondered what she could do to help Kalahn. After all, she was just a Barren. Healing and information might be helpful to some, but it wouldn't help get Prince Kason back.

The Conquest

~~~

Taryn awoke with a pounding headache. When she finally managed to open her eyes against the bright light, she saw Kason sitting on the floor of a mostly bare cell.

She tried to roll to the side, but pain exploded in her head. Kason's low voice filled the room. "Stay put, Taryn. We're in a force field cell. We'll only get out if they let us out."

"That almost sounds as if you're giving up."

"Of course not, *zyla*. I'm conserving my energy. I'll be ready when the opportune moment strikes."

She laid an arm over her eyes. "But what the hell happened? As much as Thorin disliked our plan, I can't imagine him going rogue and firing on the ship."

"Neither can I. He is first and foremost a loyal warrior. There has to be an explanation."

"And if there's not?"

"Then I trust him to help us."

She peeked out from under her arm at Kason. "That doesn't sound like much of a plan. If Geneva and the others can't find the true culprit of the attack, we may never get off this ship. That won't be good for either of our worlds."

Kason moved to her side and looked her directly in the eye. "Have faith in me, *zyla*. I have suspicions of who might've done it, but I need proof. And if I can make those assumptions here, I trust Thorin will, too, with all the resources he has at his disposal."

"Who do you think did it?"

He leaned to her ear and whispered, "Remember the disgruntled warriors we sent back to Keldera, the ones who wouldn't accept females aboard the ship?" She nodded. "If they reached out to the right people, they could've set us up."

She frowned. "But your sensors would've picked them up, right?"

"Perhaps. However, a skilled pilot knows to use satellites, planets, and other objects to hide their position, especially with a smaller ship. Or, they could've commandeered one of the two fighter ships my father sent to possibly assist us. Either way, our communications weren't shielded or secure, so once they heard about the ECA being involved, they saw it as their opportunity to strike."

"Why would they do that? From what you've told me, Keldera desperately needs a colony. Why ruin their chance on Jasvar?"

"Because they can ensure the ECA never returns to this system and then they can pounce. Many of the disgruntled warriors wanted to take Jasvar by force."

Taryn growled. "I won't let that happen. We need to get off this ship."

"And we will. For now, rest. I'm going to need your help soon. You'll know when it's time."

Searching his eyes, she wanted to ask for specifics. However, the guards posted outside their cell could be listening.

She nodded and took Kason's hand. "Stay near me, Kason, and watch over me."

"Of course, *zyla*. I will protect you with my life."

As she stared into Kason's gray eyes, she knew he meant it.

Between his trust in her, wanting to include her, and viewing her as his equal, he'd wormed his way into her heart. She was halfway in love with him already, and if he risked his life and even his sister's life to protect her people, Taryn would fall the rest of the way.

But it wasn't the time to share feelings. Too much was at stake.

So she merely raised her head to kiss him and settled back down on the bed. Closing her eyes, her mind wanted to think of ways to escape or even how to convince Geneva of Keldera's innocence in the attack.

Then Kason squeezed her hand and brushed the hair from her forehead, and a sense of peace came over her. Even in dangerous and less-than-stellar situations, her prince could ease her nerves.

After a few more minutes of his touch, Taryn fell into a deep sleep. It wasn't long before she was dreaming of a future where her planet was virus-free and she had Kason at her side.

~~~

A few months ago, Kalahn tro el Vallen, the sole princess of Keldera, never would've stood in front of a warrior with her hands on her hips and stared him down.

In the present, however, she never broke eye contact with the warrior and trainer in front of her named Jerrick. She needed his help and wasn't about to give up. She only hoped all the years of watching her brother Kason handle the warriors around him paid off. It was a bit harder for a short female with little-to-no muscle to speak of to be as imposing, but she stood taller and tried her best.

Jerrick finally sighed. "Your brother will kill me for agreeing to help you."

She ignored the flare of hope and asked, "Which brother?"

The corner of Jerrick's mouth ticked up. "Both of them."

Kalahn waved a hand. "Keltor will forgive me anything and considering Kason is no doubt now a prisoner, if we can get him free, he'll overlook it as well."

"I'm going to remember your words, in case I end up in a dungeon somewhere."

"There's no time for teasing. We need to act quickly. Are you sure you have a few more warriors who can be trusted?"

Jerrick nodded. "Yes. But to make this work, you need to meet me in shuttle bay five in fifteen minutes. The fewer people who see you, the better, especially if you're traveling with her."

He motioned toward Vala.

"I will also take care of that. I'll see you in fifteen minutes."

Before he could say another word, Kalahn guided Vala out of the training area and into a room across the corridor. Once she locked the door, Kalahn headed straight for the computer's replicator machine. "Computer, two pale blue dresses like those of a Kelderan merchant, in proportion for Vala Yarlen's measurements and my own. I also need two decorative head wraps and two sets of daggers made for female hands."

"Working," the computer answered.

Vala's voice piped up behind her. "Wearing anything but the traditional brown dress of the Barren is a crime, as is wearing anything to cover the tattoo on my forehead."

Kalahn turned toward the female she never would've paid attention to a few weeks ago. "If anyone reports you, then I will say I forced you to do it."

Vala searched her eyes. "But why?"

"Because you and I have more in common than you think. Thanks to Taryn, I now see that women can hold their own with men and succeed. I don't think I could go back to a sheltered life. I'm fairly certain you're the same." Vala opened her mouth to protest, but Kalahn beat her to it. "Making exceptions for one Barren shouldn't cause a stir. I want to help the rest, but right now, saving my brother and his bride is my top priority. Besides, if we're going to enact any long-term changes on Keldera, I think we're going to need Taryn's help. So, are you willing to risk breaking the law to help me?"

The computer finished synthesizing the dresses, head wraps, and daggers and they appeared on the replicator's panel. Vala walked over and picked up one of the dresses. "Taryn is my friend. She needs our help."

"Good. Now, hurry up and change. We don't have much time to meet Jerrick."

As Vala dressed, Kalahn picked up a set of daggers. She might have little training with them, but she'd rather be safe than sorry. After all, Taryn's advice about taking someone down when they least expected it might come in useful. As long as Kalahn could convince herself to stab someone, she would have a form of defense, even if it wasn't guaranteed because of her lack of skill.

Once all of this was over, she was going to learn how to use daggers and blast guns. Kalahn had meant what she'd said about never wanting to go back to a sheltered life at the palace. Her brothers might be a little more supportive of her dreams if she could prove she could take care of herself and handle a threat.

But first, she needed to save her brother's life. She only hoped her plan would work.

Once Vala was dressed and they'd stashed their daggers out of sight, Kalahn picked up her merchant's dress and head wrap before leading them to shuttle bay five. Thanks to Vala's disguise, no one paid much attention to them with their heads down.

As Jerrick had promised, the shuttle bay was empty. One small ship sat near the sealed exit.

They approached it and Kalahn whispered, "I hope you're as good in real life as on the simulator."

Vala missed a step. "You want me to fly a ship?"

"Yes. While I wish it was me, I acknowledge that you're better."

"But what about Jerrick and his warriors?"

"I can't risk him being seen, in case someone tries to open communications. Having two females at the helm will help our chances of being caught instead of being destroyed."

Vala frowned. "Wait, what? You want to be caught?"

"Of course. Once we find and can prove the source of the missile, we need to get aboard the ECA ship."

"That's not only risky, but I'm sure the chances of failure are greater than success."

Kalahn stopped at the shuttle and faced Vala. "If we can't prove another ship fired, then Kason and Taryn may never be let free. Whoever fired the weapon will be looking for big ships or ones piloted by males. However, a merchant and her cousin might be able to talk their way out of it, especially if we stick to the story that our pilot killed our husbands and ran off with our cargo. We then had no choice but to try to fly the ship home on our own.

"And before you protest about not being a merchant, you've worked with them your whole life. I'm sure you know enough to fool a few warriors."

"But your highness, we have no idea if the attackers are even Kelderan."

"Who else would it be? The pirates wouldn't want to alienate a potential client, and the Brevkans' honor would never allow them to frame a Kelderan ship. They're too proud and would use their own weapons."

Vala searched her eyes a second before asking, "How do you know so much about this?"

"Just because everyone thinks I'm a decoration that exists to be married off without a complaint doesn't mean I haven't used that assumption to my advantage. Keltor in particular has let me listen in on meetings when I wished. He always hoped a warrior or politician would catch my eye."

Jerrick's voice whispered behind them, "And I'm sure after today, both of your brothers will wish that had happened."

Kalahn looked at Jerrick. "After today, they may wonder why they kept forcing me to learn painting or dancing instead of using my brain to help our kingdom."

Jerrick put up a hand. "I'm not going to get involved. You can work it out with your brothers later. Let's board, and you can quickly tell me your plan before we leave because once the outer doors open, someone will come to investigate."

Thorin's voice echoed from the shuttle bay entrance. "I'm surprised you have so little faith in me. This is currently my ship. Of course I'm going to keep a close watch on it."

Kalahn turned toward Thorin. For a split second, she wondered if she could stand up to the powerful warrior who never seemed to like anyone. Then she thought of her brother and Keldera's future. It gave her the strength to stand tall and say, "Are you here to stop us?"

Thorin closed the distance between them. His gaze moved to Vala for a second and then back to Kalahn. "Putting aside the fact the Barren has broken the law, tell me what you plan to do."

Kalahn blinked. "Wait, what? Since when are you open to a female's suggestion?"

"Don't get used to it. However, I think the warriors we banished to a remote Kelderan base might be responsible. Kason may have created this problem, but I'm still determined to succeed in any way possible. The victory will secure my future."

Thorin's words were a bit cryptic, but she focused on the bigger picture. "You aren't going to like my plan."

"Tell me and I'll decide. Hurry, as my crew needs me back as soon as possible," Thorin replied.

Kalahn quickly explained her plan and said, "So? Will you let us try?"

"Your plan has merit. However, I can't guarantee your safety. I hope you realize that."

"Of course. But I need to try."

Thorin studied her a second before nodding, "Then go. I want you to record your transmissions. We'll also keep a secure line clear in case of emergency. Once we know the culprits' location, provided you find it, then we'll take care of them and access their computer logs for the fired missile while you talk with the ECA." He waved a hand toward Vala. "Once she returns, she must remove the illegal clothing. If she does, I'll overlook it."

"She has a name."

Thorin ignored her and looked to Jerrick. "The princess's life is in your hands. I trust you to do what's necessary to protect her with your life."

Jerrick made a fist and pounded it over his heart. "I will."

Thorin turned toward the door. "Then hurry. I'll send you the flight path of the missile, in case that helps you locate the ship that fired it. I have no idea who is in charge, but they may still be close, waiting to confirm the ECA ship's departure."

Thorin exited the room, and Kalahn looked to Vala. "I'm sorry he pretends you're not a person."

Vala smiled. "It's okay. I don't think he likes anyone."

Kalahn snorted. "Good point. Now, let's go before Thorin changes his mind."

~~~

Vala checked all her instruments one more time. So far, they were flying at a steady pace in the direction of one of the nearby moons.

If Jerrick and the other warriors hadn't sat in the back room, she might've been too nervous or self-conscious to do a proper job. However, with Kalahn sitting in the copilot's chair, the two of them easily controlled the ship as if they'd been doing it together for years.

As the moon drew nearer, Vala took a second to admire the glowing orb. Combined with the nearby blue-green planet and the vast field of stars, the sight outdid anything she'd ever seen on a view screen or during a simulation program. Provided they survived the mission, Vala wasn't sure she could ever go back to a life at the citadel. Hopefully, helping the princess would allow her to remain on one of the Kelderan spaceships.

She wasn't about to hope that she'd be placed on the colony transport ship if the agreement went through between Keldera and Jasvar.

One of the sensors beeped, and Kalahn spoke up. "There are two large objects behind the closest moon. They might be the two ships my father sent to assist, but I think we should investigate." Kalahn looked at her. "Are you ready to play your part?"

Kalahn was the only non-Barren she felt comfortable enough around, to tell the truth. "I'm nervous, but I should be able to do my part. I hope I don't disappoint you, your highness."

Kalahn waved a hand. "While we're onboard this ship, I told you to merely call me Kala so that no one guesses who we are."

She eyed the princess. "Even with your head wrap and different dress, you hold yourself like a princess."

Kalahn slumped a little. "Thank you for reminding me." She tapped out a sequence on the panel in front of her. "Jerrick, we're approaching some unknown vessels. Stand at the ready in case they board."

Jerrick's voice filled the space. "Understood. I'll wait for the crisis word of '*supak*' before acting."

Kalahn smiled at some memory Vala didn't know. "Good. I'm cutting off all audio to your section." She typed in the command. "Okay, 'Valyn,' take us right into their path."

She barely paid attention to her pretend name and guided the shuttle behind the nearest moon. Once they reached the far side, two Kelderan ships came into view. The instruments registered a scan before the communications light beeped with an incoming message. Taking a deep breath, Vala put on an expression of fear and hit Receive.

An unknown male's face came on the screen. His eyes widened a second before returning to an unreadable expression. "State your name and affiliation."

"I-I'm Valyn and this is my sister-in-law, Kala. We're merchants' wives from Keldera."

"You're far from home. Where are your husbands?"

Thinking of a time when she'd broken her arm, tear prickled Vala's eyes. "They were k-killed. Our cargo was stolen. We're just trying to get home but don't really understand how to fly this shuttle. We've had to rely on autopilot." She took a deep breath. "And there was some sort of missile that flew by." She sniffled. "I'm starting to think we'll never make it back to Keldera."

The sound cut off as the male talked with someone at his side. Eventually, his voice returned. "There is nothing to worry about, Valyn. The missile was fired by mistake from our ship. Come aboard and we can protect you."

Kalahn spoke up in a slightly higher-pitched voice than what she regularly had. "Th-thank you. We're in your debt."

The male smiled. "It is the duty of any Kelderan male to protect the females. I'm sorry your husbands failed. But we won't. I'll send you docking directions. If they are too complicated, I'll send someone out to help you. Our communications will respond straight away."

Vala nodded. "Thank you. We'll try, but may need your assistance."

"Good. Then I'll see you again once you're aboard my ship."

The screen went blank, and Vala typed in the command to ensure no one could hear them from one of the other ships. The instant she finished, Kalahn growled, "It's that bastard, Ilren."

"Who?"

"One of the warriors from our ship. I saw him enter the lovers' cave several times with different Barren females. If he's on a different ship, that means Kason sent him away."

"And he admitted to firing the missile," Vala added.

"I'm patching through a secure channel to Thorin. He can handle the rest so we can make our way to the ECA ship."

She noticed Kalahn's clenched jaw. "We found the guilty party. Is there something else bothering you?"

Kalahn glanced at her. "I hate how he dismissed us so easily because we were female. I suppose as a princess, I never really appreciated the liberties granted by my father."

She tilted her head. "In this case, it is a positive. Because he dismissed our intelligence, he didn't hesitate in telling us he was guilty."

"I know. But Ilren will sit for greater crimes." Kalahn took a deep breath. "Okay, I'm contacting Thorin now."

Part of Vala wanted to retreat to the back room so she wouldn't have to feel Thorin's disdainful gaze.

Then she remembered what she'd accomplished in the last few days and decided she could handle his hatred. All that mattered was saving Taryn and Prince Kason.

Chapter Twenty

Kason watched as the relief guards entered the area where he and Taryn were being held. The only time the force field came down was for meal times. He'd observed it carefully while pretending to meditate for the last day. He hoped the pattern was similar for this one as well.

The new guards carried trays, signaling meal time. Since Kason was lying next to Taryn, he moved a fraction closer to her ear and murmured, "Do as you did during the training demonstration with the females."

His words were a bit cryptic, but Taryn was intelligent. When she gave an imperceptible nod, Kason watched the guards through slitted eyelids. Once the old pair left, he bided his time. The second the force field went down, he poked Taryn's side.

She rolled off the bed and screamed as she grabbed her middle. One of the guards rushed to her side while the other pointed some type of blast gun at her.

Kason took his cue and lunged for the armed guard as Taryn rolled the other guard to the ground. While it was foolish to think they could escape, Kason had a different goal in mind.

As he finally punched the guard and secured his weapon, he pointed it at the male's head and said, "Tell your captain I want an audience. I'm tired of being ignored."

The guard growled. "The captain won't respond to your threats."

He pushed the gun harder into the male's back. "The longer she holds me here, the greater the chance of starting a war with Keldera. I'm the best hope at avoiding that, so I doubt she'll kill me. Tell her my message and your friend won't be harmed."

From the corner of his eye, he saw that Taryn had the other guard's arm behind his back as well as her knee digging into the base of his spine. She leaned some more of her weight on the man, and he grunted. The guard in front of Kason finally spat out, "I'll tell the captain. Then I'll have the pleasure of watching you be put on trial and hopefully executed."

Kason pushed the man out of the cell and toward the door. "And I look forward to you apologizing to two diplomatic representatives later for your temperament."

The man glared but exited the room. However, once the door clicked closed, the sound of another door sliding downward filled the room. No doubt, it was a safety protocol to fence them in, but Kason had expected it.

All he wanted was an audience with the captain. After a day, Thorin should have discovered the true culprits.

He turned back toward Taryn. The sight of his female holding the much larger male hostage caused pride and desire to flood his body. She was truly a worthy bride.

Taryn met his gaze. "Help me find something to tie him up so I can help once the others return. Even though I expect them to gas us and knock us unconscious, on the small chance the captain agrees to see us, I don't want this guy jumping us unaware for revenge."

Kason opened a panel. Thanks to his mandatory technical training before becoming a general, he found and ripped out some nonessential wiring. He handed it to Taryn. "If a prisoner had jumped one of my warriors, it would've garnered my attention. I hope Geneva is the same."

Taryn finished tying up the guard and stood. "She's not Kelderan, Kason. It may not work."

"She's half-alien too, from her looks. Considering she's an empath, she can see that I mean no true harm to her staff. It also should spare us being killed since death takes its toll on empaths."

Taryn opened her mouth to reply, but the inner door slid open and Geneva's form stood at the other side of the electrified gate. "Just because I feel it more than others doesn't mean I won't kill if necessary."

Kason turned toward the captain and smiled. "You came."

"Only because I sensed you had no desire to kill my staff."

Kason studied the female and stated, "And there's something else."

"Yes. Release my guard and I'll share what it is."

Kason may not have any otherworldly abilities, but he sensed Geneva was telling the truth.

He helped the guard to his feet and escorted him to the door. "You're going to have to turn off the electricity and open the gate if you want him in one piece. Although I'm more than happy to cut him down to pieces so he can fit through the openings."

Geneva tilted her head. "A Kelderan with a sense of humor. I haven't experienced that to date." She glanced to Taryn. "I'm intrigued at how much being in love with a human female can loosen a male's ways."

Kason mentally cursed at not better guarding his emotions around the empath. He could feel Taryn's eyes on his back, but he resisted looking at her just yet. "Sharing my feelings without my permission is without honor."

231

The captain met his gaze again. "It makes us even for what you did to my guards." She motioned and the gate rose. "Speaking of which, hand over my crew member."

He pushed the male forward, and Geneva guided the guard to someone at her side.

Kason raised his brows. "Well? What else aren't you telling me?"

"Come with me. Oh, and if you try anything, you'll be drugged unconscious. Keep that in mind."

Geneva turned and walked down the corridor. Taryn appeared at his side and whispered, "Once this is over, we need to talk."

He knew what it was about. In a way, Kason would be glad to tell his bride how he felt. He hated keeping secrets from her.

Placing a hand on her lower back, he followed the captain's lead. They just needed to leave the ECA's ship so he could do it.

~~~

Taryn wanted to grin at learning Kason's feelings, but resisted. As much as she might wish otherwise, her own feelings weren't the most important factor at the moment.

Captain Geneva knew something about the origins of the missile that had hit the ECA ship, she was sure of it. The sooner they discussed things with her, the sooner Taryn and Kason could clear up the misunderstanding and leave the ship.

Despite the glances some of the guards threw as they walked past, no one touched them. They clearly respected their captain's wishes.

They finally arrived at a set of double doors. Once they opened, Kalahn, Vala, and Jerrick's faces came into view. The three of them sat at one end of the table.

Kason spoke first, thankfully in CEL. "Kalahn? What are you doing here?"

Geneva jumped in. "Sit down and you'll find out soon enough."

He grunted but held his tongue. Considering Kalahn was smiling, the news couldn't be that bad.

Once everyone was seated, except for the guards posted around the room, Geneva spoke again. "Princess Kalahn, tell your brother and Taryn why you're here."

Kalahn looked at her brother. "Why, I wanted to be captured of course."

"Kalahn…" Kason growled.

"Okay, so that's not the whole of it. But I like being the one to rescue you. Let me bask for a few more seconds because I doubt it'll happen again," Kalahn replied.

Geneva folded her hands in front of her. "As much as I understand a sister's need to pester her older brother, time is of the essence. As it is, we should've left this star system by now."

Vala's soft voice filled the room in her accented CEL. "We discovered who fired the missile."

Taryn studied the Barren. She had to be wearing a translating device inside her ear. Since the Kelderans didn't have them, it had to be from the ECA.

More than that, she sat taller and her voice was firmer. Whatever had happened recently had given the woman some much-needed confidence. "Who was it?"

Kalahn answered, "Ilren."

Taryn had no idea who Ilren was, but Kason's curse signaled that he did. "Once we return to Keldera, I need to find

233

out who helped him at the remote base I sent him to." He glanced at Taryn. "He was one of the warriors who refused to work with the females and that we sent away." He looked back to Kalahn and then Jerrick. "He couldn't have orchestrated it all on his own. He has fire, but isn't a strategist."

Taryn leaned forward. "Knowing who did it is only half of it. How did you figure it out? Does Thorin know?"

Jerrick nodded, signaling he must also be wearing a translating device. He spoke in Kelderan, but Kalahn quickly interpreted. "Thorin knows. He helped once we found the fighter ship and captured the traitors. Ilren managed to take control of one of the two the king sent to help us." He gestured toward Kalahn and Vala. "These two are responsible for not only finding them but for also tricking them into confessing."

Taryn looked to Kalahn and raised her brows. "I'm intrigued."

Kalahn shrugged. "Playing a helpless female afraid of the recently fired missile worked to our advantage. To calm us down, Ilren assured us he had fired the weapon by mistake and that he would protect us."

Yes, it certainly seemed that Kalahn was destined to be more than a princess. Taryn only hoped Kalahn would have another chance to show her potential again in the future.

Kason grunted. "There is a reason Ilren was never given an officer's position."

Geneva spoke up. "All that matters is your Lt. General sent us the proof the other ship fired and I trust you to charge him accordingly since Keldera is outside our jurisdiction. If we're to investigate and possibly help Jasvar, we need to move on as soon as possible. I offer you passage on our ship, if you so choose."

234

While a part of her screamed to accept the offer and return home, she had a duty to fulfill. Taryn glanced to Kason. His people were also counting on her.

She shook her head. "Thank you, but no. I still need to settle things with the Kelderan king before going home."

Kalahn spoke up. "You might need to go to Keldera, but I'm going, along with Jerrick to ensure Ryven and the other warriors are released. We can also help set things up for when Kason and Taryn return to Jasvar."

Kason studied his sister for a second and Taryn wondered if he would outright deny Kalahn because of her recent actions. Kalahn might try something else daring while on Jasvar without her brother's presence. Since Taryn didn't really know Ryven, she had no idea if the man could keep Kalahn from getting into too much danger.

Kason finally replied, "I would try to stop you, but I have a feeling you'd go anyway."

She wanted to cheer but settled for elbowing Kason in the side. "Kason is trying to say he thinks you'll represent Keldera well." When Kason said nothing, Taryn smiled before looking to the captain. "Give us half an hour to talk with Kalahn and Jerrick and then we'll leave your ship."

Geneva nodded. "Thirty minutes. However, if you're still aboard after that, you'll be joining us for the journey." She waited for them to bob their assent before continuing, "I'm also going to give you a copy of the ECA agreement before you depart. While your final admission to the alliance is pending our investigation, I want to give you plenty of time to look it over and know what you're getting yourself into."

"Thank you," Taryn answered.

The captain stood. "My staff and I will leave you alone to use this room. Once you're done, a few guards will escort you to the appropriate shuttle bay." She bowed her head. "I hope our future working relationship proves fruitful."

"As do we," Taryn answered.

Geneva and her staff exited the room. Once they were alone, Kason turned to Kalahn. "How did you convince Thorin to let you execute your crazy plan?"

Kalahn tilted her head. "My crazy plan saved your royal behind, so you should thank me."

"Kalahn," Kason growled.

Vala spoke up. "Thorin want success. Try anything to get it."

Jerrick jumped in, and Kalahn interpreted into CEL again. "Vala is right. Thorin wants to command his own ship, and after this, headquarters will probably grant him one."

Kason wrapped one arm around Taryn's waist. "Especially when I announce Taryn is my bride and they take away my rank."

Hearing Kason's statement made her both happy and sad. She loved the thought of a future with her warrior prince, but not at the expense of his career.

Jerrick smiled. Kalahn's voice put his words in CEL. "Maybe, maybe not. I already figured that out and I can't be the only one. And yet here you are, still a general."

Hope fluttered in her chest. Maybe they could have it all.

Taryn looked between the two men. "I thought you'd said that if anyone found out, you'd lose your rank."

Jerrick shrugged, and Kalahn translated again. "Most of us have worked for years with Prince Kason. Besides, we sent away most of the dissenters with Ilren back to Keldera, after Thorin forced their surrender. I can't say if headquarters will feel the same way once it's public, but the ship is loyal to the prince."

"We'll find out what headquarters thinks soon enough," Kason said. "For now, we don't have much time. I need Kalahn to give a message to Ryven. Do you trust Vala enough to hear it, too?"

Kalahn placed a hand on Vala's bicep. "Of course I do. Without her, our mission might've failed. She's a skilled pilot. The only reason I'm not bringing her with me to Jasvar is because I want her to watch over Taryn."

Taryn rolled her eyes. "I can look after myself." Kalahn growled and she grinned. "But I admit it'll be nice to have a friendly face at my side."

Vala looked anywhere but at Taryn. She might be more confident, but the Barren wasn't used to compliments. Taryn would have to remedy that.

Kason motioned for his sister to come closer. Once she did, he whispered something in Kelderan that Taryn couldn't understand.

Kalahn answered back in the same language before switching to CEL. "Now, you two and Vala need to hurry along. I doubt Father will deny the colonization agreement now, after all Taryn has done to help us. But the sooner a formal agreement is signed, the sooner we can put everything in motion for the colony."

Taryn bobbed her head. "Of course, but if everything goes according to plan, Kason and I will arrive well before the colonists. Until we reach Jasvar, make sure no one kills each other. I'm sure the Kelderan warriors on Jasvar might be less than enthusiastic about remaining on my planet and undoubtedly under the ECA observers' watch."

Kalahn waved a hand. "I've known Ryven nearly my whole life. I can handle him."

Kason shook his head. "Ryven isn't one of your palace servants to order around, Kalahn. You'd best remember that."

Before the siblings could start an argument, Taryn stood between them. "I'm sure everyone will do a stellar job." She walked up to Kalahn and put out her arms.

The princess closed the distance and hugged her before saying, "Thanks for everything, Taryn. I'm glad you turned out to be my brother's destined bride. I'm just sad I'll miss the proclamation ceremony."

Taryn smiled. "I'm sure we'll do something back on Jasvar. Otherwise my best friend, Nova, will badger me for the rest of my life for not including her."

Especially since Taryn had probably nabbed her alien man before Nova.

Kalahn leaned forward. "I'll have to find this Nova. Any friend of yours has to be interesting."

She moved away and smiled at Kalahn. "I think you two will get along famously."

Kason wrapped both of his arms around Taryn's waist and drew her back against him. "We should go before you give any more bad ideas to my sister."

"Hey, there's nothing wrong with making life interesting. Besides, Kalahn has a lifetime of mistakes and adventures to make up for," Taryn stated.

"And I plan to make a head start before you two arrive back on Jasvar." Kalahn motioned toward the exit with her hand. "Go. As much as it pains me to say it, my brother is right. You don't have much time, and Keldera needs you two too much. I'll see you both soon enough."

The thought of not seeing Kalahn for who knew how long caused her heart to ache. She was going to miss her new friend.

Kason's low voice rumbled in her ear. "You'll see Kalahn before much longer."

She smiled up at her prince. "And to think of the trouble we can cause once we're reunited and I'm in charge of the planet."

Before Kason could reply, Vala walked up to them and bowed her head. "Excuse me for speaking out of turn, but we really should leave unless we want to remain onboard this ship."

"Feel free to say whatever you want in my presence, Vala." Once the Barren murmured she'd try, Taryn maneuvered out of Kason's grip and took his hand. "Come, Prince. I think it's time to meet the rest of your family."

When Kason said nothing, she instantly knew the meeting with the king and his older brother wasn't going to be a friendly, laidback experience.

While she'd work on repairing their family relations later, securing the agreement came first.

Waving good-bye to Kalahn and Jerrick, Taryn led Kason out of the room. Vala followed close on their heels.

As the guards escorted them to the designated shuttle bay, Kason squeezed her hand. His touch reminded her that if she ever needed strength, her warrior would lend it.

With that thought, she picked up her pace. Taryn was anxious to see Keldera, negotiate an agreement, and return to her own world.

Chapter Twenty-One

For the short ride between the ECA's ship and the one currently in Thorin's command, Kason itched to take Taryn to the back of the small space and kiss her.

With more people knowing she was his destined bride, he needed to claim her publicly. And soon.

However, with only Kason, Taryn, and Vala inside the shuttle that Kalahn had used previously, Kason had to help copilot the vessel.

And the Barren was doing a fine job. While he needed to adjust a few things every once in a while, with a little coaching, she would be as skilled as any male.

He nearly blinked at that thought. Taryn was definitely rubbing off on him. Kelderan law still forbade females from becoming pilots. Maybe after the colonization agreement was reached, Kason could talk with his older brother about changing a few things. If not for all of Keldera, then at least those who became part of the colony.

Of course, once they landed on Jasvar, Kason could help craft new rules. It would be his job to help enforce them.

Taryn's voice filled his ear. "What are you thinking about?"

He smiled at his female. "The future."

"That's pretty vague."

"Let's just say that you are rubbing off on me. I'm starting to think of how some females could have traditionally male jobs in the colony."

Taryn beamed at him, and his heart thumped harder. She would always be beautiful to him, but with excitement in her eyes and flushed cheeks, she was gorgeous.

She leaned forward. "And here I thought I would have to seduce you."

He looked to the Barren, but she pretended not to hear them. "Then maybe I'll have to hold out a little longer and see what you have in store for me."

She tapped her chin. "Let me think…no. You already said you wanted to change a few things. I'll save my skills for later."

After kissing her lips gently, he murmured, "I look forward to it."

As they smiled at one another, it was on the tip of his tongue to spill his feelings.

However, before he could go through with it, the console beeped with an incoming communication. He kissed Taryn once more before facing forward and hitting Receive.

When Thorin's face appeared on the screen, he spoke in Kelderan. "I see you made it out alive."

"Of course. Update me on the status of Ilren."

"The traitor is in custody, as are the thirty other males who helped pilot the small fighter ship," Thorin answered.

"And how did they come to occupy the ship?" Kason asked.

Thorin's eyes flicked to Vala and back. "Are you sure you wish to discuss this now?"

"Yes."

"One of the original crew alerted Ilren to the mission and put in a transfer order for him and many of his followers. We're

241

tracking down the officer who did this, although he remains elusive."

For a split second, Kason wondered how he could leave Keldera with traitors in the midst. But as he stared at Thorin and remembered Jerrick's words from earlier, about the remaining crew being loyal to Kason, he was confident they could help protect his home. "We can discuss this more in depth later. Does anyone on Keldera know of the situation? I'm concerned the wrong people could hear the charges and try to cover it up."

Thorin shook his head. "I haven't shared anything yet. I'm waiting until we're within secure communications range of Keldera before I send a report to headquarters and the king," Thorin answered. "Once you're aboard, we can discuss who to include on this case."

"Good. I'll take a look at everything in more detail once we're aboard." Kason paused before adding, "And I want you to remain in charge, even after I step foot back on the ship."

"Why?" Thorin's gaze moved to Taryn and back. "I know how to keep a secret."

"No, it's time to be truthful with the crew. I'm going to make an announcement soon after boarding, and you've proven yourself with capturing Ilren and the others as well as helping to secure our freedom. I can think of no one better to take my place."

"As you wish, your highness."

"Then prepare for our arrival and the announcement. We should be there shortly."

The screen went blank. He turned to Taryn and switched to CEL. "I hope it's okay that I told Thorin I would announce our relationship once we reach the main ship. I know I didn't ask your permission first."

"Kason, stop being so formal. While there's no way I'll ever let you make all the decisions for me nor would you allow me to do the same for you, I expect for us to have each other's backs. Speaking up for me sometimes is okay." She placed a hand on his cheek. "After all, I not only trust you, but I love you."

Kason covered Taryn's hand with his own. "Truly? I don't want you to feel pressured because of what the captain revealed."

She frowned. "If I have to tie you up and threaten you with my daggers to convince you, I will, Prince."

He grinned. "Maybe I do want that."

With a growl, Taryn stood and asked Vala, "Can you handle the controls for a few minutes?"

"Of course," she answered without taking her eyes off the main viewer screen.

"Good." Taryn took his hand and tugged him to his feet. Once they reached the rear of the shuttle, she moved her arms to behind his neck and leaned against him.

Her breasts pressing against his chest sent a rush of heat throughout his body. If not for Vala, he would pin Taryn to the wall and convince her to let him take her.

Taryn searched his eyes. "I mean it, Kason. I do love you. From your protectiveness to your skill to even your brain, all of it has done much more than impress me—it's convinced me that you are a worthy partner in life. Ruling a colony isn't easy, and few men would understand the demands. However, from your experience as both a prince and general, I think you do. And more than that, you'll probably force me to take a break when needed and to enjoy the little moments that make life special."

He placed his hands on her hips. "It almost sounds as if you want my skill as a warrior more than anything else."

She rubbed her lower body, and he resisted hissing. "Your skill is impressive in many ways, but I want all of you, Kason.

243

Faults and all. Don't ever be afraid to show them to me because each one makes you more dear."

At the vulnerability in Taryn's eyes, Kason believed her. "Even though you know how I feel, I'm going to say it—I love you, Taryn Demara. You've done more than turn my world upside down with your way of thinking. You're intelligent, stubborn, determined, and occasionally funny. All of that, combined with how easy it is to talk with you, makes you my perfect match and the one female I'd give up everything to be with."

"Kason."

"No, it's true. While starting over on Jasvar will be tough, I can handle anything with you at my side. The only question is whether you'll accept me there or not."

Taryn blinked her eyelids a few times. He hoped she wouldn't start crying.

Then she whispered, "Of course I will, you stubborn prince. I'm never letting you go."

With a growl, Kason took Taryn's lips.

~~~

As Kason's tongue slipped into her mouth, Taryn leaned her whole body against him. Hearing he cared for her from the empath captain had been one thing, but him spilling his feelings and saying he'd give up everything to be with her was quite another.

Pulling him close, she met each stroke of his tongue. If not for Vala, Taryn would've jumped up and wrapped her legs around Kason's waist.

Vala. Remembering the woman, Taryn broke the kiss. "We have company."

He nibbled her bottom lip before whispering, "She will look the other way."

She lightly scraped her nails against his neck. "I mind. Besides, what if Thorin tries to reach us again? Do you really want the crew in the command center to see you and me half naked?"

"No one sees you naked but me."

"And me, I hope."

He lightly smacked her butt. "Don't be ridiculous."

She grinned. "But it's so much fun." Kason frowned and she sighed. "Okay, okay. But I think I'm spending the night in your quarters."

"That is something I agree with wholeheartedly. I'm glad I didn't have to order you to do it."

"Yes, because that works so well."

"Then I command you to never spend the night in my bed."

She stuck out her tongue. "One day, I'm going to spite you just because I can."

"And I look forward to it, *zyla.*"

She softened at his endearment. "Can I also use *zyla*? Or is there a male form of it?"

"You can call me *zylar.* It means the same thing, but sounds more masculine."

"Almost like a fierce warlord who can breathe fire and move objects with his mind. 'I am Zylar, behold my power!'"

Kason shook his head. "Life will never be boring with you, *zyla.*"

"Damn straight." She gave him a quick kiss. "But we should probably return to our seats. We'll arrive at any moment."

"At any moment, what?"

"At any moment, *zylar*," she drawled.

He nodded. "Good. That makes me happy."

"Just make sure it doesn't go to your head, Prince. Otherwise, I may resort to calling you Mr. Fluffypoo."

He frowned. "But I don't have that much hair, and I'm always clean."

Taryn snorted. "I think the name is lost in translation. Too bad, as most native CEL speakers would've told me, it's the last thing they want to be called."

"Once you reach the same level of Kelderan as I have of CEL, then we can talk."

"I suppose." She took his hand and squeezed. "The ship is drawing closer. We should sit down, and you can tell me what to expect from this public claiming you spoke of."

They reached their seats and Kason removed his hand to buckle himself in. While it was foolish, Taryn missed his touch.

Nova was going to tease her relentlessly about being a lovesick fool once she was back on Jasvar.

As if reading her mind, Kason took her hand again once they were both secure. "It's a simple ceremony where I proclaim you as my one and only bride, and you do the same about me."

Taryn smiled. "So I call you my bride, too?"

He grunted. "No, I am your lord."

"Really? I'm supposed to call you my lord? Isn't there another term I can use?"

He stroked the back of her hand. "Not at the moment, but I'm sure you'll think of one eventually. The custom will probably remain on Keldera, but it may shift over time for the Jasvarian colony."

"Then it motivates me to think of a better title before the colony is established. I could go with 'my husband' or 'my spouse.'"

"Whatever you call me, I'll answer. Except for Mr. Fluffypoo. That is not noble enough for a warrior."

Taryn laughed, but before she could reply, Vala's voice filled the shuttle. "Ship ahead."

Kason kissed her hand before releasing it. He said something in Kelderan and Vala nodded.

As the pair guided the shuttle into the main cargo bay, Taryn's stomach flipped. She was about to become essentially married to a Kelderan warrior prince. While she wasn't nervous about spending her life with Kason, she was a little worried about the future and how both the Kelderans and Jasvarians would treat their relationship.

Still, staring at her handsome warrior, Taryn knew she could handle whatever people threw her way. After more than thirty years wondering if she'd ever find a mate, let alone love, she wasn't about to give up the precious gift because of a few sideways glances.

~~~

Kason guided the small craft into the cargo bay. Judging by the large crowd of people waiting on the far side of the large space, Thorin had called all of the nonessential personnel to hear his proclamation.

The primal part of him was pleased. Soon all the males would know to keep their distance.

Once the shuttle touched down and all the engines were disengaged, Kason undid the buckles of his seat and stood. As soon as Taryn was at his side, he took her hand.

However, before disembarking, he looked to Vala and said, "You did well. I hope you'll continue your studies and contemplate joining the colony."

Vala bowed her head. "Thank you, your highness. I will think about it."

He switched to CEL. "Is my warrior leader ready?"

"Of course. I can't wait to get this over with and head to Keldera. I'm anxious to meet your father and brother."

Taryn was far more excited than he. His father, the king, might approve of him now, but it'd been more years than he could count since he'd talked to his brother, Keltor.

Still, with his human at his side, he'd face anything.

Guiding her out of the shuttle, he scanned the crowd. Thorin was the first one to step forward and greet them. He even spoke in CEL for Taryn's benefit. "Welcome back." Thorin waved a hand at one of the crew near a console. The male tapped a few strokes, and Thorin continued, "Everything is ready."

Kason released Taryn's hand and pulled her against him. A few murmurs arose, but the second he raised a fist, the room quieted. He spoke the words in Kelderan he never thought he'd say. "Taryn Demara is my bride, and she has chosen me. Do you recognize my claim?"

A roar of affirmations went up. He looked down at Taryn. She stood tall and said the phrase he'd made her memorize in Kelderan. "Kason tro el Vallen is my lord, and he has chosen me. Do you recognize my claim?"

While her accent was strange and stilted, the crowd yelled their assent.

Kason took his cue. "Then per the laws governing Keldera, I willingly give up my commission and acknowledge Thorin Jarrell as my successor. He will take over control of this ship."

He motioned toward Thorin and the male spoke up. "I respectfully accept command. And my first order as general is for you and your bride to return to your quarters and rest up. We're going to push hard to return to Keldera as soon as possible. You're going to need your strength, especially since training will continue as usual, for both the males and females." A few murmurs rolled through the crowd, but Thorin ignored them. "If not for Princess Kalahn, Vala Yarlen, or Jerrick and his warriors, we could've been at war with the Earth Colony Alliance. Cooperation may be our future, especially for any who wish to join the colony. Everyone is dismissed."

As the crowd dispersed, Thorin turned toward Kason and switched to CEL. "I hope both of you will still help with training. But take a day to celebrate."

No sooner had Taryn said, "Thank you," than Thorin turned and exited the cargo bay. His female looked up at him. "I'm almost starting to like him."

Kason had a feeling Thorin wished to join the colony and maybe find his own bride among the Jasvarians, who wouldn't care about his father's heritage. But talking of Thorin's future was the last thing Kason wanted to do in the present. He hauled Taryn up against his body and whispered, "Right now, you should only think of me. I am your lord."

The corner of her mouth ticked up. "More like, 'Oh, lord, what did I get myself into?' as they said in old Earth times."

He frowned. "You think you are funny, but I don't always understand."

Taryn shook her head before raising her chin. "For now, my lord, I think you need to kiss me and make me forget about everything but your touch."

Nuzzling her cheek, he answered, "Anything to please my bride."

Taryn moved to kiss him, but he stepped to the side and scooped her up. She barely had time to blink before he added, "Not here. The second I kiss you I won't be able to stop. And I meant it earlier when I said I don't want anyone else to see your naked body."

"But me."

"Yes, stubborn woman, no one but you and me."

Taryn tilted her head. "Then you'd better start running, *zylar*, because I'm going to kiss you in two minutes no matter where we are."

He growled before running. Taryn had thrown down a challenge that he fully intended to win.

Chapter Twenty-Two

Several days later, Taryn lay next to her warrior and listened to his even breathing. While the sex had been great, she'd also enjoyed working with Kason to train the women onboard the ship. He may no longer be general, but his innate desire to lead would never fade. The Kelderans on the ship still listened and looked to him for guidance.

Taryn yearned to be back home to also guide her people through the new changes. The ECA ship should have arrived by now and the talks should've begun. However, communications from Jasvar would be delayed because of the distance. Taryn wouldn't find out how things were going until after her meeting with the Kelderan king, which would be happening in about two hours, if Thorin had kept the ship on schedule.

She snuggled into Kason's side and traced the markings on his chest. They flickered between purple and red, which meant he was happy and lustful.

And also awake.

Running a hand back and forth over his pecs, she murmured, "I'm not going to stroke your skin forever."

He smiled but kept his eyes closed. "Of course not because I'm about to roll over and cover you with my body."

Before she could reply, he did what he said and she squeaked. "What are you doing?"

As he played with her breast, Taryn found it hard to concentrate on his reply. "Easing your tension before you leave this room."

She bit her lip to keep from moaning as he lightly tweaked her nipple. "I really should prepare some more. I can barely say a few sentences in Kelderan and I want to memorize the formal greeting for your father perfectly."

He switched to Kelderan and said, "You'll do fine, *zyla*."

Taryn answered in CEL. "Probably, but a little extra prep work wouldn't hurt."

"Then I'll make this quick."

Kason ran his hand down her abdomen and between her legs. When he teased her opening with his finger, she spread her legs wider.

He chuckled. "It doesn't take much to convince you, bride. You're nice and wet for me."

"Maybe I'm just humoring you, Prince."

"We'll see about that."

He moved away and flipped Taryn onto her belly before raising her hips. Even though there were a million reasons why she should discourage him, she wiggled her bottom. "So far, you're not very quick."

With a growl, she felt Kason's hard cock rub up and down her folds before he plunged into her core. She moaned and arched her back at the fullness.

He brushed her shoulder blade before moving his hand to her breast.

She'd never tire of his rough palms against her skin.

Kason moved his hips and Taryn's thoughts fled her head. Each of her warrior's thrusts rubbed just the right spot inside, and she clutched the sheets. "Faster."

"Anything for my bride."

Kason increased his pace and somehow managed to pinch and roll her nipple as he did so.

She was close to coming.

Then he removed his hand and stilled his movements. Taryn looked over her shoulder and growled, "Why did you stop?"

"Because I wanted to see your beautiful face before you shatter."

Her anger faded. "Now you see me, so don't keep me waiting, *zylar*."

Wrapping one arm around her waist, he lifted her up to lean against his chest. "Kiss me and I'll do as you wish."

Kason took her lips, and she welcomed his tongue. She loved the spicy male taste that was Kason tro el Vallen.

He broke the kiss but didn't release her waist as he moved again. His free hand went between her thighs and lightly brushed her hard nub.

She rested her head on his shoulder as her prince found the pace she liked. Each pass of his fingers brought her closer to the edge. Lights danced before her eyes before pleasure finally raced through her body as she came.

Kason continued his thrusts until he stilled with a roar and spilled inside her.

As Taryn came down from her high and her heart rate slowly returned to normal, Kason nuzzled her neck. His hot breath danced against her skin as he said, "I love you, Taryn."

She looked up to meet his gaze and placed a hand on his cheek. "I love you, too, Kason." Amusement danced in his eyes and she frowned. "Why is that funny?"

"It's not. But I think you're relaxed enough to face anything now."

"Yes, your magical penis eases all of my problems. Oh, baby," she said in a flat voice.

Lightly pinching her nipple, he answered, "Of course it does. Don't forget it."

At his deadpanned tone, she laughed. "I think my lord has definitely loosened up since our first meeting."

"I'm glad to see you're calling me 'lord' now."

She rolled her eyes. "I'm still thinking of an alternative. 'Lovey poo' doesn't quite have the same ring."

"Isn't poo another name for excrement? Why would you want to call me that? I assure you I don't stink."

She grinned. "Only in a good way." He opened his mouth, but she beat him to it. "I'll explain it later. I need some time to prepare for your father. However, I do need to shower." She caressed his jaw. "And I may need some help in there."

"Anything for my female."

"You need to stop saying that or I'm going to take it at face value."

He nibbled her earlobe. "There are limits, but the fun part is watching you discover them."

"Kason."

He bit her neck and licked the sting. "Come. I know how you like to shower."

Lifting her off him, he stood and hauled Taryn to her feet. She barely had a second to think before he pulled her into the bathroom and proceeded to slowly caress every inch of her body, including his tongue between her thighs.

~~~

THE CONQUEST

Two hours later, Kason stood with Taryn outside his father's meeting room. While his bride was gaping at the high ceilings with their view screens displaying the stars, he breathed evenly to focus his mind.

He had no idea whether his father would accept Taryn or not, let alone if Keltor would even agree to meet with them. Since Keltor was merely the heir, Taryn could negotiate her agreement with just the king and the major players of government.

Then he remembered his promise to Kalahn during their brief exchange back on the ECA ship, to make sure Keltor was doing okay. For some reason, his sister was concerned about their brother. Something about him not wanting to be king, but grudgingly accepting the fact.

The doors finally slid open. Inside was a large rectangular table surrounded by murals of Keldera's history and past monarchs. At the far end of the table was an intricately carved chair on a raised dais. His white-haired father sat tall in his gray and black robes as he assessed first him and then Taryn. When his father waved them forward, Kason guided Taryn to the place a few seats down from the dais.

As he drew closer, Kason noticed even more lines etched into the king's face than he remembered from their conversation via the comm units. His father looked older than he should. Before he left Keldera, he needed to find out what was going on. Even if his father wouldn't tell him, maybe his brother would.

However, there was no sign of Keltor. Kason would have to track him down.

His father finally spoke up in CEL. "Welcome home, my second son and his bride."

Taryn bowed her head. In her rough Kelderan accent, she said, "The honor is mine. Thank you for allowing me to set foot on your planet."

The king answered in CEL. "Your official greeting is appreciated. Please, sit down and let's discuss the agreement."

As they took their places, Kason scrutinized his father. In his much younger days, King Kastor would've required more pomp and ceremony before they took their seats.

For the first time in a long time, Kason was anxious to speak alone with his father to find out the truth.

One of the males to the king's right, the head of government named Hinvel Mayta, spoke next in thickly accented CEL. At one time, the male had been Kason's tutor in the language. Hinvel said, "We have reviewed the basics of the colony agreement you sent late last night via secure communications. There are a few details that need to be ironed out, but we don't foresee any problems in agreeing to most of them."

Taryn folded her hands in front of her. "Which aspects do you wish to change?"

The king spoke up. "We will go into details after the evening meal. My council merely wanted to reassure you that we desire to reach an agreement with you. Now that's done, they are dismissed."

Kason barely resisted his jaw dropping open as the council members filed out of the room. King Kastor was a fair king, but he had never worried about soothing the feelings of an alien before, not even those who occasionally traded with Keldera.

Thankfully, Taryn didn't miss a beat as she scrutinized the king. "I know our two worlds are different, but I wish to reach an agreement as soon as possible so that I can return to my people. Surely you can understand how I don't like to leave them alone longer than I have to."

The king laid his hands on the arms of his chair. "Spending one evening and night on my planet seems a fair enough request.

After all, my son has proclaimed you his bride. For your future children's sakes, you need to understand our ways and traditions."

Kason finally spoke up. "So you accept my choice?"

"Of course. The human has proven herself worthy. It's nice to see one of my children find their partner."

While I'm still alive was left unsaid.

Not wanting to address his father's mortality just yet, he asked, "Where is Keltor?"

"He is visiting some of our loyal communities, as any future king should do in these troubling times."

While Kason had intended to talk with his father alone, Taryn's hand on his knee reminded him that he could share anything with his bride.

Kason cleared his throat. "I sense you are skirting the true issue. Father, are you ill?"

For a few seconds, Kastor remained silent. Then he sighed. "I tried to hide it as long as I can, but I'm dying, Kason. There is no medicine that can save me."

Taryn squeezed his knee, and he placed his hand over hers. Kason and his father may not have been close in years, but Kastor was still his father. With his mother gone, Kastor was the only tie remaining between him and his two siblings.

His female spoke up in a soft voice. "How long do you have, your majesty?"

Kastor smiled. "You may call me Kastor. And half a year at most. I'm grateful for the time as it allows me to prepare both the planet and Keltor for the transition, especially after the recent scare. The ECA's sudden appearance reminded me that we need to prepare better in case the Brevkan attacks our planet again." The king leaned forward. "But rest assured the agreement will be reached, and you can return to your planet soon enough. I just wanted one last evening with my son."

All the years of pain and disagreements faded away. Kason wasn't about to tarnish his father's remaining weeks with hatred or past petty disagreements.

Taryn smiled at his father. "I hope I'm invited, too. I'd like to spend some time with you. That way I can see for myself who you are rather than relying on what Kason tells me."

His father smiled back. "A straightforward female. I can see why my son chose you. After all, he never likes to do things the easy way."

Kason frowned. "I did not pick her solely because of the challenge."

Taryn raised an eyebrow. "I hope not."

He leaned toward his female. "But it does make things interesting, *zyla*."

Not caring his father was in the room, he kissed Taryn gently.

Once he finished, his father chimed in again. "I will give you two a little time for yourselves. There will be a dinner in your honor in the main hall this evening."

Taryn looked to Kastor. "Are you sure? We can stay with you if you like."

Kastor waved a hand in dismissal. "I need to rest or I won't last the evening." He looked to Kason. "It will also give you time to find Keltor."

To help protect his sister's true location, Kason added, "And Kalahn."

The corners of his father's mouth turned upward. "I know she's not on the planet, Kason, so you don't have to lie to me."

"How...?"

"I have eyes and ears everywhere. Kalahn always wanted to do more than wear pretty dresses and attend dinners. In my old

258

age, I finally realized that, but not before she took matters into her own hands. She reminds me of your mother before she became my queen."

"Mother was rebellious?" Kason asked.

"To a point," Kastor answered. "Although she eventually accepted her place and forgot about her scandalous dreams once she had Keltor. The children meant everything to her."

As Kason digested the new information about his mother, his father rubbed his forehead and added, "I must retire. I look forward to this evening."

Kastor pushed a button, and two Barren nurses came into the room. Kason took his cue and stood. "Until tonight, Father."

Taryn was at his side. "Nice to meet you, Kastor."

The king nodded. Kason guided Taryn out of the meeting room, and she whispered, "I'm so sorry, Kason."

"He has lived a long life and kept his planet together, with many years of peace after the war with the Brevkan ended. That is enough for any Kelderan monarch."

Taryn threaded her arm through his. "Still, it's okay to show your emotions to me at any time. I hope you know that."

"Of course, *zyla*. But for the moment, let's find our quarters and prepare for tonight."

She stopped in her tracks. "Not until we find Keltor."

"Taryn, my brother is busy. We can talk with him later at the dinner."

She scrutinized him before replying, "That may actually be better. With a crowd watching, you two will have to act civilly."

"My brother and I may not get along well, but we're no longer children. I have no desire to hit him."

"I'm going to believe you. However, you must promise me you'll resolve some of your issues before we leave."

He glanced at her. "Why are you so determined to repair relations with my brother?"

"The truth? Well, I'm an only child. I always wished for siblings, but my mother miscarried too many times after me and never had another. Probably because they were all male embryos attacked by the doom virus. So, whenever someone dear to me has siblings and arguments, I want to repair them and remind them that siblings are a blessing some of us were denied. Provided they didn't do something awful such as steal or kill, or something like that. But in most cases, it's just a petty reason for the fighting. I have a feeling the feud between you and Keltor is of the petty variety."

"I suppose so." He cupped her cheek. "I will try my best for you. However, I can't guarantee Keltor will welcome the reconciliation."

"Then I'll just have to display a lot of charm. Maybe then he'll love me as a sister and realize he needs to fix things with you in order to see me again."

He growled. "I don't like the thought of you charming my brother."

She turned and laid a hand on his chest. "I love you, Kason, so stop with the jealousy crap. It's going to get old fast."

He blinked. "What?"

"I don't want to have the same conversation a million times. Next time, I'll aim my dagger at your balls."

He smiled slowly. "I'd like to see you try."

She sighed. "Everything is a turn on for you." She tugged his arm and started walking. "Let's get ready and prepare for tonight. Maybe I can relax you a little beforehand, provided you promise not to act jealous around your brother."

"Will it involve your tight leather outfit from your first interrogation?"

She flashed a mischievous smile. "It can."

"Then let's hurry up. I need a lot of calming before I face my brother."

As Kason guided Taryn through the maze of corridors to his old room, he tried his best not to think of the evening ahead. He wanted to focus solely on his bride for the next few hours. Maybe then he could survive the evening without punching his brother in the nose.

Chapter Twenty-Three

Taryn had done a good job of ignoring the stares in the corridors, but as she and Kason approached the towering double doors to the main hall, her heart beat double-time. Being on the arm of one prince and trying to charm another was going to put her in the center of attention. And not all of it was going to be good, especially as Evaine had remained on the Kelderan ship and Taryn would be the only Jasvarian at the event.

You can do this, Taryn. Remember, you're representing your planet.

Taking a deep breath, she gripped Kason's arm a little tighter. He glanced down at her. "What's wrong? With the interpreting device in your ear that you received from the ECA, you'll at least be able to understand what's going on. And I will translate when needed."

She shook her head. "I'm not too worried about that. Me not being able to speak Kelderan means I won't have to suffer too much small talk." Kason raised his brows and Taryn continued, "I can handle people staring at me, that's not the issue. The problem is many are going to hate me for forcing you to retire your commission. From what I've gathered, you're quite notorious as a warrior here."

He took her free hand. "I doubt they will hate you, *zyla*. Your planet is going to ease the overpopulation of mine."

"Rationally, I'm sure they realize that. But an alien stealing one of their princes? I'm sure some will see that as a traitorous act. I'm also worried about the antimonarchy groups using us as a means to promote their own causes."

"They may try. But that is for my father, brother, and the council to handle. Tonight, you represent Jasvar. You need to show the people of Keldera what I already know—that you are a strong, intelligent, and caring leader."

She smiled at her prince. "I'll try, although I did leave all but one of my daggers back in the room so I can't impress them with my dagger-flinging skills."

He snorted. "That might be for the best. Otherwise, you might give the females some bad ideas."

"I'll let that slide for now. But eventually, they should learn how to defend themselves. It'll come in handy if and when your enemies attack."

"I'll make sure to mention it to Keltor. But first, we need to find him." Kason motioned toward the doors. "Are you ready?"

She nodded and the two males at either side of the hall opened the doors.

The room was nearly as big as the cargo bay back on the Kelderan ship, but there was one major difference—the walls and ceilings were made entirely out of view screens. Currently, they displayed dancing lights and patterns. The Kelderans in the room paid them little attention since most of the eyes were on her and Kason.

Keeping her head high, she allowed Kason to guide her through the throng of people up toward the front of the room. King Kastor sat in a huge, intricately carved chair and to his right was a male who looked a lot like Kason with golden skin and dark blue hair, although he was leaner and not quite as muscled.

Kason whispered, "That's Keltor next to my father."

Keltor met Taryn's gaze. The man's face was expressionless. He and Kason had that ability in common.

But the closer they drew to him, the more differences she noticed. Yes, they both had the same golden skin and dark blue hair, but Keltor's nose was more like Kalahn's and his eyes were like Kastor's. Kason must have inherited his from their mother.

And even though Keltor was handsome in his own right with his square jaw and broad shoulders, he didn't quite live up to her own prince. Of course, Taryn was a bit biased. Nova would no doubt find Keltor sexy.

They finally ascended the dais and stood next to Keltor and Kastor. Both remained seated, but it didn't bother Taryn. She bowed her head and said in Kelderan, "Nice to meet you."

Keltor's deep voice answered in CEL, "So this is the human leader of our future colony planet."

Kason wrapped an arm around her waist. "She is also your sister now, too."

As the brothers stared at one another, Kastor spoke up. "Once I announce Taryn as Kason's bride, you three may go to the room behind us to talk."

"There's nothing to discuss, Father," Keltor stated.

"There is. And you will talk."

Even Taryn could hear the steel in Kastor's voice.

Both Kason and Keltor mumbled their assent and the king nodded. "Good." He motioned to his left side. "Then take your places next to me. I'm going to announce Kason's proclamation."

Taryn asked, "What about the future colony?"

"I will do that once you are on your way to Jasvar. I don't want to risk any sort of sabotage beforehand."

Taryn nodded. She and Kason moved to Kastor's left.

THE CONQUEST

The king signaled one of the guards on the dais and a boom reverberated through the room. The voices died down and all eyes focused on Kason's father.

Kastor raised his voice and spoke in Kelderan. Taryn was grateful for the device in her ear as he said, "Tonight we are here to celebrate the proclamation of my second son, Kason. He has found his bride." Kastor motioned toward Taryn. "Her name is Taryn Demara. While human, she has proven herself. Just recently, she helped to avoid war with the Earth Colony Alliance. I wish her and my son a fruitful union and eternal happiness."

The king made a fist and pounded it over his heart. Most of the people in the crowd did the same, although not quite all.

To be honest, more people had followed the king's blessing than Taryn had anticipated.

Kastor continued, "Many of you have questions and want to bless the couple. They will make the rounds in a short while. In the meantime, enjoy the food and drink. It's not often we have such a special event to celebrate."

With a wave of his hand, Kastor signaled the music to resume. Once the crowd settled back to enjoying the evening, he turned toward Kason and Taryn. "You must go now to talk with Keltor." He looked to his oldest son. "Settle your differences."

The two brothers merely grunted. Keltor led the way. Kason and Taryn followed.

She wondered what had happened between the two brothers. If things got out of hand, she only hoped she could help.

~~~

Kason wanted nothing more than to take a few minutes to plan escape routes in case things went awry when he and Taryn accepted congratulations and mingled with the people in the great hall.

Instead, he was following his older brother into the back room. And once the door shut, everyone stood in silence.

At least, until Taryn spoke up. "So? What's the cause of your big fallout?"

He'd rather have had the discussion in Kelderan, but he wouldn't shut out his bride; the translator in her ear could always make a mistake. "Keltor tried to shirk his duty."

Keltor's face remained impassive, which was a surprise given his brother's emotional nature as a teenager. "I was nineteen and in love. Maybe now you understand why I wanted to give up the crown."

Kason took a step forward. "You are the heir and honor bound to secure the royal line with a suitable bride. The daughter of a shop assistant would have torn the kingdom in two."

"In the end, I had no choice but to give her up. Although I will never forgive you for scaring her away."

Taryn chimed in. "Wait, what did you do, Kason?"

Keltor looked to Taryn. "He told her that I was betrothed to another and that if she didn't want her father to lose his position, she needed to forget I existed."

"It was for the best of the kingdom," Kason gritted out.

"It still wasn't right, Kason," Taryn pointed out.

"If I hadn't already been enlisted in the armed forces, we might be having a different conversation right now, Keltor. But I was set on my path and there was no room for an abdication, especially since females can't take over the crown." Kason forced his anger down a notch. "If it had happened later in life, then perhaps I would've acted differently. But it was over fifteen years ago. It's time to let it go. What with Father's health and the troublemakers trying to overthrow the monarchy, we have bigger problems."

"I hear you're going to head the colony?" Kason kept the confusion from his face as he nodded. Keltor continued, "Then we shall stay out of each other's way. I know more about the kingdom than almost anyone alive. All I have is duty now, with Kalahn gone. Only contact me when it's related to our people on Jasvar. Now, excuse me, I have people to meet with."

Keltor brushed past them and out the door.

Kason sighed. "I knew this wasn't going to be easy. I hope my father doesn't try to meddle anymore."

Taryn faced him. "Why did you do it, Kason? I understand duty and that you were young, but Keltor should've had his chance to decide his future."

"At sixteen, duty was everything to me. The war with the Brevkan was just dying down and everyone was afraid our society would crumble. I didn't want to disappoint our recently departed mother. So, full of arrogance and pride, I went to father and tried to handle the situation."

"So your father knew about this?"

"Yes, although Keltor always blamed me. Father probably never would've known about the female until it was too late if it weren't for me."

"You need to apologize, Kason. Even if Keltor brushes it off, it might help your brother heal a little."

Even a few months ago, Kason would've ignored the request. Too much time had passed. Keltor should've moved on.

But as Taryn searched his eyes, he was afraid of disappointment filling her gaze.

Besides, the small voice in his head told him it was the right thing to do.

He brushed her cheek with his forefinger. "While you hammer out the negotiations later tonight, I will find Keltor and apologize."

"Good. Although that's only the first step. At some point, we're coming back to Keldera to win over your brother. After all, he will be responsible for supplies and people coming to Jasvar. From a diplomatic standpoint, we need to have good relations."

"He will never abandon Kalahn, who will probably end up joining the colony, so I doubt he will forsake us."

"Kason."

He sighed. "Okay, I will try. Although the female he once loved has disappeared, so if he still wants her, I can't help him reconnect."

She smiled. "So you tried to track her down? That tells me you regretted your actions."

He grunted. "I never would've meddled in someone's love life as an adult."

"Then tell Keltor you tried to find her. It may make all the difference in the world to him."

He put out an arm. "I don't know what will happen with my brother, but I do know that if we don't head out into the main hall soon, people will feel neglected. Come, *zyla*. The sooner we finish this duty, the sooner you can hash out your negotiations and I can try to sort things out with my brother."

Taryn threaded her arm through his. "Okay, but try to keep our time mingling as short as possible. I'd much rather have more time to discuss the colony agreement. Besides, smiling and fluttering my eyelashes really isn't my thing."

"Just be yourself. Well, for the most part. We'll save your fighting skills for later. It'll give you an element of surprise in case something goes wrong before we leave."

THE CONQUEST

His female nodded, and Kason escorted her into the main hall. He did a quick scan but didn't see Keltor anywhere. Finding his brother was going to be interesting since all the royal siblings were good at hiding when they didn't want to be found.

Still, he would seek out Keltor and try to make things right. Yes, for the colony, but more importantly, for his bride. He wasn't about to disappoint her.

Chapter Twenty-Four

Three hours later, Taryn flexed her feet under the table in yet another conference room and resisted slapping her cheeks to stay awake. Negotiations were slow because of the language barrier. The king had retired for the night, and it was just Taryn and a few members of the council. Hinvel Mayta, the head of government, had resorted to interpreting or allowing the computer to do so.

Once the computer finished translating Taryn's latest point, Hinvel answered in CEL, "After a year, the colony will be given more autonomy in terms of changing the laws. While anyone who violates one of yours will be prosecuted by a joint team of Kelderans and Jasvarians, the basics of Kelderan law will be enforced on the Kelderans living in the settlement. It's the only way to ensure order."

The computer interpreted and Taryn answered, "Let's revisit it in six months, and you have a deal."

As Hinvel told her answer, a few of the others shrugged. She pushed on. "This is the last point, gentlemen. We both want the colony. Unless you have so little faith in your people that you don't think they can adjust to a new way of doing things, then let's call it a deal."

THE CONQUEST

The Kelderan council members talked among themselves. Taryn caught bits and pieces. Although limited by the device in her ear, most seemed ready to cave.

Hinvel finally met her gaze again. "We will agree to six months provided Kason and the general we send to oversee things on Jasvar provide positive reports on progress. If there is worry and dissent, it will extend to one year."

Taryn knew that was probably the best she could get. Kason would be on her side already, so she'd just have to work on winning the unnamed general's favor as well.

She nodded. "Deal. Are we ready to sign?"

The young man at Hinvel's side tapped a few things on his tablet and a few seconds later a copy printed from the far wall. Once he retrieved the documents, he laid them in between Hinvel and Taryn. Two pens followed suit.

Hinvel gestured toward the document. "Confirm the changes and sign."

She raised her brows. "I'd like time to study it first."

"We thought of that." Hinvel took a piece of paper from behind the agreement. "This is a temporary agreement. It says you agree to allow a Kelderan colony, but no ships will be sent until you sign the official document."

Scanning the CEL portion of the one page document, she didn't see anything out of the ordinary or deceitful. Taking the pen, she signed the temporary agreement. "I'll look over the other one and hope to sign it before I leave."

Hinvel signed the one-sheet paper and nodded. "I will meet you right before your departure to check on your progress. I look forward to working with you, Taryn Demara of Jasvar."

"And I you, Hinvel Mayta of Keldera."

The much older man smiled. "It's late and I think we should all go to bed. Keep me abreast of your departure time. Your lord will know how to contact me."

At the term "lord," Taryn decided her next order of business was finding a new word for her spouse. "Husband" might be too bland. Maybe Nova could help her back home.

Thinking of her friend, a small sense of homesickness overcame her. She needed Kason.

She made her final good-byes and exited the room. She expected to see Kason, but it was just the guards and an unfamiliar Barren assigned to her. Since neither the guards nor the Barren female spoke her language, Taryn smiled and motioned for them to go with her hands. The woman nodded and Taryn followed her lead.

As they turned down one corridor and the next, it became harder and harder for Taryn to stay awake. It'd been nearly twenty-four hours since she'd slept and a lot had happened in the interim. Maybe she should cut back sex on the days she knew she'd be busy with negotiations and meetings.

After what seemed like an hour but was probably only five minutes, they entered a corridor more poorly lit than the rest. It was then that Taryn noticed the Barren woman was gone and it was just her and the two guards. She slowed her pace to get a better look at them. However, they stopped and faced her.

Both of them had swords in their hands.

Just as she reached for her dagger, a blur jumped from one of the doorways in the hall and tackled one of the guards to the ground. Taryn didn't miss a beat drawing her weapon and rushing the other one. From the stunned expression on the man's face, he hadn't expect a female to fight back.

But it was too late for him. Taryn knocked him off balance and grabbed his genitals with one hand and positioned her dagger at his penis with the other. "Move and I'll cut it off."

He probably didn't understand CEL, but he understood the threat and went eerily still.

Keltor's voice filled her ears. "So the rumors are true."

She didn't dare look away from the guard beneath her. "I have no idea what people are saying about me. But if you could help me tie this guy up, I'd appreciate it."

Keltor grabbed the guard's straps across his chest and hauled him upward. Taryn barely had time to scoot away without making him much more than a eunuch.

A quick glance told her the other guard was already detained. Keltor made quick work of the other one before facing her.

They stared at each other for a few seconds before Keltor finally spoke up, "I'm sorry you were attacked. No matter what is between my brother and me, you are part of my family now and should be protected."

So Kason must not have found Keltor and apologized. "It's not your fault those two men were jerks."

Keltor went to the nearest console in the hallway, placed his hand, and spoke something in Kelderan. Since she couldn't understand it, she assumed the tussle must've jarred her interpreting device.

When finished, he answered her. "They will be tried and imprisoned for a very long time. Kason should be here soon to collect you."

Taryn should let Kason and Keltor hash out their problems. However, she couldn't help but blurt, "Kason tried to find the woman you loved. I think he knows he wronged you."

"It does not matter."

273

"Liar."

He raised his brows. "It can be considered treasonous to question the heir."

"Well, then it's a good thing I'm family now, isn't it? Convicting one of your own as treasonous would be quite the scandal."

One corner of Keltor's mouth ticked up. "You are clever for a female."

"I'm clever, period."

Keltor shook his head. "You are intriguing, human. You might actually keep my brother on his toes."

"Of course I will. But that isn't important. Give him five minutes, your highness. I don't want to start a new life, let alone a new colony, with the past hanging over our family's heads. I know Kalahn wouldn't want it."

He studied her. "How do you know what my sister wants?"

She shrugged. "We became friends onboard Kason's ship. She snuck on, you see, and we were roommates."

"So that's where she disappeared to."

"Yes. But what's more important is that she wants her brothers to at least talk with each other. If not for Kason, then try for her."

He paused for one long minute before replying, "I will listen and see what he has to say."

Taryn clapped her hands. "That's all I ask."

Kason's voice echoed down the hallway. "What's going on? Are you okay, *zyla*? Did they hurt you?"

She turned just as Kason reached her. He took her face in his hands and scanned every inch. She finally smiled. "I'm fine. Keltor and I make a good team."

Kason looked to his brother. "Thank you for helping her, Keltor. I am forever in your debt."

"It was nothing. It's partially my fault for not better vetting the guards. Not everyone is as welcoming as Father when it comes to your bride."

"And you, brother? What do you think of Taryn?" Kason asked.

Keltor smiled. "I think she will be a valuable asset."

Silence fell. It took everything Taryn had not to speak up. She wanted the two brothers to talk to each other without her constant nudging.

Kason's voice finally filled the corridor, but it was in Kelderan. All she could do was watch their facial expressions and wait for an update later from Kason.

~~~

Keltor's words, about Taryn being an asset to the family, finally convinced him he needed to try to make things right. Not just for Taryn, but also for himself. It had been a long time since he thought about how horrible his actions had been in the past. If someone had ripped Taryn from his life once he'd fallen in love with her, Kason may not have recovered.

And yet, his brother was doing his best to gear up for taking over the planet without the benefit of a bride. Keltor may not be a warrior, but he was strong in other ways.

Kason finally said, "My words will never bring her back, but I now understand the full extent of your loss, brother. I am profoundly sorry for what I did all those years ago. If I could bring Azalyn to you now, I would."

"Your female mentioned that you tried to find Aza. If you were so determined to keep us apart, what convinced you to try to reconnect us?"

"Because as you grew up and shouldered more responsibilities, I saw that you did little for yourself. A female of your own choosing might help alleviate the loneliness that comes with being a monarch."

Keltor assessed him a second before replying, "We may never be close, but we can try to be a little less guarded around each other going forward. For both Kalahn's and your bride's sake."

"So you forgive me?"

Keltor glanced to Taryn and back. "I think you finally understand the extent of my loss. I will always be hurt by what happened, but I don't wish to be petty. Your female shouldn't suffer for something that happened long before she came into your life."

It may not be all-out forgiveness, but Kason would take it. "Thank you."

Keltor moved toward the restrained guards. "I will handle these traitors. Go. Your bride looks about to fall over, even if she's trying to hide it."

Kason nodded. "I hope to see you again before we depart."

"You will. I have messages for you." He motioned toward the guards. "I'll tell you more later."

Taryn swayed a little and Kason gripped his female's shoulders. "Until then, brother." He switched to CEL. "And it's time to take you to bed."

"I would protest, but the adrenaline is wearing off and I'm going to crash."

THE CONQUEST

He scooped up his bride. When she didn't protest, he knew she was exhausted. "I will always have your back, Taryn Demara." He waited until they were far enough away from Keltor and the two prisoners before he added, "Keltor and I are on better terms now."

She leaned her head against his chest. "I'm glad. The bigger our family becomes, the better."

"So, you're ready to have ten children."

She frowned up at him. "Family means more than children. And given my age, I'd have to have twins one set after another to have that many kids anyway. Unless you want a constantly pregnant woman with mood swings and a steady stream of weird cravings, you might want to rethink the idea."

He kissed her forehead. "You and my siblings are enough, *zyla*. Any children we have will just be extra people to love."

Her expression softened. "I love it when you let your tough exterior down for me, *zylar*. It makes me love you even more."

"Then I will keep trying, my bride, to win as much of your heart as possible. We're going to need love to survive the coming years. Setting up the colony won't be easy, but together we can accomplish anything."

She laid a hand on his cheek. "Our future may be unwritten, but I say we can craft a great one."

"Not great, *zyla*. It will be perfect."

She smiled. "I think it's time to get you to bed. You're starting to sound romantic."

"I can be romantic."

She snuggled into his chest and murmured, "Of course you can."

As Taryn's breathing slowed and she fell asleep, he held her tighter in his arms. He couldn't write the future, but with Taryn's love and the support of his family, Kason knew it would be a great one. If he were lucky, it might even be perfect.

Epilogue

Two Weeks Later

Taryn shuffled her feet as the shuttle made its way to Jasvar's surface. "Why are they taking so long? We should've landed by now."

Kason slowly stroked his hand up and down her back. "The shuttle is taking the normal amount of time to land."

She frowned up at him. "Are you sure?"

He smiled. "Yes, *zyla*. Maybe carrying my child has made you lose all sense of time."

"You only had me tested because of my impatience. It's odd, though, knowing so early. I'm not the only one who's going to have to get used to your technology." She paused and lowered her voice, "My only hesitation about returning to Jasvar is that if I'm carrying a boy, he'll be taken from us."

He hauled her against his side and cupped her jaw. "The scientists have been working nonstop to find a cure to the doom virus. You've already been given everything deemed safe." He kissed her gently. "Besides, if there was anyone who could fend off the virus, it would be you, my bride. Your stubbornness has its merits."

She lightly slapped his chest. "I wouldn't tease me right at this moment, Kason. I'm impatient, homesick, and pregnant with a probably stubborn child warrior. That combination doesn't bode well for your soft bits."

He chuckled. "I've already designed special armor, just in case."

"Kason."

He stroked her cheek with his thumb, and some of her tension eased. "I believe our child will live and be born healthy. I refuse to accept anything else." He pulled her against his chest, and she melted into him. "Whatever may come, we can face it together."

She sighed and wrapped her arms around him. "I know. It's just been hard the past two weeks. While the initial reports from Jasvar have been promising, I'm anxious to see it with my own eyes."

"And you will. We're here."

Amidst her discussion with Kason, Taryn hadn't noticed the shuttle touching down. She turned and Kason released her.

Grabbing his hand, she tugged him toward the rear hatch and waited for the light to blink twice. The second it did, Kason typed in a command on a flat panel and the hatch opened at the same time as the stairs lowered to the ground.

As she waited for the stairs to finish descending, she noticed Nova, Kalahn, Jerrick, and a Kelderan warrior she didn't recognize waiting a safe distance away. Nova and Kalahn waved, and Taryn did the same. Once the stairs were ready, she released Kason's hand and raced down them.

She rushed into Nova's arms first and then Kalahn's. "I've missed you both."

Nova's voice was full of amusement. "Me most of all, I hope. Otherwise, the wine I've been holding back I'm going to share with Kalahn instead."

THE CONQUEST

She and Kason had decided earlier to keep the news of her pregnancy a secret until they could inform their most trusted friends in private. Taryn didn't want any of the Kelderan warriors to think she was weaker because of the child growing inside her.

As much as it pained her to keep it from her friends, she merely raised her brows and said, "Maybe I've given up drinking wine. The Kelderan equivalent isn't that palatable."

Kalahn spoke up. "That isn't fair. Once you grow accustomed to it, you can't live without it."

Nova looked to Kalahn. "But you have for the past few weeks. And consumed quite a bit of Jasvarian wine in the meantime."

Kalahn shrugged. "I was just trying to follow your customs."

The three of them chuckled. Nova was the first to speak again. "So it looks like things have worked out between you and the sexy alien. Does he have any friends or brothers? I haven't had any luck with the lot here."

"In time, Nova. We might, I don't know, want to prepare for the colonists first? That'll increase your choices, so you should be willing to work day and night to get everything ready," Taryn stated.

"I've been working already. I could just use a little release, if you know what I mean," Nova said as she winked.

Kalahn's cheeks turned pink. As Nova teased the princess about being innocent, Taryn noticed Kason talking with the unknown warrior. She caught her prince's eye and he walked toward her, his friend right behind him. As soon as Kason was close enough, she put an arm around his waist. "Nova, may I introduce my husband, Prince Kason tro el Vallen of Keldera? Kason, this is Nova Drakven, my best friend and chief strategist."

Kason bowed his head. "Nice to meet you."

Nova smiled. "That's a bit formal. Taryn is my sister in all but blood. Come here."

Nova hugged Kason's free side, and Taryn bit her lip to keep from laughing at Kason's startled expression. Once Nova released him, Taryn decided to ask, "Who's your friend, *zylar*? We haven't been formally introduced."

Kason cleared his throat and motioned toward the Kelderan male with silver hair and lavender-tinged skin. "This is my oldest friend and best trainer, Ryven Xanna. Ryven, this is my bride, Taryn Demara."

Ryven's CEL accent was thick but understandable. "I've heard a lot about you, Taryn. Kalahn speaks highly of you."

She looked to Kalahn. "Good things, I hope."

Ryven answered, "By Jasvar's standards, of course. I'm still dubious about your dagger wielding capabilities."

Kason grunted. "Don't challenge her, Ryven. It's not worth it."

Taryn ignored him. "We could hold a contest right now if you like?"

Kason squeezed her gently. "Later. First, you need to show me our home and introduce me to your people. There's a lot to learn before the colony ship arrives in a few weeks."

Remembering her duty, Taryn nodded. "Then let's hurry. As much as I enjoy the replicator on your ship, I can't wait for a home-cooked meal. Once you try it, you'll never want to go back."

"All I remember is the cold, tasteless food I ate here as a prisoner."

"Are you really going to keep reminding me about that?" Taryn asked.

"Of course." Kason winked. "But I may forget if I have a good meal and can spend the rest of my nights in your bed."

Despite her best efforts to resist, her cheeks heated. "Kason."

He chuckled. "Come, *zyla*. Show me our new home."

At hearing "our home," Taryn's eyes prickled.

However, she was aware of everyone's gazes on her, so she cleared her throat and held her head high. "Well, if Keldera's official governor on Jasvar asks, I should oblige. I need him on my side if our people are to live together in peace."

Kason leaned down and whispered, "And I'm sure you'll find many creative ways to keep me on your side, *zyla*."

Ignoring his innuendo, Taryn motioned toward the entrance to the mountain settlement in the distance. "We'd better hurry or the entire settlement will ambush us. Word travels fast here."

As they made their way toward the entrance, Taryn leaned against Kason's side. Between the familiar purple trees and pink sky, as well as the comforting presence of Kason and her friends, Taryn was truly home. The future might be challenging, but as long as she had her friends and family at her side, she would be able to face anything.

And as Kason kissed the top of her head, she resisted placing a hand over her lower abdomen. She had much to fight for and damn anyone who tried to stand in the way of her happiness.

Blaze of Secrets
(Asylums for Magical Threats #1)

After discovering she has elemental fire magic as a teenager, Kiarra Melini spends the next fifteen years inside a magical prison. While there, she undergoes a series of experiments that lead to a dangerous secret. If she lives, all magic will be destroyed. If she dies, magic has a chance to survive. Just as she makes her choice, a strange man breaks into cell, throws her over his shoulder, and carries her right out of the prison.

To rescue his brother, Jaxton Ward barters with his boss to rescue one other inmate--a woman he's never met before. His job is to get in, nab her and his brother, and get out. However, once he returns to his safe house, his boss has other ideas. Jaxton is ordered to train the woman and help her become part of the anti-magical prison organization he belongs to.

Working together, Kiarra and Jaxton discover a secret much bigger than their growing attraction to each other. Can they evade the prison retrieval team long enough to help save magic? Or, will they take Kiarra back to prison and end any chance of happiness for them both?

Excerpt from *Blaze of Secrets*:

CHAPTER ONE

First-born Feiru *children are dangerous. At the age of magical maturity they will permanently move into compounds established for both their and the public's protection. These compounds will be known as the Asylums for Magical Threats (hereafter abbreviated as "AMT").*
—Addendum, Article III of the *Feiru* Five Laws, July 1953

Present Day

Jaxton Ward kept his gaze focused on the nearing mountain ledge ahead of him. If he looked down at the chasm below his feet, he might feel sick, and since his current mission was quite possibly the most important one of his life, he needed to focus all of his energy on succeeding.

After all, if things went according to plan, Jaxton would finally see his brother again.

He and his team of three men were balanced on a sheet of rock five thousand feet in the air. To a human, it would look like they were flying. However, any *Feiru* would know they were traveling via elemental wind magic.

Darius, the elemental wind first-born on his team, guided them the final few feet to the mountain ledge. As soon as the sheet of rock touched solid ground, Jaxton and his team moved into position.

The mountain under their feet was actually one of the most secure AMT compounds in the world. Getting in was going to be difficult, but getting out was going to take a bloody miracle, especially since he'd had to barter with his boss for the location of his brother. In exchange, he had promised to rescue not just Garrett, but one other unknown first-born as well.

Taka, the elemental earth first-born of Jaxton's team, signaled he was ready. He nodded for Taka to begin.

As Taka reached a hand to the north, the direction of elemental earth magic, the solid rock of the mountain moved. With each inch that cleared to form a tunnel, Jaxton's heart rate kicked up. Jaxton was the reason his brother had been imprisoned inside the mountain for the last five years and he wasn"t sure if his brother had ever forgiven him.

Even if they survived the insurmountable odds, located Garrett, and broke into his prison cell, his brother might not agree to go with them. Considering the rumors of hellish treatment inside the AMT compounds, his brother's hatred would be justified.

Once the tunnel was big enough for them to enter, Jaxton pushed aside his doubts. No matter what his brother might think of him, Jaxton would rescue him, even it if took drugging Garrett unconscious to do so.

Taking out his Glock, he flicked off the safety. Jaxton was the only one on the team without elemental magic, but he could take care of himself.

He moved to the entrance of the tunnel, looked over his shoulder at his men, and nodded. After each man nodded, signaling they were ready, he took out his pocket flashlight, switched it on, and jogged down the smooth tunnel that would lead them to the inner corridors of the AMT compound.

If his information was correct, the AMT staff would be attending a site-wide meeting for the next hour. That gave Jaxton and his team a short window of opportunity to get in, nab the two inmates, and get back out again.

He only hoped everything went according to plan.

~~*

Kiarra Melini stared at the small homemade shiv in her hand and wondered for the thousandth time if she could go through with it.

She had spent the last few weeks racking her brain, trying to come up with an alternative plan to save the other prisoners of the AMT without having to harm anyone. Yet despite her best efforts, she'd come up empty-handed.

To protect the lives of the other first-borns inside the AMT, Kiarra would kill for the first and last time.

Not that she wanted to do it, given the choice. But after overhearing a conversation between two AMT researchers a few weeks ago, she knew the AMT would never again be safe for any of the first-borns while she remained alive.

The outside world might have chosen to forget about the existence of the first-born prisoners, but that didn't make them any less important. Kiarra was the only one who cared, and she would go down fighting trying to protect them.

Even if it meant killing herself to do so.

She took a deep breath and gripped the handle of her blade tighter until the plastic of the old hairbrush dug into her skin. Just as she was about to raise her arm to strike, her body shook. Kiarra closed her eyes and breathed in and out until she calmed down enough to stop shaking. Ending her life, noble as her reasons may be, was a lot harder than she'd imagined.

Mostly because she was afraid to die.

But her window of opportunity was closing fast; the AMT-wide meeting would end in less than an hour. After that, she would have to wait a whole other month before she could try again, and who knew how many more first-borns would suffer because of her cowardice.

Maybe, if she recalled the conversation between the two researchers, the one which forebode the future harsh realities of the other AMT prisoners, she'd muster enough nerve to do what needed to be done.

It was worth a shot, so Kiarra closed her eyes and recalled the conversation that had changed the course of her life forever.

Strapped to a cold metal examination table, Kiarra kept her eyes closed and forced herself to stay preternaturally still. The slightest movement would alert the researchers in the room that she was conscious again. She couldn't let that happen, not if she wanted to find out the reason why the researchers had increased her examination visits and blood draws over the past two weeks.

Most AMT prisoners wouldn't think twice about it, since they'd been conditioned not to ask questions, but Kiarra had gone through something similar before. The last time her visits had increased with the same frequency, the AMT researchers had stolen her elemental magic.

Since then, no matter how many times she reached to the south—the direction of elemental fire—she felt nothing. No tingling warmth, no comforting flame. She was no different from a non-first-born, yet she was still a prisoner, unable to see the sky or feel a breeze, and forced to live in constant fear of what the guards or researchers might do to her.

Of how they might punish her.

THE CONQUEST

Dark memories invaded her mind. However, when the female researcher in the room spoke again, it snapped Kiarra back to the present. The woman's words might tell her more about her future, provided she had one after her treatment.

She listened with every cell in her body and steeled herself not to react.

"Interesting," the female researcher said. "Out of the ten teenagers, nine of them still can't use their elemental magic, just like F-839. Dr. Adams was right—her blood was the key to getting the Null Formula to work."

It took all of Kiarra's control not to draw in a breath. Her serial number was F-839, and all of the extra blood draws finally made sense—the AMT was using her blood to try and eradicate elemental magic.

The male researcher spoke up. "They're going to start a new, larger test group in a few weeks and see if they can stop the first-borns from going insane and/or committing suicide. If we don"t get the insanity rate below ten percent, then we'll never be able to implement this planet-wide."

"Don't worry, we'll get there. We have a few million first-borns to burn through to get it right."

Kiarra opened her eyes and embraced the guilt she felt every time she thought about what had happened to those poor first-born teenagers.

Because of her blood, not only had five teenagers already gone insane, but their insanity was driving an untold number of them to suicide.

And the researchers wanted to repeat the process with a larger group.

She couldn't let that happen.

They needed her blood, drawn and injected within hours, as a type of catalyst for the Null Formula to work. If they didn't have access to her blood, they wouldn't be able to conduct any more tests.

There was a chance the researchers might find another catalyst within a few weeks or months, but it was a risk she was willing to take. Stopping the tests, even for a few months, would prevent more people from going insane or committing suicide.

Kiarra needed to die.

I can do this. Think of the others. Taking a deep breath, she tightened her grip around the shiv's handle and whispered, "Please let this work,'" before raising the blade with a steady hand and plunging it into the top half of her forearm.

Kiarra sucked in a breath as a searing pain shot up her arm. To prevent herself from making any more noise, she bit her lip. Despite the AMT-wide staff meeting, a guard would come to investigate her cell if she screamed.

You can do this, Kiarra. Finish it. With her next inhalation, she pulled the blade a fraction more down toward her wrist. This time she bit her lip hard enough she could taste iron on her tongue.

While her brain screamed for her to stop, she ignored it and gripped the handle of the blade until it bit into her palm. Only when her heart stopped beating would the other first-borns be safe—at least from her.

An image of a little girl crying, reaching out her arms and screaming Kiarra's name, came unbidden into her mind, but she forced it aside. Her sister had abandoned her, just like the rest of her family. Her death wouldn't cause anyone sadness or pain. Rather, through death, she would finally have a purpose.

This was it. On the next inhalation, she moved the blade a fraction. But before she could finish the job, the door of her cell slid open.

Kiarra looked up and saw a tall man, dressed head to toe in black, standing in her doorway and pointing a gun straight at her.

Shit. She'd been discovered.

The Conquest

_____

Want to read the rest?
Blaze of Secrets is available in paperback

For exclusive content and updates, sign up for my newsletter at:

http://www.jessiedonovan.com

Author's Note

Thank you for taking a chance on my new series. I grew up watching *Doctor Who*, *Star Trek* (Original, Next Generation, and Deep Space Nine), and *Red Dwarf*. I've always had a love of sci-fi mixed with humor and close relationships. In fact, my first attempt at writing my dragon series took place on an alien planet. However, that eventually changed to a contemporary paranormal romance, but I always wanted to try writing a sci-fi romance someday. Then the idea hit me—what if there was a shortage of men instead of women? And *The Conquest* was born.

This book took a lot of world-building and work, but I think it turned out well. Of course I couldn't have done it without help or feedback from others. I wish to thank the following people:

—Becky Johnson and her team at Hot Tree Editing. They caught quite a few of my inconsistencies and made the story better. Thank you!

—Clarissa Yeo of Yocla Designs. Every cover she makes for me is amazing and this one is no different. She knows exactly how to portray the genre without making it look like ever other sci-fi romance out there. I really appreciate her talent!

—My three beta-readers: Donna H., Iliana G., and Alyson S. These three ladies found a few more inconsistencies and typos. They helped me polish it up and I appreciate their help immensely.

I also wish to thank my readers. You make my dream of writing full-time possible. I know some of you wish I wrote faster, but know deep down that long, quality stories take time. Thanks for your patience and support. It means the world to me.

My plan is to have the second book in this series out sometime in 2017. It will be about Vala and Thorin and should prove extremely interesting. It may not seem so on the surface, but they really do suit each other. While I always post updates on my website or Facebook, you can make sure you hear all the latest news by joining my newsletter on JessieDonovan.com.

Thanks and I hope to see you at the end of the next story.